Radical Mansfield

Double Discourse in
Katherine Mansfield's Short Stories

Pamela Dunbar

Lecturer in English
University of Warwick

First published in Great Britain 1997 by
MACMILLAN PRESS LTD
Houndmills, Basingstoke, Hampshire RG21 6XS and London
Companies and representatives throughout the world

A catalogue record for this book is available from the British Library.

ISBN 0–333–68782–5 hardcover
ISBN 0–333–68783–3 paperback

First published in the United States of America 1997 by
ST. MARTIN'S PRESS, INC.,
Scholarly and Reference Division,
175 Fifth Avenue, New York, N.Y. 10010

ISBN 0–312–17467–5

Library of Congress Cataloging-in-Publication Data
Dunbar, Pamela.
Radical Mansfield : double discourse in Katherine Mansfield's short
stories / Pamela Dunbar.
p.   cm.
Includes bibliographical references (p.) and index.
ISBN 0–312–17467–5 (cloth)
1. Mansfield, Katherine, 1888–1923—Criticism and interpretation.
2. Literature and psychology—New Zealand—History—20th century.
3. Psychological fiction—History and criticism.   4. Modernism
(Literature)—New Zealand.   5. Radicalism in literature.   I. Title.
PR9639.3.M258Z6354 1997
823'.912—DC21   97–7010
                                                              CIP
                                                              r97

This book is printed on paper suitable for recycling and made from fully managed and
sustained forest sources.

10   9   8   7   6   5   4   3   2   1
06   05   04   03   02   01   00   99   98   97

Printed in Great Britain by
The Ipswich Book Company Ltd, Ipswich, Suffolk

To
M.B.D. and the
memory of J.H.D.,
and
to Holly

Contents

Acknowledgements

In the autumn of 1988 I was fortunate enough to have been able to take part in both the Katherine Mansfield Centenary Symposium at the Newberry Library, Chicago, and the Centennial Conference at Victoria University in Wellington, New Zealand, where I also had the opportunity of examining the Mansfield collection at the Alexander Turnbull Library. All these activities contributed significantly to the writing of this book, and I wish here to express my gratitude to the Librarian and Trustees of the Turnbull Library and to Warwick University's Research and Travel Fund committee for grants which enabled me to undertake the trip.

I should also like to thank the conference hosts, the Librarian and Trustees of the Newberry Library, and Professor Roger Robinson and his colleagues at Victoria University of Wellington, as well as Anne Else and her fellow organisers of the Wellington women's seminar on Mansfield, for the warmth and generosity of their welcome; as well as other Mansfield scholars and friends new and especially old encountered at the conferences, for warm hospitality and stimulating company. Thanks in particular to Dr Kirsty Cochrane for helpful suggestions on the manuscript and on other Mansfield matters; and to Professor Jeremy Treglown, who also made helpful suggestions on the manuscript and who was instrumental in ensuring that it reached the light of day. I am grateful as well to my editor, Charmian Hearne, and agent, Duncan McAra, for advice and assistance.

Grateful acknowledgement is made to the Society of Authors as the literary representative of the Estate of Katherine Mansfield for permission to reproduce a previously unpublished story of Mansfield's, 'His Sisters' Keeper'; also to the University of Otago Press and the Women's Studies Association of New Zealand, and Messrs G.K. Hall & Co., a division of Macmillan Publishing Co., for permission to reproduce material based on an article of mine entitled 'What *Does* Bertha Want? A Re-reading of Katherine Mansfield's "Bliss"', published in the *Women's Studies Journal*, IV, ii, December 1988, pp. 18–31, and reprinted in *Critical Essays on Katherine Mansfield*, ed. Rhoda B. Nathan, New York, 1993, pp. 128–39.

Preface

In January 1921, just two years before she died, Katherine Mansfield wrote to a painter-friend: 'I try and make family life so gorgeous – not hatred and linoleum – but warmth and hydrangeas.'[1]

Yet beneath the 'hydrangeas' – the material prosperity, the emotional fulfilment, the sense of contentment conveyed by such well-known pieces as 'Prelude', 'The Garden-Party', or 'The Doll's House' – there is a persistent sense of malaise; a preoccupation with alienation, with premature death, with sexual maladjustment; above all a disposition to challenge received assumptions about human relationships and the nature of individual identity.

Mansfield then is far from being the 'safe' writer the lyrical surfaces of her most famous stories proclaim her to be. She radically questioned all the most compelling myths of personal and public life – the romance of marriage, family happiness, child purity, the grandeur of the artist's task, the coherence and integrity (in both senses) of the individual self, the immutable nature of sexual identity. And she dealt frequently in dangerous, or taboo, subjects relating to the underside of these myths – child abuse and neglect, prostitution and procuration, murder within marriage, wife-beating, sexual deviation, child sexuality. She also broke fresh literary ground by interrogating subjects like sexual bliss, or conveying a woman's subliminal perception of her pregnancy. And she was among the first of the post-Victorians to chip away at received taboos on recording sexual experience.

These two aspects of Mansfield's writing, the lyrical and the subversive, are in some of the best-known stories presented in a layered or contrapuntal manner, with the surface lyricism serving as a cloak for more subversive themes and attitudes.[2] Mansfield adopts this method, in part because of the dangerous nature of the material – much of it autobiographical – with which she was dealing; in part in order to reflect the doubleness of the way in which according to her, society and indeed the human mind itself are organised.

It is of course possible to read the stories without acknowledging their subtexts; and indeed this has until recently been the usual approach. But such a partial reading ignores an essential, perhaps

the essential, aspect of Mansfield's writing. It has also led to un-
founded criticism – that she is a writer of mere 'chocolate-box' pieces,
or that her works exist only on the margins of history, unaffected
by contemporary literary trends and divorced from the great social,
political and cultural events of her time. And it has resulted in the
formation of an unofficial Mansfield canon which favours apparently tranquil pieces like 'Prelude', 'The Garden-Party', and 'The
Doll's House' while neglecting other, more patently disturbing works
like the satirical *German Pension* sketches, the confessional mono-
logues, and the early colonial tales – pieces just as accomplished
and innovative as the better-known stories.

Mansfield's writings were in fact deeply affected by two events
– one cultural, the other social and political – which radically altered
early-twentieth-century Europe's perception of itself, and in so doing
contributed signally to the formation of the Modernist movement.

The Great War affected Mansfield herself most immediately
through the death of her beloved brother Leslie – something which
triggered an imaginative return to the early life, and hence the writing of her most accomplished stories. But she also travelled several
times through wartime France noting in her letters and journal the
disruption that it caused even far from the battle-front. One of her
stories is set in the war zone, and several others focus on the devastation it caused in the lives of those bereaved by it.

The second 'event' reflected in her writings was less dramatic but
just as fundamental in its effect on the European consciousness –
the publication by Freud of his early works on sexuality and the
mechanism of repression. Mansfield must have known something
of these: in the café society she frequented on first returning to
London it would have been impossible to avoid hearing about them.
But in any case several members of her circle were deeply engaged
with his ideas. A.R. Orage, for a time a close friend of hers as well
as editor of the journal *New Age* which published some of her early
stories, was a passionate disciple; and Leonard and Virginia Woolf,
also friends of Mansfield and the original publishers of 'Prelude',
produced the first English edition of Freud's works.[3] D.H. Lawrence
and Frieda were acquainted with his radical views as well.[4]

In keeping with the general British coyness about acknowledging
any acquaintance with Freud, Mansfield nowhere mentions his name.
But in 'Psychology' (1919?), one of her most intriguing stories, she
does refer to the then revolutionary technique of 'psycho-analysis'
– and in a context which makes clear she had an understanding of

what it involved. And whilst her declared approach to her art was devoutly anti-theoretical the content and layered structure of many of her stories show what appears to be a considerable debt to the lead metaphor and insights of depth-psychology.

Mansfield was also deeply influenced by writers like Oscar Wilde – literary figures of a generation or so before her own, whose radicalism was as much a matter of lifestyle as of literary innovation. In fact her own life became, like Wilde's, largely the result of a conscious decision to challenge restrictive social and sexual norms in the interests of broader experience and a deeper 'truth'. There was an early break with her conventional family, and a solitary voyage to the far side of the world to make her name as a writer. There were lesbian affairs, the wild early years in England – including a marriage which only lasted an afternoon, the glamour (and hardship) of what used to be called a Bohemian lifestyle, flirtations with stage and film work. And, though there was eventually a lasting – if unconventional – relationship with the editor and critic John Middleton Murry, there were other affairs, trips across wartorn France – later because of failing health but in her younger years for the sake of passion, an eleventh-hour commitment to Gurdyeyev's mystical teachings.

Though she never abandoned her quest for 'truth' this child of respectability did sometimes acknowledge and even pay tribute to those structures which to her obstructed or concealed it. The unconsummated marriage to a friend of only three weeks' standing seems, for instance, to have been a panicky attempt to legitimise a pregnancy; and when she became unable to sustain the deception she allowed herself to be whisked off to Bavaria – out of reach of scandal – by her formidable mother. Alone and desperately unhappy she nevertheless remained there for six months after Mrs Beauchamp's departure.

The closeness of Mansfield's writings to the circumstances and details of her own life – as well as the forthright way that closeness is declared (the names of her most famous family the Burnells, for instance, identify their originals as members of her own family) – also must have constrained her to 'write double'. Her technique thus accommodates her own need to find some dialogue, however uneasy, between the conventional social manner of her family and her own fiercely independent attitudes, a dilemma caught in Laura Sheridan's plight in 'The Garden-Party'.

Almost all Mansfield's stories deal with the family: even those which highlight her characters' isolation contain implicit criticism of it as an institution which marginalises and derides those who fail to conform to its norms. And, while paying apparent tribute to the idealised notion of the family as serene and united, most of the stories in fact dismantle this belief. To Mansfield the family unit is basically a site of conflict and tension, threatened both by the individual's unwillingness or inability to conform to the role assigned them within it, and by the dark complexity of the individual consciousness and of family members' relationships with each other. She shows particular concern for connections in which there is striking inequality of power – typically those between child and adult, or between lovers. In almost every case her focus is upon the more vulnerable of the pair.

The traditional notion of the patriarchal father as a benevolent overlord is challenged: but so too is that of his authority, for time and again the woman is found to be the stronger partner in a relationship. And the conventional assumption – made in many Victorian novels – that true significance is to be found outside the home, in the 'male' domains of work and public affairs, is also challenged. It is woman's experience and the woman's domain that, as in other key Modernist works, are at the heart of Mansfield's vision.

She frequently represents women as the victims of men. One is battered, several murdered, by their husbands. On a less dramatic level they are consistently subjected by their partners either to social humiliation or to incessant sexual demands. Occasionally it is the men who are the victims. But in almost all cases the illusion of the happy marriage is effectively dispelled: there is hardly a contented couple in the whole of Mansfield's works.

She dismantles the Romantic notion of childhood innocence as well. Many of her children are mistreated or emotionally neglected. They are also shown to be prey to their own inner anxieties, aggressions and sexual fantasies. In a piece so daring that it has remained unpublished to this day, for instance, she evokes a young girl's fantasy of brotherly rape. In her interpretation of the adolescent girl's maturing as the confining of the mobility and imaginative openness of her consciousness within the fixed structure of the adult psyche she also looks beyond the idealised – and developmentally static – child-woman dear to Victorian novelists.

Mansfield challenges not only the Victorian notion of the family but also the humanist's belief in the self as a coherent and unified entity; one open to rational argument, and of fundamental moral probity. In her stories she frequently focuses on the duality and on the perversity of the human mind. And she deconstructs the traditional notion of the creative artist as a bearer of moral authority, in total control of his handiwork, and by tradition male; putting up against this view a democratic notion of the creativity of 'ordinary' people – for instance, of women engaged not in high flights of the imagination but in everyday tasks connected with the domestic round.

She also dismantles conventional beliefs about rigid gender-roles and 'normal' sexual orientation. This she does both by suggesting that these are at least to some extent the product of acculturation and experience, and by interrogating the rigid nature of accepted male and female roles and identities. In the macho world of the colonial outback, for instance, women display 'masculine' aggression; but male settlers too are placed under strain by being forced to live up to an exaggerated notion of the strong-man stereotype. Mansfield's courage in dealing with the complexity of sexual orientation is also shown in her concern with the attraction between members of the same sex – a taboo subject particularly in the years following the Wilde trial of 1895 – and with the general mobility of human desire.

Mansfield's writings show a profound appreciation of English and continental literary tradition – including the nineteenth-century French and Russian prose realists. (The Russians were just then coming to the attention of the British reading public through the translations of Constance Garnett, a literary figure associated like Mansfield herself with Bloomsbury.) From them, as well as from the French Symbolists and English Romantics and *fin-de-siècle* aesthetes, she obtained insights regarding the transformative significance of the Romantics' 'moment' of intense feeling, the lyricism of prose-poetry, the potency of myth and symbol, the complexity of the self and the crucial importance of subjective experience, the alienation of the artist, and the interrelatedness of the arts.

One of her most significant formal innovations was to marry the preoccupations of nineteenth-century aestheticism and *fin-de-siècle* fatalism to a pessimism and sense of cultural, historical and social fragmentation that were brought about (or reinforced) by the experience of the Great War. This resulted in short pieces which with their apparent combination of open-endedness and taut structuring and their use of the subjective lyrical voice, caught both the poignancy and the purposelessness of life as it was perceived in the aftermath of the War. They also contributed signally to the 'invention' of the Modernist, or 'literary', short story.[5]

Mansfield's vital role in the creation of the Modernist short story has recently been acknowledged in seminal works by Clare Hanson, Kate Fullbrook, and Sydney Janet Kaplan[6] amongst others. The earlier neglect of her contribution was in part the result of a general neglect of the English short story, and a lack of esteem for it. But it also owed something to the nature of the relationship Mansfield as an individual enjoyed with the British cultural establishment. She and her husband John Middleton Murry moved on the fringes of Bloomsbury, welcome no doubt for their talents, their liveliness and their charm. Yet – the one a 'little colonial' of unverifiable pedigree, the other irredeemably lower middle-class – they were never entirely accepted by the 'Bloomsberries'. Scholars and historians of the period have also privileged Bloomsbury.

This bias has particularly affected the relative literary reputations of Katherine Mansfield and Virginia Woolf. Where it was in fact Mansfield with her innovative talents and her stylistic brilliance who was a profound influence upon the writing of her friend ('I was jealous of her writing – the only writing I have ever been jealous of')[7] it is Woolf, the more socially and culturally established figure, who has generally been credited with these innovations. So the similarities between their writings – Mansfield's almost always predating Woolf's – are referred to by critics as if they were the product of an affinity of minds instead of the influence of one mind upon another.[8]

The key works here are Mansfield's long stories 'Prelude' and 'At the Bay'. Their preoccupation with female and domestic experience, with a multiple heroine, with the gendered aspects of male and female, with the mother's protection of her own identity in the face of her husband's overbearing conduct, with intimations of death in life, with symbolic structuring, all have their equivalents in Woolf's *To the Lighthouse* (1927) and *The Waves* (1931). In particular the key structural device of 'At the Bay', the imaging of life as a single day, is replicated in *The Waves*. And even the central section of *To the Lighthouse*, which evokes the death and devastation caused by the Great War, may be seen as an attempt by Woolf to meet Mansfield's criticism of her earlier novel *Night and Day* for failing to take account of the Great War and its effect on the contemporary consciousness.[9]

The history of Mansfield's development as a writer is in large part the story of her lifelong attempt to dramatise socially unacceptable insights into the irrationality of the human mind and the perceived fatality of the human situation. Her struggle both to reveal and to conceal this material led to the development of sophisticated techniques of indirection – subtextual discourse (including the use of fairytale and mythic parallels at odds with their chronicle–realist surfaces), linguistic ambiguity, complex and system-free symbolism[10] – which in turn assisted her evolution of a Modernist rhetoric.

My study of Mansfield focuses closely upon the stories and their subtexts, in an attempt both to emphasise the extent of their originality and subtlety, and to trace the evolution of one of the great Modernist innovators of twentieth-century English literature.

1

Alienation

Katherine Mansfield's earliest stories[1] show a precocious awareness of the market. Produced for her school magazine[2] and written when she was only nine or ten, they are pious tributes to the received myth of the happy, well-regulated, and socially concerned middle-class family; a family which – like that of many later Mansfield stories – bears a distinct resemblance to her own.

These childish pieces however show no trace of the tension and malaise that disturb the lyrical surface of the mature stories: it is partly this that makes them so dull. But in the way their young author attempts to equate 'normal' life with special treats for the children one suspects that – despite the piety – she herself also found dull the life that they reflect. Certainly their picture of family life is close to that which is eagerly forsaken by Pearl Button in the later story which bears her name.

'Mary',[3] confided to a personal notebook some four or five years after the school sketches were written, also centres on Mansfield's own family – as the characters' names, as well as its painful lack of objectivity, makes clear: the heroine Kass bears the author's nickname; Mary the second given name of Charlotte, an elder sister; and their surname Beetham is an aural near-transcription of Beauchamp, Mansfield's own family name. But 'Mary' tells a different story from the school pieces. It focuses on private feelings rather than on events, and in place of the bland contentment of the early sketches projects a mood of keen resentment.

The story shows the heroine, the 'unloved child' of the family, allowing her less-gifted sister Mary to win the school prize which should by rights have been hers. This appears to be a ploy on Kass's part to recover, not only her parents' regard but also the self-esteem which she has lost thanks to their attitude towards her. However, when the plan succeeds and Mary is acclaimed, Kass feels – perversely – cheated: 'The sacrifice was too great. . . . Nobody loves me, nobody understood me, and they loved Mary without the [prize], and now that she had it I decided they loved me less.'[4] So distressed is she that she even considers coming clean about what she has done. But the noble impulse which inspired her scheme reasserts itself, and she stays silent.

'Mary', then, devotes itself to revealing Kass's 'true' generosity of spirit – as well as her inner confusion and lack of self-esteem. It is the distance between its preoccupations and those of the magazine pieces – between troubled psychology and serene appearance – which the later Mansfield will negotiate so successfully in her mature writings.

Most of Mansfield's biographers hint that she was emotionally neglected as a child. Her mother Annie – the Linda of the Burnell stories – had the disposition of an invalid, and baby Kathleen, as Mansfield had been christened, was given over to her grandmother's care. But a younger sister Gwendoline, a sickly infant born just two years after Kathleen herself, usurped her sister's place in the grandmother's arms. Mansfield's earliest memory became one of exclusion: 'All day, all night grandmother's arms were full. I had no lap to climb into. . . . All belonged to Gwen.'[5]

Though she kept herself at a distance from all her children, Annie Beauchamp seems to have been particularly aloof towards the young Kathleen. A contemporary of Mansfield's, who met the parents on shipboard during a return voyage from England, recalled Annie's chilling words of greeting to her third daughter: ' "Well, Kathleen, . . . I see that you are as fat as ever." '[6] (In 'Mary' this offending plumpness is reinscribed so it becomes ground for approval – though on the part of the grandmother rather than the parents: 'I was a strong, fat little child who burst my buttons and shot out of my skirts to Grandmother's entire satisfaction, but Mary was a "weed".')[7] The father Harold Beauchamp by his own confession scarcely remembered Mansfield as a child – 'too much absorbed in building up the business'.[8]

In her writings Mansfield was to return constantly to the depiction of a heroine or hero hopelessly at odds with their parents. Soon after completing 'Mary' she began to project this theme onto the traditional structures of myth and fairytale. These allowed her both to avoid the self-pitying emotional nearness of 'Mary' and to offer a broader ground against which to display the complex emotions of her child-protagonists. They also enabled her to translate her own emotional estrangement from her parents into the traditional one of literal absence – a condition starker yet less emotionally compromised than that set out in 'Mary'.

'His Ideal'[9] was written a year or so later than 'Mary' – and probably after Kathleen and her elder sisters had themselves experienced estrangement from their parents by being sent for three years to Queen's College in London, a girls' school run on advanced lines.

Like others of the early tales, 'His Ideal' owes much to the liberal education Mansfield received at Queen's – in this case a familiarity with the *fin-de-siècle* fantasy of the allure of death:[10] but it also conveys the intensity of its hero's desire for a succouring mother-figure.

The sketch centres upon the earthly visitations of a ministering lady robed in white. This lady appears to the hero only when he is ill. He spends the intervals between illnesses longing for her return. Eventually, having grown old, he decides to throw himself into the river so that in its depths he will be reunited with his ministering spirit for ever. As he does this the woman '[holds] him in her arms as she would a little child', and he feels 'his bitterness fade away into the past, become buried with the past'. At the same time the woman reveals, both to us and to him, that 'her name was Death'. The hero's desire for permanent union is granted only in death.

Mansfield's fairytale 'The Green Tree'[11] also deals with parent–child estrangement. The young hero is given a plot of ground by his father, and devotes himself to tending the tree which is planted there. Its beauty moves him to compose songs about it. Eventually he neglects his parents for the tree; and when they in revenge plot its destruction they are killed by one of its falling branches. Similarly the hero's lover, attracted to him by his songs, is driven away because of his passion for the tree. In the end the Boy himself gets killed trying to reach the golden fruit which grows on its topmost bough, and the tree is cut down and burnt.

The story clearly draws on the fairytale 'Jack and the Beanstalk', in which the young hero similarly asserts his independence from his parents, and the beanstalk – like Mansfield's Green Tree – brings him great gifts but also bad trouble. However, where Jack's story alludes briefly to a golden harp as one of the magical objects which the hero plundered from the land at the top of the beanstalk, Mansfield's tale places the obsessive pursuit of artistic excellence at its centre. In this respect 'The Green Tree' reflects the new gulf which the adolescent Mansfield – with a father 'only interested in money and [a] mother [only] in social climbing'[12] – felt her artistic interests opened up between herself and them. Significantly, though,

the emphasis has changed: where in the earlier story 'Mary' it is
Kass who was neglected it is now the parents who are the injured
parties.

The fairytale mode in which Mansfield's 'Green Tree' begins
appears to promise not some joyless child–parent power-struggle
but a magical escape from the whole field of familial discontent. Yet
as the narrative continues, its dimensions narrow to those of a moral
fable on familial discord and the follies of the solitary and obsessional
fin-de-siècle artist. Where Jack emerged victorious from his quest,
helping himself to the golden objects of the dream and then cutting
down both giant and beanstalk, Mansfield's Boy is killed trying to
reach the golden fruit. The subsequent felling of the tree serves as
a kind of re-enactment of this death – an underlining of the hero's
fate.

With her fragmentary novel 'Juliet' (1906–7), also begun while
she was at Queen's College, Mansfield reverts to the family chronicle mode. With the reversion goes an attendant loss of newly-
acquired perspective and control.

The heroine of the piece is a thinly fictionalised portrait of the
young author herself, moody and at odds with her family, and
caught in transition from girl- to womanhood – a condition which
fascinated Mansfield more or less throughout her writing career:

> Juliet was the odd man out of the family – the ugly duckling. She
> had lived in a world of her own, created her own people, read
> anything and everything which came to hand, was possessed
> with a violent temper, and completely lacked placidity. She was
> dominated by her moods which swept though her and in number
> were legion. She had been as yet, utterly idle at school . . . and all
> the pleading of her teachers could not induce her to learn that
> which did not appeal to her. She criticised everybody and every-
> thing with which she came into contact, and wrapped herself in
> a fierce white reserve.[13]

The subject of 'The Green Tree', rebellion against the family, has
been taken up and embedded in a realistic social context. In 'Juliet'
too the heroine defines her difference from her parents, not in terms
of their rejection of her but as an act of rejection on her own part.
And as in 'The Green Tree' rebellion has its inevitable final consequence. The early death of the heroine – presumably in childbirth – looks like either a punishment for waywardness or else the

inevitable consequence of an inability to negotiate the transition between child- and adulthood. However, death is here followed by symbolic rebirth, for the child born to the heroine's girlfriend and her former beloved is named for Juliet herself. Mansfield employs this ironic double-ending in something the same way she would later employ her technique of counterpointing discourse – in order to manage the gulf between social expectation and personal desire.

Often regarded as the first of Mansfield's mature pieces, 'The Tiredness of Rosabel' (1908) was written during its author's brief return stay in New Zealand after her time at Queen's College, when her dissatisfaction with the family appears to have been at its height and while she was pressing her father for permission to return to London. Though set in the metropolis, the tale conveys not a delighted anticipation of freedom but an apprehension of loneliness which so far as is known she nowhere openly expressed.

Like 'Juliet', 'Rosabel' attempts to render both the workings of a distinctively female consciousness and the distress of a heroine subject to the social pressures which bear upon the adolescent girl. Both also deal in alienation – not now from the family but in something approaching the term's classical Marxist sense, as it relates to the dehumanising aspects of a shopgirl's working life.

Where Juliet's remedy for her situation lay in death, Rosabel finds hers in dreaming. 'The Tiredness' focuses in particular upon how that dream is constructed – not according to the mysterious influx of the divine imagination but as the product of happenstance and of commercial manipulation. Its heroine Rosabel is – like Juliet – a descendant of all the Romantic heroines and heroes who came out from under Don Quixote's cape; compensating for the inadequacies of reality by attempting to remake the world in the image of their dreams. And just as Madame Bovary, a country doctor's wife who aspires to the Parisian high life, was a democratised version of Don Quixote so Rosabel herself is an updated, and popularised, Emma Bovary – an exploited and penniless shopworker who dreams of transformation into the privileged consumer.

The piece evokes Rosabel's lonely and unrewarding life by tracing both her actual journey, from the fashionable milliner's store where she works, to her digs, and her fantasy of a more glamorous existence through marriage to the rich and arrogant escort of a customer.

The whole tale is based on the conventional Romantic opposition between reality and dream. The gap between them is emphasised from the start. Rosabel, who is short of money, is faced with a choice between buying a bunch of violets or a square meal. Needing the meal she opts for the violets, then boards a bus for 'home'. Her journey exposes similar contrasts – the allure of the objects in which the heroine invests her dreams is set against the banality and sleaziness of everyday reality: 'Westbourne Grove look[ing] as she had always imagined Venice to look at night' (p. 514) is set against the 'black, greasy [pavement] mud' (p. 514) that has collected on her skirts; an excerpt from *Anna Lombard*, the cheap romance that her neighbour on the bus is reading, against the way she reads it – 'mouthing the words in a way that Rosabel detested, licking her first finger and thumb each time that she turned the page' (p. 513).

Once inside her room Rosabel kneels in front of the window. This gives, symbolically, not onto the outside world but into her own dream-consciousness. (It is partly for this reason that the dream-maid closes the curtains: you don't fantasise *within* the dream.) Our heroine then begins to daydream about her client's escort, the cavalier Harry. He falls for her, and after a rapturous courtship they are married – fantasy subsiding back into 'reality' at the moment of consummation.

Unsurprisingly, Rosabel's fantasies are built around the desired elements that her life lacks – sumptuous clothes, appetising food, luxurious surroundings, security, status and (most compelling of all) a highly desirable lover who desires *her*. The fantasy is also presented as a kind of universal feminine dream – one which combines a wish for luxury with a longing for homeliness; a hunger for romance with the need for affection.

Like her predecessors in the *Bildungsroman* tradition, Mansfield emphasises the secondhand nature of her heroine's imaginings; the way they are not her own but the product of others' fantasies. Unlike Cervantes or Flaubert, however, she is also concerned with the way these dreams are constructed. Here the key is the cheap romance another passenger is devouring:

> She glanced at the book which the girl read so earnestly. . . .
> She could not see very clearly; it was something about a hot,
> voluptuous night, a band playing, and a girl with lovely, white
> shoulders. (pp. 513–14)

The impressionable heroine reacts instantly to the passage: she feels 'almost stifled' (p. 514), and unfastens the two top buttons of her coat. Later the extract is built into her dream:

Rosabel knew that she was the most famous woman at the ball that night; men paid her homage, a foreign Prince desired to be presented to this English wonder. Yes, it was a voluptuous night, a band playing, and *her* lovely white shoulders.... (p. 518)

Besides indicating the derivative nature of the dream, the episode also hints at the extent to which its source, *Anna Lombard*, itself draws upon traditional feminine fantasies. Its author is successful in manipulating her readers because her material forms the stuff of popular fantasy which they have already imbibed. So Mansfield shows the way the dream is built up: at the same time she hints at the complexity of the mind-structure which builds it.

She also breaks new ground by applying her theme of the manipulation of fantasy to the modern urban world. References to an 'electric staircase' and to motorised transport, as well as the air of conspicuous display and purchase in the 'millinery establishment' where Rosabel works, place the story within the context of the 'dream-factory', the retailing industry which – like the writers of pot-boiler fiction – seeks to maximise its sales by titillating the fantasies of the prospective (female) consumer. The point is underlined when Rosabel, on her way home, finds herself drawn to – and no doubt subliminally influenced by – the advertisements in the bus. And by describing the jewellers' shops seen through the rain-spattered bus windows as 'fairy palaces' (p. 513) Mansfield further underlines the sense of bewitchment and the hope of social advancement to which the consumerist dream appeals.[14]

Offsetting these contemporary references are the story's subliminal allusions to the Cinderella story. These are numerous and witty. The fairy godmother's function is taken over by the romance that Rosabel reads from; the glass coach in which she is transported from 'reality' to 'dream' is a commuter bus; Cinderella's fabulous glass slipper becomes a black hat, an object of fashionable consumer purchase; and the upper-class miss who bears the hat away is an Ugly Sister – the ugliness a measure of Rosabel's envy. The folk habit of duplication which gave rise in the original tale to Cinderella's Ugly Sisters has here ceded to a more intricate and conscious psychological doubling: Rosabel has both a false double – Harry's girl-friend, to whose position and status she aspires, and a true – the girl on the bus, absorbed in her reading for precisely the reason that Rosabel is bewitched by the dream – neither of them has the remotest chance of having their fantasies translated into 'reality'. The true double is pointed up for us when Mansfield indicates that the second girl is 'very much [Rosabel's] own age'.

The Cinderella parallel also highlights the way the young Mansfield is still learning to manage a key danger of autobiographical writing – lack of objectivity – by displacing her early preoccupation with alienation from the family onto larger and less intimate structures. It is perhaps for this reason that both Rosabel's own fictional family and early experiences, and the vestigial (and of course lamentable) family of the Cinderella fairytale have been erased.

Rosabel's dream ends with an abrupt reversion to 'reality': she '[throws] out her arm to feel for something which was not there' (p. 518), and awakens . . . to the cold grey light of morning. Mansfield concludes by launching a bid for pity for her heroine. This she does somewhat clumsily – by adopting a stance she almost never used, and which is out of kilter with the story's aim of emotional identification with its heroine, that of the all-knowing, and morally authoritative, nineteenth-century narrator: 'because her [Rosabel's] heritage was that tragic optimism, which is all too often the only inheritance of youth, still half asleep, she smiled, with a little nervous tremor round her mouth' (p. 519).

Paradoxically perhaps, this may be the very point in the story where Mansfield comes to think more of her own situation than of her heroine's. The key phrase is certainly identical to one she applied elsewhere to herself – in a letter written more or less contemporaneously with 'The Tiredness of Rosabel', when she was back in New Zealand after the Queen's College years . . . but desperate to return to the metropolis: 'I cannot live with Father, and I must get back because I know I shall be successful – look at the splendid tragic optimism of Youth' (4 March 1908).[15]

Within a few months of writing 'The Tiredness of Rosabel' Mansfield had got her way with Harold Beauchamp, and set sail for the Old World; within a year of her return she had undergone a series of unhappy and deeply unsettling experiences. In as much as these form the 'matter' of her first collection of stories they also helped to precipitate her coming-of-age as a writer.

The events of the time, their chronology in particular, is not fully known: but it would appear that Mansfield became pregnant in late 1908 by Garnet Trowell, a son of her old cello-teacher from

Wellington. The family had moved to London to enable Garnet and his twin brother to continue their musical education, and Kathleen renewed her friendship with him there. The pair became engaged, but before long went their separate ways. Then in March 1909 Kathleen got married – not to Trowell but to George Bowden, a friend of only a few weeks' standing. She deserted him on the day of their wedding.

When rumours of these happenings reached the family back in New Zealand, Annie Beauchamp promptly set out for England, to sort out her wayward daughter. On arrival she escorted Kathleen to Bad Wörishofen, a spa-town in Bavaria, abandoning her there after only a few days. She then returned to England and caught the next boat home – all this within a fortnight of her original arrival in London. On reaching Wellington she made the Victorian gesture of cutting Kathleen out of her will. Mansfield's later story 'The Stranger', an imagined evocation of Mrs Beauchamp's wharfside re-union with her husband, celebrates without bitterness the mother's formidable character.

Kathleen herself stayed on in Bad Wörishofen for six months – though she moved within days of Mrs Beauchamp's departure from their expensive hotel to a cheap boarding-house. Journal entries made during the rest of her pregnancy reveal extreme loneliness, even desolation: 'Some day when I am asked [by the unborn child]: "Mother, where was I born?" and I answer: "In Bavaria, dear," I shall feel again, I think, this coldness – physical, mental – heart coldness, hand coldness, soul coldness.'[16] When her child miscarried shortly afterwards her wretchedness intensified. There was artistic compensation though – the boarding-house, the Pension Müller, was to provide her with both title and setting for her first collection of stories.

In a German Pension was published in 1911, though most of the pieces in it were written within six or seven months of Mansfield's return to England in January 1910 and had already appeared in A.R. Orage's magazine *New Age*. The collection enjoyed considerable acclaim when it first appeared, and the volume sold well – although until recently most Mansfield critics virtually ignored it, presumably because it does not conform to its author's signature of lyrical evocation. The placing of the volume at the back of the standard Constable edition of the collected stories (which has been in print continuously since 1945) also reflects the lack of esteem in which it was once held. In recent years, however, it has received substantial attention from feminist critics.[17]

All thirteen pieces in *In a German Pension* are set – though with
varying degrees of explicitness – in Germany. Six are told in the
third person, most of these offering semi-naturalistic accounts of
German family life. The remainder are satirical first-person sketches
of a group of German 'cure-guests' temporarily resident at the
pension of the title. These tales derive much of their vigour from
characterisation which is sharply-defined and highly simplified but
which does offer hints of a more complex underlying reality.

The cure-guests of the sketches appear at first to be little more
than modern-day personifications of vice: they display vulgarity,
snobbery, greed, aggression, hypocrisy, condescension, touchiness,
crude lustfulness, and sexist prejudice unrelieved by a single positive quality. The names of some of them – Herr Rat, Frau Oberregier-
ungsrat, the Vegetable Lady, and so on – offer a clue to the principles
of simplification and animosity that informed their creation. Antony
Alpers suggests in his *Life of Katherine Mansfield* that Mansfield took
as her inspiration for some of these sketches cartoons from the contemporary Bavarian magazine *Jugend*: 'All her Bavarian characters
are there – the Baron, the Modern Soul, the Advanced lady, young
women dressing by windows or smoking alone at café tables.'[18]
And certainly the satirical tone of these pieces as well as their taut
dialogue, the caption-like quality of some of their final lines, and
the forceful two-dimensional quality of their characterisation, invite
comparison with the topical cartoon.

Most of the sketches offer minor revelations regarding their
key characters. Yet these revelations simply expose beneath some
two-dimensional apearance an equally two-dimensional reality: the
reason for the Baron's mysterious unsociability turns out to be a
literally all-absorbing greed; the young woman fêted as sister to
a baroness is exposed as the daughter of her dressmaker; the so-
called 'Modern Soul' is revealed in spite of her claims to spiritual
purity to have thoroughly earthly desires.

In two of these cases, however, the texts also offer, through apparently throw-away asides, alternative constructions of character that
are both more complex and more problematic than those dictated
by the forcing logic of the plot. Both involve a humorous defla-
tion of the figures concerned. The Baron turns out to be a standard
'case' of insecurity: he eats obsessively, and neurotically avoids the
company of the other cure-guests: he hoards; he is nervous of pretty
well everything (up to and including lamp-posts); he humps his
luggage around with him in a little black bag for fear of servants

and the damp. And the 'Modern Soul' Sonia Godowska is a second-rate actress who cultivates 'sapphism', a modish nineties narcissism, and mother-love as props to her artistic genius:

> ... the modern soul and I found ourselves together under the stars.
> 'What a night!' she said. 'Do you know that poem of Sappho about her hands in the stars. ... I am curiously sapphic. And this is so remarkable – not only am I sapphic, I find in all the works of all the greatest writers, especially in their unedited letters, some touch, some sign of myself – some resemblance, some part of myself, like a thousand reflections of my own hands in a dark mirror.'
> 'But what a bother,' said I.
> 'I do not know what you mean by "bother"; is it rather the curse of my genius. ...' (p. 719)

> '. ... I love my mother as I love nobody else in the world – nobody and nothing! Do you think it is impossible to love one's tragedy? "Out of my great sorrows I make my little songs," that is Heine or myself.' (p. 720)

In both these examples the simple, two-dimensional construction of personality is the only one to be admitted to the sketches' official ideology: the second, more complex aspect is released only in apparently throw-away asides. It is by these means that Mansfield manages to hint at problematic aspects of the key characters' personalities and social relationships – while choosing not to engage fully with them.

The Narrator of the first-person sketches is also a cure-guest at the pension, and it is in fact she who offers the most striking example within the sketches of complex, and incompletely disclosed, identity.

This complexity of identity and its partial disclosure are crucially linked to the question of the Narrator's relationship with her author. Living on her own at a pension in a Bavarian spa-town she is in just the position Mansfield herself had been in during the months preceding the writing of the sketches. Furthermore there is ample testimony from Mansfield's acquaintances that the Narrator's demeanour, in particular her tartness of manner, was reciprocated in the author's own. And recent events in Mansfield's life – her pregnancy and miscarriage, the termination of her engagement with the presumed father of her child, her abandonment in Bavaria by Mrs Beauchamp – would more than account for the mood of bitterness, confrontationism and pained vulnerability that dominates the *German Pension* volume, and which is particularly sharply focused in the more autobiographical first-person sketches. They would also give a context to the volume's obsessive subliminal preoccupation with childbirth and with death, and to the hostile relations between the sexes that it depicts. Even Mansfield's pregnancy, the 'illness that is no illness', could be construed as the covert subject of one exchange between the Narrator and a fellow cure-guest. This takes place in the sketch entitled 'Frau Fischer':

> '. . . What complaint are you suffering from? You look exceed-ingly healthy!'
> I smiled and shrugged my shoulders.
> 'Ah, that is so strange about you English. You do not seem to enjoy discussing the functions of the body. . . .' (p. 699)

In the *Pension* sketches, then, we are dealing with a narrator whose persona is imperfectly dissociated from that of her creator – and who cannot therefore be regarded as a fully-formed fictional con-struct; a 'character' enjoying autonomous and self-contained exist-ence within the fiction. Instead, her nature has to be measured in terms of her relationship to her creator – and of the necessities and compulsions that governed her creation.

Like their narrator the sketches as a whole have a slight and unshaped, even at times an 'unfinished', quality which invites com-parison with reportage rather than with imaginative fiction as the term is normally understood.[19] The name of the boarding-house in which Mansfield stayed for three months, the Pension Müller, is for instance bestowed unchanged upon its fictional equivalent. So too are the names of several other places and individuals encountered by the author during her Bavarian period: the village of Schlingen, for instance, and the characters Frau and Herr Brechenmacher and Frau Fischer.[20]

The Mansfield/Narrator identification is supported by the ori-ginal version of the first-published of the Pension tales, 'Germans at Meat' (*New Age*, 3 March 1910). This contains clues to the Nar-rator's identity that were suppressed in the book-edition of the story: she herself is referred to as 'Kathleen', Mansfield's original given name, and when the Widow asks her whether she has any family she 'assured herself', we are told, 'that it was the heated atmosphere which was making her flush'.[21]

This identification between Mansfield and her Narrator is not, moreover, simply an extreme case of a writer drawing for copy upon herself and her own experiences. Ambiguities have been planted in the sketches, and relevant information withheld from them, so that problems or mysteries created within the texts can only be solved outside – by reference to the author's life.

In contrast moreover to her frankness about the cure-guests, the Narrator exercises very considerable discretion where her own background is concerned. We do not learn her name, for instance, nor anything about her appearance. We are also told almost nothing either about her past in general or about how she came to be staying in a foreign boarding-house, and on her own.

All this might at first glance seem to 'place' her simply as the anonymous mouthpiece-narrator of tradition. And certainly the tales, with their emphasis on dialogue and on sharply-observed visual detail, lay some claim to being objective records, purged of any reporting bias, of the doings and sayings of the cure-guests.

But here too appearance is countered by a sharply opposed 'reality': all the sketches are strongly marked by the Narrator's own jaundiced asides, her mordant wit, her animosity towards the German nation in general and the other cure-guests in particular. At bottom her apparent objectivity functions merely as a filter for the display of prejudice: indeed a profitable reading of her function in the tales would be as that of the observer–recorder whose apparent objectivity is an illusion – a warning, as it were, against the claims of the old nineteenth-century school of authoritative narration.

In the final instance, then, the Narrator herself is not so much anonymous as problematically evasive. In 'The Advanced Lady', for instance, she 'acknowledges' that she is English (p. 754) – which is indeed the logic of the thread of German–English antagonism that binds the sketches together. Elsewhere, however, she implicitly distances herself from the English. For instance, in 'The Modern Soul', when the Herr Professor asks, ' "Have you any swallows in England?" ', she replies, ' "I believe there are some at certain seasons. But doubtless they have not the same symbolical value for the English. In Germany –" ' (p. 714). And in 'The Luft Bad', when cross-questioned as to her nationality, she denies being American – but adds that she is 'hardly' an Englishwoman either. To which her companion retorts, ' "You must be one of the two; you cannot help it . . ." ' (p. 732).

The issue of the Narrator's nationality is not resolved within the sketch. But if it be accepted that her identity does have a dimension which derives directly from that of the author she serves to mask, then the import of the 'Luft Bad' conversation becomes clear. For the Narrator's 'concealed' nationality then emerges as that of a New Zealander; someone who because of the relative obscurity of her country, its distance from Europe, its cultural and geographical location between Britain and the United States, might well be regarded in the German view – at least as this view is perceived by a New Zealander – as 'having to be' either American or English. So the Vegetable Lady's ' "you cannot help it" ' reflects both Old World disregard for a small, 'new' country and a New Zealander's ruefulness at this disregard.

The Narrator's 'husband' is another case in point. A conversation from 'Germans at Meat' casts doubt, at the very least, on the intimacy of her relationship with him:

> 'What is your husband's favourite meat?' asked the Widow.
> 'I really do not know,' I answered.
> 'You really do not know? How long have you been married?'
> 'Three years.'
> 'But you cannot be in earnest! You would not have kept house as his wife for a week without knowing that fact.'
> 'I really never asked him; he is not at all particular about his food.' (p. 686)

The Widow may even be insinuating that she does not believe the Narrator has a husband at all: certainly she encourages doubt on the subject. And there is of course a still deeper element of subversiveness in her charge – that lack of a husband and shoddy housekeeping are offences of comparable magnitude.

In the final section of 'Frau Fischer' the Narrator responds to the prying enquiries of the title-character – another meddlesome widow – by inventing an identity for her husband that confers a socially acceptable explanation for his absence from her side: 'I said he was a sea-captain on a long and perilous voyage' (p. 702). But this, the only substantial piece of information she reveals anywhere about him, also turns out to be a fabrication: the piece ends with her referring pointedly to the husband as a 'virgin conception', and vowing

to 'send him down somewhere off Cape Horn' (p. 703). Her invention of this particular identity, and her swift and gleeful – if rather
tight-lipped – scuppering of it, inevitably cast further doubt on the
question of the husband's existence. One fiction elicits another.

The question of this husband's existence or non-existence is inevitably related to that of the Narrator's own identity. And she, having
created a persona for the husband, goes on to create, somewhat
sardonically, a (reciprocal) identity for herself.... Or rather, she
creates *two* identities – one corresponding to the romantic persona
with which she has endowed her 'husband', the other conforming
to Frau Fischer's conception of the role she ought to be playing for
him. This is itself an extrapolation from the Frau's own assumptions about what the husband must be like. The Frau herself duly
amplifies the portrait:

> This husband that I had created for the benefit of Frau Fischer
> became in her hands so substantial a figure that I could no longer
> see myself sitting on a rock with seaweed in my hair, await-
> ing that phantom ship for which all women love to suppose
> they hunger. Rather I saw myself pushing a perambulator up the
> gangway, and counting up the missing buttons on my husband's
> uniform jacket. (p. 703)

This cluster of invented identities provides an ironical affirmation
of Mansfield's views regarding the elusiveness of the self and the
extent to which it is socially constructed. It also contains a hint of
her belief (made more explicit later) that the role normally played
by the self in the construction of its own identity is a defensive one
whose aim is the protection and preservation of that self. The most
salient distinction between the persona which the *German Pension*
Narrator creates for herself and that set up by a later, more obviously
vulnerable character like Miss Brill is that the Narrator's has all the
appearance of being a self-conscious and sardonic fabulation – and
a spur-of-the-moment retort to Frau Fischer's intrusive probings –
whereas Miss Brill's is part of her own 'permanent' self-image; an
illusion crucial to her survival as a personality.

The uncovering of this little act of construction and invention
may tempt us to investigate how much more of the 'matter' of
the *Pension* sketches has to do with stratagems of concealment.
Certainly 'Frau Fischer', which begins with the Narrator focusing
on the title-character but ends with the Frau's curiosity becoming a

'device' with which to probe the Narrator's own vulnerabilities and uncertainties, suggests a double impulse – one towards both self-revelation and self-concealment.

The last section of the sketch begins with the title-character holing the Narrator up in her bedroom. Hostilities are opened with an admission that has more than a hint of menace in it: '"... When I meet new people I squeeze them dry like a sponge..."' (p. 702). Then, after cross-questioning the Narrator about her husband, the Frau takes it upon herself as an older woman and a widow – she insists upon her widowed status throughout the conversation – to articulate the loneliness that she 'knows' the younger woman must feel. This provokes the Narrator to retort that she 'like[s] empty beds' (p. 702).

After drawing attention to the 'duties' of a wife, Frau Fischer starts to excavate another of the Narrator's danger areas – that of babies and childlessness. The younger woman again closes the conversation down – this time through insult: '"But I consider childbearing the most ignominious of all professions"' (p. 703).

Frau Fischer herself is represented as thoroughly unsympathetic. But this merely makes her, in the perverse play that marks the rhetoric of the *Pension* sketches, an appropriate figure to attempt an intimate relationship with the Narrator. And it is indeed she, and she alone, who dares to offer what might in another context be taken to be sympathetic advice – advice which is here construed as tiresome interference, and rejected:

> Frau Fischer reached down and caught my hand.
> 'So young and yet to suffer so cruelly,' she murmured. 'There is nothing that sours a woman so terribly as to be left alone without a man....
> 'Handfuls of babies, that is what you are really in need of,' mused Frau Fischer. 'Then, as the father of a family he cannot leave you. Think of his delight and excitement when he saw you!'
> The plan seemed to me something of a risk.... (p. 703)

That section of 'Frau Fischer' which records the title-character's skirmish with the Narrator is framed by references to the Frau's habit of 'squeezing people dry'. The slightly leery sexual undertone of the metaphor makes it clear that, for the Narrator, Frau Fischer's overtures are not just an interference: they are an act of violation.

On another level, however – that at which the fiction engages
with biography – Frau Fischer plays the role not of snoop but
of catalyst (and of 'truth-teller') for the embattled Narrator–author.
Failing to provoke her adversary into frank speaking she goes on to
assert a series of possible truths which, so far as can be gathered,
Mansfield does not care (or dare), even within the fiction of the
sketches, to confront directly. It is no doubt for this reason that she
has the Narrator put Frau Fischer down so sharply. And by insist-
ing on the Frau's status as a widow Mansfield also draws attention
to the parallel between herself and the Narrator, whose own husband is either absent (as the Narrator claims) or else (as the reader
assumes) problematically non-existent. Here too the situation of the
author, whose own 'husband's' existence was doubly problematic,
looms behind that of her narrator.

In 'The Luft Bad' the Narrator emphasises, through what has
since been named the sexual politics of the gaze, her general sense
of alienation from her own sex. These feelings express themselves
in acute self-consciousness.

The sketch, which is set inside a women's sunbathing enclosure,
is one of several works in which Mansfield uses an all-female enclave to explore the subject of relations between women. It focuses
on the bathers' appearance and physical condition, clarifying some
of the implications of the other *Pension* pieces by making the body
a site of explicit unease.

Unusually, the Narrator is here the object of her own direct
attention. She begins by blaming her sunshade for the acute self-
consciousness she feels. But as the piece proceeds the reader is left
in little doubt that the real ground for her embarrassment is her
own (and perhaps her companions') near-nakedness:

> I think it must be the umbrellas which make us look ridiculous.
> When I was admitted into the enclosure for the first time,
> and saw my fellow-bathers walking about very nearly 'in their
> nakeds,' it struck me that the umbrellas gave a distinctly 'Little
> Black Sambo' touch.
> Ridiculous dignity in holding over yourself a green cotton thing
> with a red parroquet handle when you are dressed in nothing
> larger than a handkerchief. (p. 729)

Self-consciousness comes about when an individual internalises
another's appraising regard. There being no men in the women's

enclosure the gazes to which the Narrator of 'The Luft Bad' is exposed are those of her none-too-friendly (female) fellow 'air-bathers'.

The male principle does however figure in the sketch, on the level of symbol. It takes the form of trees which, lofty, majestic and disdainfully unselfconscious, appear to be gazing down into the women's quarter: 'A high wooden wall encompasses us all about; above it the pine trees look down a little superciliously, nudging each other in a way that is peculiarly trying to a debutante' (p. 730). But the precise significance of the trees cannot be assessed in isolation from a subsequent portrait of some 'merely' human males, to be heard indulging in vigorous – and sometimes destructive – activities in their own section next door:

> Over the wall, on the right side, is the men's section. We hear them chopping down trees and sawing through planks, dashing heavy weights to the ground, and singing part songs. Yes, they take it far more seriously. (p. 730)

This notion of an identity irrevocably split between disengaged observation and strenuous activity points, like other aspects of the sketches, to a conception of character based not on any graduated range of possibilities but on a narrow and confining dualism. It recalls an earlier reference to a couple of clubs lying around in the *luft bad* – 'one, presumably the lost property of Hercules of the German army, and the other to be used with safety in the cradle' (p. 729). The Vegetable Lady's chiding of the Narrator for presumed gluttony (' "You overeat yourself dreadfully . . . shamelessly! How can you expect the Flame of the Spirit to burn brightly under layers of superfluous flesh?" ' [p. 731]) highlights another aspect of this sterile dualism, that between Spirit and Flesh – even if in this context the realm of the spirit proves elusive.

The Narrator, then, is under pressure from the cure-guests' comments, as well as from their hostile regard. The final straw turns out to be some cross-questioning from the Vegetable Lady regarding the touchy subject of her nationality. She flees the little circle, and heads for a nearby swing. Rushing through the air on this swing she has an ecstatic experience which releases her briefly from her torturing self-consciousness. The action also bestows a sense of liberation and immateriality that involves a communion – rare in this volume, though not in Mansfield's later writings – with the natural world. Just as significant is a parallel transformation in the nature

of the pine trees – from supercilious overseers to harbingers of
ecstasy. Sanctified by this new Other the Narrator can now afford
to spurn the group that has rejected her:

> From the pine forest streamed a wild perfume, the branches
> swayed together, rhythmically, ponderously. I felt so light and
> free and happy – so childish! I wanted to poke my tongue out
> at the circle on the grass, who, drawing close together, were
> whispering menacingly. (p. 732)

Her moment of ecstasy is, however, swiftly undercut by an inner
voice warning her of the body's imperious demands: such excitement 'is very upsetting for the stomach' (p. 732). At this she retires
to the bath shelter for a hosing down.

While dressing she is told, 'there is a man who *lives* in the Luft
Bad next door. . . . He buries himself up to the armpits in mud and
refuses to believe in the Trinity' (p. 732). Here then is the ultimate
antithesis to the freedom and loftiness signified by the pine trees
– materialism both philosophical and literal; bound by the earth,
categorically rejecting the things of the spirit. (As an 'earthbound'
air-bather, this figure is also representative of the spirit of contradiction that pervades the sketches.)

The piece ends ironically, with the Narrator taking a leaf out of
his book:

> The umbrellas are the saving grace of the Luft Bad. Now, when
> I go, I take my husband's 'storm' gamp and sit in a corner, hiding
> behind it.
>   Not that I am in the least ashamed of my legs. (p. 732)

Where once she blamed the umbrellas for her self-consciousness
she now retreats behind her husband's.

If taken at face value the concluding remark is a fairly explicit
acknowledgement that the Narrator is no longer in any mood to
hide from the appraising regard of the other women. What she is
now retreating from is any repetition of the expansive experience
of a few moments ago.

'The Luft Bad', then, deals with the Narrator's self-consciousness
and her ambivalent relations with both men and women. Particularly
complex are her, and the sketch's, feelings towards men and the
male principle – desired yet shunned; excluded from the women's

sunbathing shelter yet reintroduced and confronted indirectly, on the level of symbol.

The elements of opposition and conflict observed in 'Frau Fischer' and 'The Luft Bad' are representative of personal relations in the *German Pension* sketches as a whole. The causes of these adversarial relationships are several, and shifting: sometimes they appear to be embedded in the human personality itself, and therefore to be antecedent to any particular ground for conflict. Generally, however, specific causes *are* attributed to the opposition and conflict the tales record. The most obvious, though not necessarily the most germane, are those which arise from national and cultural differences between the young woman and the other, German, cure-guests.

These guests are depicted, not as a random group of individuals but as representatives of the German national character seen through the xenophobic eyes of the Narrator. Their unattractiveness therefore becomes that of their race. References to unlovely traits traditionally deemed to be Teutonic pepper the sketches, and presumed German types – the gross materialist, the bogus philosopher–idealist – figure prominently, sometimes within the same character.

The differences in point of view between the Narrator and her fellows reach their sharpest in hints of the possibility of armed belligerence between 'their' two nations (the Narrator being assumed in this regard to be English): for the sketches reflect not only Mansfield's unhappy personal experiences in Bavaria but also the tense relations between England and Germany in the years preceding the outbreak of the Great War.

The Narrator's most persistent complaint against her fellow cure-guests concerns their ceaseless preoccupation with bodily processes – eating, evacuation, sex, childbirth; a preoccupation which seems at times to take on the status of a *credo*: in the tale named after her Frau Fischer demands of the Narrator, ' "How can we hope to understand anybody, knowing nothing of their stomachs?" ' (p. 699). Two at least of these preoccupations are also represented as characteristically German – although they could equally have been conceived as concerns quite natural to a group of semi-invalids . . . or for that matter to a pregnant woman.

In fact, however, the traits are rendered as a set of obsessions or gratuitous fixations which themselves approach the condition of a malady. It is even implied that they are the true 'illness' from which the Pension guests are suffering, for whatever the complaints which brought the most prominent of them to the Bavarian spa, these are kept very firmly off the page. (Minor characters, on the other hand, are frequently defined by their illnesses: 'There was a lady from the Spanish Court here in the summer; she had a liver.' [p. 688, etc.].)

The sketches focus obsessively on food. In particular, several contain mealtime scenes beset by references to food and drink: the four-page 'Germans at Meat', for instance, contains well over forty of them, and even its title – in which 'at Meat' displaces the more colloquial 'at Table', 'at Dinner', or 'at Mealtime' – helps to underline the presumed carnality of the German national character.

The cure-guests' obsession with food is represented as distasteful in itself. But consumption also serves as a figure for the more risqué – and, as presented here, even more distasteful – topic of rampant male sexuality.[22]

'Germans at Meat', which is made up almost wholly of dialogue, traces the progress of a mealtime conversation at the pension. The talk consists of a series of hostile 'engagements' between the Narrator and her fellow guests. Its structure, which appears casual, has in fact been carefully contrived. It falls into five sections or informal 'scenes', each beginning with the arrival on the table of a new dish, and concluding with an attempted putting-down of the foreigner. Furthermore each section revolves around an issue of conflict between the Narrator and the Germans – the eating habits of the English; the relative sizes of English and German families; German cultural life; Anglo-German military hostilities; and the Narrator's presumed inadequacy as a wife. Every 'scene' takes place to the accompaniment of hearty eating, and all contain figurative references to food. Again the discourse is double, and again it is on the figurative level that the Narrator, generally worsted in open conversational skirmish, gains her victories.

The sketch begins with Herr Rat boasting in practically the same breath of his exploitation of women, his self-sufficiency, and his feats of gluttony. But while he gives us only a brief direct insight into his sexual experiences and proclivities he goes into his appetite for food at length, and in detail:

'... As for me, I have had all I wanted from women without marriage.' He tucked his napkin into his collar and blew upon his soup as he spoke. 'Now at nine o'clock I make myself an English breakfast, but not much. Four slices of bread, two eggs, two slices of old ham, one plate of soup, two cups of tea – that is nothing to you.' (p. 683)

The Narrator, faced here with an implicit challenge regarding her own sexual appetite, protests that she can at least make good tea – something which neatly turns the subject from woman's sexuality to her role as carer . . . but the skill is mocked by Herr Rat as he swiftly forces the topic back to his own ground: ' "What do you warm the teapot for? Ha! ha! that's very good! One does not eat the teapot, I suppose?" ' (p. 684). The sex/eating equation is given a further, and even more grotesque, twist when the Widow, recounting an episode in which newborn children replace food on the supper-table,[23] flirts with the notion of metaphoric cannibalism:

I have had nine children . . . [but a] friend of mine had four at the same time. Her husband was so pleased he gave a supper-party and had them placed on the table. Of course she was very proud. (p. 685)

The sketch ends with the Narrator confessing she does not know her husband's favourite meat – an admission not merely of general lack of intimacy but, on the level of metaphor, of a total lack of 'carnal' knowledge of him. And just before this she had to parry a challenge regarding the presumed military weakness of England. (In 'Germans at Meat' she is for once identified unambiguously with the English: indeed, as we have seen, she was in its original version referred to as 'the Englishwoman'.) So the Germans manage to insert both the threat of aggression and an insinuation of rejection into the exchange, and its language – like that of the sketch's opening confrontation ('[Herr Rat] fixed his cold blue eyes on me with an expression which suggested a thousand premeditated invasions' [p. 684]) – doubles as the rhetoric of sexual posturing:

Said the Traveller: 'I suppose you are frightened of an invasion too, eh? Oh, that's good. I've been reading all about your English play in a newspaper. Did you see it?'
   'Yes.' I sat upright. 'I assure you we are not afraid.'
   'Well, then, you ought to be,' said the Herr Rat. 'You have got no army at all – a few little boys with their veins full of nicotine poisoning.'
   'Don't be afraid,' Herr Hoffmann said. 'We don't want England. If we did we would have had her long ago. We really do not want you.'
   'We certainly do not want Germany,' I said. (p. 686)

Food also serves as a figure for sex in 'The Modern Soul'. The 'Herr Professor', eating cherries with gusto, boasts to the Narrator about the robustness of his trombone-playing:

> 'There is nothing like cherries for producing free saliva after trombone playing, especially after Grieg's "Ich Liebe Dich". These sustained blasts on "liebe" make my throat as dry as a railway tunnel. . . .' (pp. 711–12)

And later, when she refuses to partake with him, he patronises what he takes to be her womanly modesty: ' "Psychologically I understood your refusal. It is your innate feminine delicacy in preferring etherealised sensations. . . ." ' (p. 712). His subsequent observations make it clear that the food–sex equation is a conscious one:

> '. . . All cherries contain worms. Once I made a very interesting experiment with a colleague of mine at the university. We bit into four pounds of the best cherries and did not find one specimen without a worm. But what would you? As I remarked to him afterwards – dear friend, it amounts to this: if one wishes to satisfy the desires of nature one must be strong enough to ignore the facts of nature. . . .' (p. 712)

The innuendo is later picked up and taken to further excess by the Narrator/Mansfield, who uses the Professor's own weapon by reducing his musical talents to the level of reflex sexual stimulation: 'The Professor appeared with his trombone, blew into it, held it up to one eye, tucked back his shirt cuffs and wallowed in the soul of Sonia Godowska' (p. 718).

As well as taking up a position of opposition towards the cure-guests the Narrator of the *Pension* sketches makes a point of distancing herself from every one of their fixations. She lets it be known that she is a vegetarian, and of small appetite; she claims a preference for 'empty beds'; she treats with scorn the merest hint of romance between any of the other guests, and is for her own part plainly unavailable; she declares herself lacking in 'those sparks of maternity which are supposed to glow in great numbers upon the altar of every respectable female heart' ('The Advanced Lady', p. 753); and, as we have already seen, she professes to consider childbearing 'the most ignominious of all the professions' ('Frau Fischer', p. 703).

She also pours scorn on what she regards as teutonic fertility –
the 'custom', much admired by her fellow guests, of having babies
by 'handfuls'. And when in the company of these other guests, she
intervenes both through acerbic commentary and telling silences to
suppress any dwelling upon the grosser of their revelations:

> 'I eat sauerkraut with great pleasure,' said the Traveller from
> North Germany, 'but now I have eaten so much of it that I cannot
> retain it. I am immediately forced to –'
> 'A beautiful day,' I cried, turning to Fraulein Stiegelauer, 'Did
> you get up early?'
>
> ('Germans at Meat', p. 684)

> '. . . But you never have large families in England now; I suppose
> you are too busy with your suffragetting. Now I have had nine
> children, and they are all alive, thank God. Fine, healthy babies
> – though after the first one was born I had to –'
> 'How *wonderful*!' I cried.
>
> (ibid., p. 685)

However, a consistent thread of emphasis in the sketches makes
it clear that the Narrator is deeply committed to the very subjects
which (she claims) revolt her. The edginess of her rejection of certain of them may itself be some indication of this. More positively,
it is implied several times that there may be common ground between her point of view (or that of the English) and the attitudes of
her fellow cure-guests (the German nation). In 'Germans at Meat',
for instance, the English as well as the Germans are implicated in
charges of gluttony and militaristic belligerence, and in 'The Modern Soul' Frau Godowska, by describing the English as '"Without
soul, without heart, without grace"' (pp. 714–15), and by quoting
her late husband's remark that '"England is merely an island of beef
flesh swimming in a warm gulf sea of gravy"' (p. 715), attributes to
the English nation defects which the Narrator/author herself assigns
to the Germans.

So the diametric opposition that the Narrator has painstakingly
set up between herself and the other, German, cure-guests is not sustained. Occasionally it breaks down quite openly – as for instance
when the Vegetable Lady accuses her (and others) of overeating
'shamelessly' ('The Luft Bad', p. 731). Furthermore she shows a
marked interest – masked of course by the usual hostility – in the

amours of the Germans; and in 'The Advanced Lady' she develops an antagonistic relationship with the title-heroine that itself has undertones of intimacy. (Indeed this heroine, a writer with a sense of mission who is acutely sensitive to the roles and destinies of women, and who also has a 'secret sorrow' and 'little time' for her husband, appears to be a satirical self-portrait of Mansfield herself. The same could well be claimed for the heroine of 'A Modern Soul'.) And the Narrator's stereotyping of the Germans has its precise counterpart in the way they regard her.

Nor is her posture of entrenched opposition to the cure-guests wholly consistent. Even if we discount the times she associates herself ironically with them – and in the context of the complex rhetoric of the *Pension* sketches these perhaps ought not to be entirely disregarded – there are also times when she seems no more than a reluctant ambassador for the English point of view. This is to say nothing of the occasions on which she appears to resent being 'branded' by the Germans as a foreigner. So what had at first appeared to be clearcut opposition collapses into a much more complex set of antipathies and allegiances.

This ambivalence, or uncertainty, is in fact the reflection of a more profound paradox – that the cure-guests do not serve merely as a focus of opposition for the Narrator: they are also a kind of repository, or dumping-ground, for rejected aspects of her own attitudes (or prejudices) and experiences, particularly those her controlling spirit the author appears to have engaged with but was either unwilling or unable to confront directly.

The author/Narrator, then, displaces her own negative feelings, including her sense of unbelonging, onto a group of characters who are objects to her of intense hostility – thus doubly distancing them from her own self. So the cure-guests' antipathetic Germanness comes to serve as a kind of screen for her own attitudes and recent experiences. And the antipathy with which these Germans are depicted – an apparent, perhaps actual, chauvinism which in the pre-War climate of 1911 almost certainly contributed to the volume's success – becomes some measure of the intensity with which she herself rejected these attitudes and experiences. The strategy also enabled Mansfield to engage with socially taboo subjects whilst distancing herself from them.

We are left then with an unsettling sense that the Narrator is to be identified with that rejected and detested Other from which she most sharply distinguishes herself – her fellow cure-guests. Or, to put it another way, that to which she is fundamentally opposed contributes in good measure to her own definition.

This definition covers the Narrator's brittleness and apparent emotional shallowness, her air of enigma, the fixed nature of her viewpoint, the mixture of aggressiveness and defensiveness which characterises her reactions, the way all attempts to approach her are construed as hostile advances.

So the construction of her personality is critically related to the confrontationism on which she seems always to be engaged. She thus provides an early but striking example of Mansfield's Romantic and Modernist belief that character is largely formed out of its relations with its environment – in this case a narrow, and limiting, world of entrenched confrontation.

In *In a German Pension* it is principally through this Narrator that Mansfield conveys her dualistic conception of the personality as both superficial and profound. Here this takes the form of an entity split between a combative and coruscating social surface and a neurotically obsessive private self: though it will be presented in the later, more ostensibly lyrical stories and in the *Journal* as the recording consciousness versus the sacred and mysterious soul.

The uneasy oscillation in the *Pension* sketches between revelation and concealment, detachment and engagement, is of course in part a consequence of the fact that the Narrator is made to bear the psychological 'load' of her author. This helps too to account for a further dichotomy – that between witty and malicious satirical energy and tight, almost relentless control. The energy and sparkle result from the impulse to expose; the trenchant brevity, the evasiveness, the firm grip – and the uncertainty of focus – to the determination to repress. The issue also relates to yet another problem in the reader's apprehension of these spiky and unsettling pieces – that their author may, despite a surface impression of relentless control, not be fully the mistress of her material; further that the significance of certain passages may be either not fully known or else not fully acknowledged by her.

The Narrator's ambivalent characterisation, her prejudice, and the wholly uncorroborated nature of the accounts she gives of herself, also invite a more general scepticism as to how much 'truth' they convey. That which originally presented itself as documentary reportage – something beyond the inevitable mendacity of fiction – turns out to be the site of absolute uncertainty. Mansfield the writer has the last laugh.

Unlike the first-person pieces, the third-person *German Pension* stories have the basic ingredients of autonomous fiction – plots of a certain intricacy, and characters of some depth. They are also without the sketches' signature of the author's direct personal experience – the pension and cure-guests, the documentary, 'slice-of-life' flavour, the embattled figure of the Narrator herself. Even the Germanness of the characters, intrinsic to the 'meaning' of the sketches, here becomes incidental – part simply of the particularity of fiction. And the stories project more sympathetic attitudes, and a greater range of emotional experience generally, than the sketches: though elements of irony remain the tight satirical grip of the Narrator no longer holds.

The most considerable of the stories – 'A Birthday', 'At Lehmann's', 'Frau Brechenmacher Attends a Wedding', and 'The Child-Who-Was-Tired' – cover the same subjects as the Narrator-sketches. Yet for the most part the stories' greater fictionality appears to have allowed Mansfield to deal with these issues centrally and explicitly, rather than in asides or on the level of the subtext. Nevertheless some areas of concealment do remain – areas which bear a coded relationship to Mansfield's own experience but which are nevertheless presented as the hang-ups of the characters themselves.

The *Pension* stories exhibit another point of difference from the first-person pieces in that they deal with the hardships the woman experiences within her traditional wife-and-mother role rather than her rejection of it. And where the sketches offered, somewhat tongue-in-cheek, an implicit challenge to the notion of the family as the social norm by presenting women in many other situations than that of married life – widowhood, a career, 'sapphism', mother-love (but not, interestingly, the despised state of spinsterhood) – the stories take the family as their ground of engagement. They deal in familial power-relations, in the perceived harshness of woman's destiny, and in the contradictory roles that are forced upon women within the family – sex object, nurturer, mother, domestic drudge. But they suggest no solution to these dilemmas: indeed events tend to exacerbate rather than ameliorate the women characters' fates.

'A Birthday' is the only one of the *German Pension* tales to inhabit almost throughout the consciousness of a male character. That character is Andreas Binzer, a businessman rendered with a Tolstoyan combination of authorial sympathy and self-incrimination. He is pampered, vain, and self-regarding; prejudiced and irritable; exacting in what he expects of others, and indulgent towards himself.

When the story opens he is awaiting the birth of his third child. But throughout his wife's labour he remains preoccupied with his longing for a 'son and heir' and with his own comfort and anxieties – though a reference to the breakwater he sees from his window hints at his subliminal preoccupations. Most tellingly, he turns on the bathroom taps in order to drown the sound of his wife's screaming. Yet the reader is not entirely alienated from him – partly perhaps because despite his apparent complacency there is some evidence that his is a personality under stress. In a touch which could have been bestowed on one of the Pension guests, for example, he is represented as the victim of a cleanliness complex. He objects vehemently to the maid spitting on his boots as she cleans them, to the stench of fennel and of refuse from the gully behind his home, to the slopping of water over the doorstep of the nearby public house. More substantially, he is also much less secure and more dependent on his wife than he initially appears.

Binzer is Mansfield's first concerted attempt to capture the psychology of the paterfamilias figure – officious, conceited, touchy, and outwardly domineering; yet inwardly timorous and dependent. Her father Harold Beauchamp (like Binzer a businessman of sound commercial instinct) was clearly the model: the nature of Binzer's relationship with his wife and all but one of the statistics regarding his parentage – three children within four years, the elder two of whom are girls – are further proof of the connection. Furthermore several aspects of the story's setting – the view over the harbour, the deep gully and iron suspension-bridge at the back of the house, the restless wind – identify it as Wellington, and the house as No. 11 (now 75) Tinakori Road, Mansfield's own birthplace and first home.[24]

Though Anna Binzer is in the end safely delivered of a son the unease generated for the reader by the hero's (or perhaps the Narrator's) own anxieties and sense of inner defeat seem to outlast Binzer's own. We remember his anguished thoughts of a few moments earlier, and the startling image of death with which the doctor conveys his views on the doubtful benefits of having nurses present at a birth: ' ". . . I'm not keen on nurses – too raw – raw as rumpsteak. They wrestle for a baby as though they were wrestling with Death for the body of Patroclus . . ." ' (p. 738).

The happy delivery of a son with which the story ends is also deeply compromised by its covert autobiographical connection: for the third child of Annie and Harold Beauchamp, born to them after precisely four years of marriage, was of course not a boy but a girl-child – Kathleen Beauchamp herself, and it is in a sense *her* birthday that the tale recounts. The real-life father's disappointment at the birth of yet another daughter,[25] no secret within the family, appears to have been superimposed upon Mansfield's grief for the loss of her own child; then transmuted in the fiction into joy at the arrival of a son. It is through celebration that Mansfield has here dramatised her own sense of alienation.

'At Lehmann's' also tells the story of a birth – this time to the wife of a café-proprietor. However, the main thread of the narrative is focused not upon the birth itself but upon the naïve young serving-girl Sabina and her initiation into sexual knowledge. Sabina is shown trapped between her desire for a child and her wish to become an object of sexual desire.

Through her the story examines the problems and contradictions of the young woman's situation. It also demonstrates considerable covert unease about the birth-process itself. Where the narrative freely admits the reader to the rooms on the ground floor it almost wholly excludes her from the bedroom. And events in the bedroom, though the object of fascination for almost all of the story's major characters, are concealed from the customers.

This division of the Lehmann establishment into 'public' and 'private' areas, and the separation of events into a (partially acknowledged) courtship and a labour that is hidden from all eyes, of course reflects the taboos that traditionally surround the process of childbirth. But the most significant function of this courtship/labour division is to symbolise the lack of relationship in the innocent Sabina's mind between childbirth and sex. Her innocence is highlighted at the end of the story, when the Frau's labour is juxtaposed with Sabina's seduction, bewilderment, and subsequent flight:

> He let go her hands, he placed his on her breasts, and the room seemed to swim round Sabina. Suddenly, from the room above, a frightful, tearing shriek.
> She wrenched herself away, tightened herself, drew herself up.
> 'Who did that – who made that noise?'
>
> .   .   .   .   .   .
>
> In the silence the thin wailing of a baby.
> 'Achk!' shrieked Sabina, rushing from the room. (p. 729)

As well as suggesting an emotionally painful conclusion to her first seduction, Sabina's shriek both echoes and confirms that of the Frau. The characters are in fact doubles: the Frau's lot is that of the girl, while Sabina offers a glimpse of a more youthful Frau. The ending also conveys the hopelessness of Sabina's position – the way in which she, trapped like Blake's mythic figure Thel by a destiny she cannot bear to confront, responds in the same way as Thel herself. In the realistic context of Mansfield's story this refusal must point, as Blake's perhaps does not, to future social or psychic alienation.

Much of 'At Lehmann's' is devoted to investigating how Sabina's destiny has come about, and how inevitable it really is. The girl is open to exploitation on many counts – her youth, her sex, her lowly employment, her good nature, her ignorance. However, it is her own desires – for sexual experience, and to mother a child – which finally seal her fate. The embedding of her emphatic rejection of the Frau's condition within the story's assertion of the dual nature of her desire emphasises the way she is trapped between the conflicting demands of social conditioning and her own instincts:

> She wanted to look at him [her seducer] again – there was a something about him, in his deep voice, even in the way his clothes fitted. From the room above she heard the heavy dragging sound of Frau Lehmann's footsteps, and again the old thoughts worried Sabina. If she herself should one day look like that – feel like that! Yet it would be very sweet to have a little baby to dress and jump up and down. (p. 724)

Here Mansfield is investigating the nature of Sabina's desire. She appears to regard it as deepseated, possibly innate (the Young Man's 'restless gaze wandering over her face and figure gave her a curious thrill deep in her body, half pleasure, half pain. . . .' [p. 724]), but also as the product of a strong, even forcing, process of acculturation. The key episodes are those in which Young Man shows Girl a soft-porn sketch of a naked woman and suggests that the picture resembles her, and a later incident in which the flattered Sabina reflects on how nice it would be to have a 'great big looking-glass' to admire herself in. The implication is that this narcissism may simply be an acculturated response to being the habitual object of the male gaze.

Sabina follows up her wish for a mirror by a further expression of horror at the idea of looking like the 'unappetising' (the word is Herr Lehmann's) Frau:

> 'I wish,' she whispered, smiling sleepily, 'there was a great big looking-glass in this room.'
> Lying down in the darkness, she hugged her little body.
> 'I wouldn't be the Frau for one hundred marks – not for a thousand marks. To look like that.' (p. 726)

Here Mansfield reveals how Sabina is torn not only between her own desires and the demands of patriarchal society but also between the conflicting roles that are visited upon her by that society – those of being both the shapely object of man's desire, and the swollen receptacle of his seed.

Unease about the processes of pregnancy and birth in 'At Lehmann's' is by no means restricted to the adolescent consciousness of the heroine. It can also be found in Hans the scullery boy's tale about his dirty fingernails having been stained from birth because of his mother's inky fingers, and the cook Anna's speculation as to how the Frau's swelling might have 'got into' her varicose veins (significantly perhaps, Anna herself has varicose veins as well); in the story's references to the Frau's confinement as her 'bad time', and the confinement-room as the 'ugly room'; and of course in the heroine's final inability to confront her 'destiny'.

Furthermore there are a couple of passages which contain hints – themselves tellingly obscure – about pregnancy and childbirth. The first serves to implicate Anna in the universal female 'fate' of pregnancy:

> Anna, the cook, had grown so fat during the summer that she adored her bed because she did not have to wear her corsets there, but could spread as much as she liked, roll about on the great mattress, calling upon Jesus and Holy Mary and Blessed Anthony himself that her life was not fit for a pig in a cellar. (pp. 721–2)

Sabina's apparently random association of birth and death – a connection she hitches to a reference to her deceased grandmother – also requires explanation:

> Birth – what was it? wondered Sabina. Death – such a simple thing. She had a little picture of her grandmother dressed in a

black silk frock, tired hands clasping the crucifix that dragged between her flattened breasts, mouth curiously tight, yet almost secretly smiling. But the grandmother had been born once – that was the important fact. (pp. 723–4)

Both in their subjects and in their less-than-complete articulation of them these passages are reminiscent of the first-person *Pension* sketches – no doubt because Mansfield would here, as she was there, have been writing out the deep-seated and conflicting feelings she must have had about the miscarriage of her own child.

But where in the first-person sketches the pathologising of childbirth appeared to be the product of the Narrator's obsessions, in 'At Lehmann's' it is presented as of general relevance – another result of the contradictions invested in woman by prevailing social attitudes.

'Frau Brechenmacher Attends a Wedding' also casts a younger and a more mature woman as doubles. Here the perspective is that of the mature character, the Frau of the title; who after attending a local wedding comes to reflect on her own 'difficult' bridal night and the life of drudgery that has succeeded it. The story shows women as the prey, and the plaything, of men. But it also reveals their own complicity in schooling the younger generation in this role.

The tale opens with the Frau getting ready to go to the wedding – or rather, with her getting her absent husband's party-clothes ready for him to wear. As she does so she grooms her nine-year-old daughter Rosa as a 'little mother':

After supper Frau Brechenmacher packed four of the five babies to bed, allowing Rosa to stay with her and help to polish the buttons of Herr Brechenmacher's uniform. Then she ran over his best shirt with a hot iron, polished his boots, and put a stitch or two into his black satin necktie. (p. 704)

In having Rosa accept her mother's offer of her black shawl to wear while she is out, Mansfield is indicating her readiness to take on the role of wife and mother – even if this 'mantle' and the status associated with it are presented merely as a consolation: 'After all, she reflected, if she had to go to bed at half-past eight she would keep the shawl on' (p. 704).

When Herr Brechenmacher eventually arrives home from work

(there are hints that he himself is under pressure, the victim of a more general system of exploitation), he is immediately showered with attention and respectful admiration by his wife and daughter. He repays the Frau by sending her to dress in the dark passage outside. This of course reflects her low status relative to his; but it also indicates the way in which the (male) gaze, so importunate in the case of Sabina, has no regard for the ageing woman: now she is no longer an object of desire Frau Brechenmacher must become invisible. No wonder she has (to judge by the medals on the brooch she is wearing) dedicated herself to the service of the Virgin.

The bride at the wedding, who clearly *is* still sexually desirable, and who was also until recently a rebel against social constraint (her illegitimate daughter, poignantly wearing a wreath of forget-me-nots, sits beside her at the feast), is subjected to ribaldry both by Herr Brechenmacher and by her own husband:

> Herr Brechenmacher alone remained standing – he held in his hands a big silver coffee-pot. Everybody laughed at his speech, except the Frau; everybody roared at his grimaces, and at the way he carried the coffee-pot to the bridal pair, as if it were a baby he was holding.
> She lifted the lid, peeped in, then shut it down with a little scream and sat biting her lips. The bridegroom wrenched the pot away from her and drew forth a baby's bottle and two little cradles holding china dolls. As he dandled these treasures before Theresa the hot room seemed to heave and sway with laughter. (p. 709)

The imagery of this passage is complex and highly ironical. The coffee-pot, for example, suggests both baby and mother, 'vessel' of that baby and source of its nourishment. The baby can also be equated with the contents of the coffee-pot – that which is to be devoured – just as the bride is herself ready to be offered up as a kind of sacrifice to her groom:

> At the head of the centre table sat the bride and bridegroom, she in a white dress trimmed with stripes and bows of coloured ribbon, giving her the appearance of an iced cake all ready to be cut and served in neat little pieces to the bridegroom beside her, who wore a suit of white clothes much too large for him and a white silk tie that rose half-way up his collar. (p. 706)

The implication is that both women and children are the prey of the 'devouring' male. However, the groom's conduct in 'Frau Brechenmacher' appears no less than the woman's to be the product of conditioning: his over-large wedding clothes, for instance, are a hint that he has not yet grown into his new, more self-important, role.

Frau Brechenmacher reacts to her husband's coffee-pot prank as if she herself were the target of it – as indeed in a sense she was:

> She stared round at the laughing faces, and suddenly they all seemed strange to her. She wanted to go home and never come out again. She imagined that all these people were laughing at her, more people than there were in the room even – all laughing at her because they were so much stronger than she was. (pp. 709–10)

This sense of alienation stems from her feeling of helplessness; the helplessness from the subservient role she has been assigned.

As Frau Brechenmacher and her husband return home, the Frau recalls their first night together. Despairingly she asks herself, ' "Na, what is it all for?" ' (p. 710). But her husband has a different purchase on the events of that night: he remembers only, and with considerable relish, the virginal reluctance of his bride.

The story concludes with a shot of the Frau, passive and vulnerable, in their bedroom on the night of the local wedding: 'She lay down on the bed and put her arm across her face like a child who expected to be hurt as Herr Brechenmacher lurched in' (p. 711). Such (it is implied) will be the fate of the rebellious bride.

Like 'The Tiredness of Rosabel', 'The Child-Who-Was-Tired' is a Cinderella story without a fairytale ending; another version of the tale of the deprived child who seeks consolation in fantasy. But where in 'Rosabel' the distinction in the heroine's mind between unlovely 'reality' and delicious fantasy is reasonably clear – even if details from 'reality' do intrude into the fantasy – here the confusion between them is radical, and disturbing. And where 'Rosabel' was more or less in the realist mode, 'The Child' combines stark naturalism with the simplicity and resonance of legend.

Its title-figure is a servant-girl who also takes care of her employer's four children. Her situation points up both the vulnerability of the child and woman's true position within the family – her lack of power, and the drudgery which is her lot.

The Child herself is perhaps the most deprived and put-upon of all Mansfield's heroines. Stripped of the formal status of wife and mother she becomes the ultimate victim – exploited by reason of her youth, her sex, her lowly birth, her illegitimacy, and her simple-mindedness. Though an outsider she is also at the bottom of the family heap – and at the symbolic centre of all its antagonisms as well: child vs adult, servant vs employer, child vs child, female vs male. The tale concludes when, weary, desperate, harassed beyond reason by the crying of the youngest child, she finally smothers him: the quintessential victim has finally claimed a victim of her own.

The ironies of the Child's position are reflected in the intricate pattern of 'doubling' in which she is implicated. Just before she smothers the crying baby she walks him in her arms, in an effort to comfort him. The candle-light throws up on the wall a shadow which distorts – and transforms – her identity:

> As she walked up and down she saw her great big shadow on the wall like a grown-up person with a grown-up baby. Whatever would it look like when she carried two babies so! (p. 751)

Both the shape of the shadow and the verb 'carried' are neatly ambivalent: the Child has become the symbolic bearer of her (the Frau's) next child.

Other details in the story identify the heroine, not with the mother but with the baby she is looking after. Most significantly, her smothering of the young child is presented as an act of desperation through which she extinguishes – or possibly releases – her own suffering self. The baby stands, then, both for the Child *and* for the Child's opposing Other. Such a device hints at the title-figure's complicity in her own fate. The hint is backed up by the implication that there is a connection between the killing and an episode from the Child's past in which her mother attempted to do away with her by squeezing her head into a wash-hand jug.

The murder proves to be an act of disturbing ambivalence in other ways as well. It is rendered as a deed of ultimate violation: her comparison of her struggling victim to ' "a duck with its head off, wriggling" ' (p. 752), captures the repulsive nature of the act as well as the revulsion of the aggressor for her victim. But it is an act of gentleness too; even one of mercy. And while it is the Child's sole deed of self-assertion, her one attempt to gain a measure of control over her own life, it is also a suicide bid. It contains overtones both of hope and of despair. It implies a longing for release – both on the Child's own account and on that of the baby – but it suggests too an impulse towards revenge. It is a single, swift and jubilant action in which the heroine manages to avenge herself on all the people (and categories of people) who have 'put upon' her – adults, employers, children, the mother who attempted to kill her, the whole male sex. (Much of the story's power rests incidentally on Mansfield's skilful handling of perspective – the way she claims our sympathy for the Child by adhering for the most part to her point of view, while at the same time invoking a passing impression of how she appears to the Frau – as a depraved idiot.)

The story also contains persistent references to the teeth which the baby – a boy-child – is cutting. It is in fact his eye-teeth which are emerging – something that popular legend associates with the gaining of worldly wisdom. Mansfield appears to be equating this particular event with a different aspect of maturation – entry into the domain of destructive male sexuality.[26] (As has already been observed, she repeatedly associates eating with the assertive and predatory aspects of male behaviour.) An indication of the malignity associated with the process is conveyed in the brother Hans's reference to the teeth as 'evil eye-teeth' (p. 747). The final 'act' of the story, then, is rendered both as the killing of a baby and – something which the image of the beheaded duck may imply – a symbolic castration.

At intervals throughout the story the Child retreats into an hallucinatory dreamworld whose main feature is 'a little white road with tall black trees on either side, a little road that led to nowhere, and where nobody walked at all' (p. 743 etc.). It may at first appear to represent some desired relief from the stress and turmoil of her daily life; but the starkness of its imagery, its association with isolation, and the fact that the journey is without issue, point to negation and oblivion rather than release. They also hint at the desperation of the situation which engendered such a fantasy; perhaps too at the doubtful value of fantasy itself. A less ambivalent focus for the Child's desire resides in a meadow with 'grass blowing like little green hairs' where she remembers having 'heard of a child who had once played for a whole day . . . with real sausages and beer for her dinner – and not a little bit of tiredness' (p. 749).

The story ends, not with the killing but with the heroine retreating once again into her dream:

> She heaved a long sigh, then fell back on to the floor, and was walking along a little white road with tall black trees on either

side, a little road that led to nowhere, and where nobody walked at all – nobody at all. (p. 752)

It is presumably the silencing of the baby – her other, suffering self – that finally allows the Child to enter into this fantasy-world.

Yet the story also *began* with the dream. And on that occasion the Child was aroused from sleep by the heavy hand of the Man on her shoulder. It is with an anticipatory sense of the return of this hand – now become the righteous hand of patriarchal justice – that we confront the story's conclusion. And so it comes about that the conclusion itself heightens rather than resolves the contradictions and stresses of the heroine's position.

There has been a good deal of scholarly discussion about the extent to which Mansfield based 'The Child-Who-Was-Tired' on Chekhov's short story 'Sleepyhead', and the justice of the charge of plagiarism that has in this respect been levelled against her.[27]

Mansfield's debt to Chekhov, both in the general outline of 'The Child' and on points of detail, is indeed considerable. Yet one of the most striking features of her story, the network of relationships that centre upon the heroine, is indebted not to Chekhov himself but to her own preoccupation with familial relationships and tensions. And her experience of miscarriage a short time earlier may well have helped to weave the web of negative feelings – guilt, loss, anger – which the story traces. It may also be relevant that the killing is at one and the same time starkly rendered – the heroine murders a child who stands symbolically both for her own child and for herself – and given its greatest possible mitigation: the Child is barely responsible for her actions. It is in this psychological investigation of the Child's situation that her author can lay claim to genuine originality.

'Bains turcs' (1913) was written a year or two after the publication of *In a German Pension*. Yet with its sharp-eyed Narrator, its obsessional material, its preoccupation with social alienation and with the presumed peccadilloes of German culture and character, it is in all but setting one of the *Pension* sketches.

The setting is in this case a women's Turkish bath – an exclusively female enclave even though one which, unlike its more traditional version, the harem, appears to have been freely chosen. It is also a domain, moist and warm, of sexual liberation – one in which women's fantasies, repressed in the countervailing culture outside the baths, are permitted to flower – in the same way as their bodies, concealed in the larger world, are here exposed. And by the same token it becomes a place of discovery in which certain 'truths' and prejudices, denied in the outside world, are exposed.

The sketch is woven around observations made by the Narrator on a visit to the baths. The first person she encounters, the (female) cashier, is a decadent figure and a sort of gatekeeper to this alien realm – and clearly someone to be reckoned with:

> Her black skirt swished across the scarlet and gold hall, and she stood among the artificial palms, her white neck and powdered face topped with masses of gleaming orange hair – like an over-ripe fungus bursting from a thick, black stem. (p. 590)

By contrast the (male) lift attendant is a parodic and thoroughly insignificant figure. He has a midget's stature, and the status of a transient; he is compared to a dead bird; he has a perpetual – and surely lubricious – sniffle; he adopts a submissive attitude towards the cashier and, where she flaunted herself through her clothes, conceals himself behind his:

> She rang and rang. 'A thousand pardons, Madame. It is disgrace-ful. A new attendant. He leaves this week.' With her fingers on the bell she peered into the cage as though she expected to see him, lying on the floor, like a dead bird. 'It is disgraceful.' There appeared from nowhere a tiny figure disguised in a peaked cap and dirty white cotton gloves. 'Here you are!' she scolded. 'Where have you been? What have you been doing?' For answer the fig-ure hid its face behind one of the white cotton gloves and sneezed twice. 'Ugh! Disgusting! Take Madame to the third storey!' The midget stepped aside, bowed, entered after me and clashed the gates to. We ascended, very slowly, to an accompaniment of sneezes and prolonged, half-whistling sniffs. I asked the top of the patent-leather cap: 'Have you a cold?' 'It is the air, Madame,' replied the creature, speaking through its nose with a restrained air of great relish, 'one is never dry here. Third floor – *if* you please,' sneezing over my ten-centime tip. (pp. 590–1)

In the 'deviant' realm of the Turkish bath it is the men who are the alienated ones: the attendant is the only male figure in the sketch, and his position as lift-keeper, his behaviour, and his attributes all suggest a preliminary ritual humiliation – and dismissal – of the male sex.

Gaining entry at last to the Warm Room the Narrator embarks on a free-association daydream which transports her, first to that popular location for fantasy the jungle: 'Yes, it might have been very fascinating to have married an explorer... and lived in a jungle, as long as he didn't shoot anything or take anything captive. I detest performing beasts' (p. 591). This demonstrates how within the relaxed and relatively unrestrained ambience of the baths she allows herself to acknowledge the attractions of male assertiveness... provided of course that it is safely confined. Next she turns to 'circuses at home' (p. 591) – in particular the ambivalent figure of the clown making himself up, and the suggestive one of a steam organ 'playing the "Honeysuckle and the Bee" much too fast... over and over' (p. 592). Finally she alludes to 'a game of follow-my-leader among the clothes hung out to dry' (p. 592) – a reference that may well be less innocent than it initially appears.

A new section of the sketch begins with the entry into the Warm Room of two tall blonde women – 'very stout, with gay, bold faces, and quantities of exquisite whipped fair hair' (p. 592). Laughingly they set about offering mandarin oranges to each other, apparently as a sexual overture. They then fall to criticising the unattractiveness of their fellow bathers. The lesson is that of 'The Luft Bad' – even in an 'alternative' domain, and even to other women, woman is still spectacle:

'But I cannot imagine... why women look so hideous in Turkish baths – like beef-steaks in chemises. Is it the women – or is it the air? Look at that one, for instance – the skinny one, reading a book and sweating at the moustache – and those two over in the corner, discussing whether or not they ought to tell their non-existent babies how babies come – and... Heavens! Look at this one coming in. Take the box, dear. Have all the mandarins.' (p. 592)

The newcomer, a 'short, stout little woman with flat, white feet, and a black mackintosh cap over her hair' (p. 592), does indeed cut an unprepossessing figure. A foil to the couple in attitudes as well as in appearance, she is presented as the guardian and exemplar of conventional views. She has a large family, upholds the virtues of 'kuche und kinde', makes much of personal modesty, subscribes wholeheartedly to the notion of male authority... and expresses intense contempt for the female couple. Furthermore she is German, and as the only identified German in the sketch (which seems to be set in France) attracts to herself some of the animus that was heaped in the *Pension* sketches proper upon the cure-guests. Her alienation is further underlined in the fact that, speaking only German, she cannot communicate readily with the 'natives'. Indeed the confrontation between her and the presumed Frenchwomen has the makings of a nationalist allegory, with German stolidity set against French decadence.

Mackintosh Cap is also the target of the Narrator's own considerable, and frankly-expressed, distaste: in the alternative – and alienated – world of the Turkish bath those who uphold the 'normative' institution and values of the family readily become a target for ridicule.

So strong in fact is the animus towards her that the straightforward expression of grief over a stillborn child (something not found in any of the other *Pension* pieces) is assigned to her. Mansfield seems to have considered her uncongenial persona and the satirical context in which she is placed sufficient in themselves to distance her from the dangerous arena of feeling:

> '. . . Four children I have living, and it was really to get over the shock of the fifth that we came here. The fifth,' she whispered, padding after me, 'was born, a fine healthy child, and it never breathed! Well, after nine months, a woman can't help being disappointed, can she?' (p. 594)

The sketch ends with an image that states more or less explicitly what has already been implied – that Mackintosh Cap's obsessive preoccupation with the couple, and the strength of her hostility towards them, arise from frustrated longing: 'as the two walked out of the ante-room, Mackintosh Cap stared after them, her sallow face all mouth and eyes, like the face of a hungry child before a forbidden table' (p. 595).

More problematic is the Narrator's own attitude towards the couple. She is clearly alive to their attractiveness; she endorses their distaste for the other women; and she is forceful in contrasting them favourably with Mackintosh Cap:

> I could not get out of my mind the ugly, wretched figure of the little German with a good husband and four children, railing

against the two fresh beauties who had never peeled potatoes nor chosen the right meat. (p. 595)

Yet her own tentatively expressed feelings of allegiance towards the couple are disturbed by a subliminal hostility that finds expression in something which approaches burlesque. Her attitudes throughout the story are typically complex: she is single-minded only about her detestation of the conventional, and conventionally prejudiced, figure of Mackintosh Cap. Her own desires, though always at issue within the text, are not brought fully to its surface. She remains therefore doubly alienated – both from the 'orthodox' world outside and from the 'deviant' one within.

So Mansfield's Turkish bath turns out to be an alternative, female realm – perhaps even a lesbian enclave; moreover, one in which the repressed (female) libido can allow its fantasies free rein. It is of course both separate from, and critically opposed to, a supposedly normal world outside.

Like Mansfield's other representations of alienation the bath is shot through with contradiction. It offers, even to some extent aligns itself with, the prejudice that attaches to such arenas: but it also suggests the liberating possibilities of separatism. Most notably, its perspective is one from which the normative world is to be assessed . . . and, if necessary, judged. It represents too a kind of spatial extension of the *Pension* Narrator's stance of oppositionality – and one which shows a shaft of self-knowledge that is absent from the *Pension* sketches proper.

In 'How Pearl Button Was Kidnapped' (1911) Mansfield again treats directly the subject of a child's alienation from her family. But she also to some degree at least, does what she had already done in the *Pension* tales – displace this sense of alienation onto a larger and less intimate entity. In 'Pearl Button' the larger entity is that of the Maori community, itself opposed to – and alienated from – New Zealand's dominant white culture. In a Romantic and Lawrentian contrast the emotional warmth and colour of the Maoris' lives are set against the dull and regimented existence of those who belong to established society.

'How Pearl Button Was Kidnapped' is on one level a child's fantasy of adventure; of escape from the safety – and dullness – of a suburban childhood. It is also a simple lament for a day at the seaside that ended too soon. Yet at the same time it too reaches back to fairytale, and to the fairytale hero's attempts to gain independence in the face of his parents' will.

Pearl, the heroine of Mansfield's story, is abducted from her own garden by a couple of semi-itinerant women – clearly Maoris although the tale, recounted from the perspective of the racially and culturally innocent Pearl, does not disclose this directly. The women take her to meet their own extended family, then on a trip to the seaside. There Pearl encounters and grows to love the unfamiliar – though at first sight threatening – element of the sea. While at the seaside she is discovered and 'rescued', screaming in protest, by a posse of police. Her estrangement resides – it turns out – not in the kidnapping but in her relations with her own family: she feels instantly 'at home' with her abductors, alienated only when compelled to return to her parents.

Pearl's abductors offer her both emotional security and freedom. Used to a narrowly regimented existence she asks them in disbelief, '"Haven't you got any Houses of Boxes?". . . . "Don't you all live in a row? Don't the men go to offices? Aren't there any nasty things?"' (p. 522). The deep contentment she experiences on being caressed, and the nature-imagery which accompanies the description, suggest reversion to some original, ideal state. The effect is intensified by the implication here, though not elsewhere in the story, that Pearl is a very young child. The experience is powerfully evoked – and reiterated for good measure:

> One of the women . . . caught Pearl Button up in her arms, and walked with Pearl Button's head against her shoulder and her dusty little legs dangling. She was softer than a bed and she had a nice smell – a smell that made you bury your head and breathe and breathe it. . . . (p. 520)

> Birds were singing. She nestled closer in the big lap. The woman was as warm as a cat, and she moved up and down when she breathed, just like purring. Pearl played with a green ornament round her neck, and the woman took the little hand and kissed each of her fingers and then turned it over and kissed the dimples. Pearl had never been happy like this before. (pp. 521–2)

Mansfield's own early sense of exile from her mother's and grandmother's laps comes to mind.

In 'Pearl Button' the Maori women form a telling contrast to Pearl's own mother, who is preoccupied with household chores – 'In-the-kitching, ironing-because-its-Tuesday' (p. 520) – when her daughter is snatched. The child's surname, and her carefully schooled behaviour, also help to conjure up a life of dull, restrictive and alienating domesticity.

The 'green ornament' which one of the women is wearing is without doubt a greenstone *tiki*, regarded by the Maori people as a fertility charm. This supports the notion that Pearl has found in the woman a primal mother-figure. The sea also appears to have a signification similar to that of the abductors themselves and their lifestyle – that of an 'unknown element' which becomes a focus of desire. Appropriately, it is the women who teach her to love and to enter into this new element. It is also appropriate that the sea should be opposed in its evanescent colour to those truly threatening agents of undissolving blue – the police who come to take Pearl back to her 'old' family.

As has already been suggested, Pearl's surname alludes to her family's 'buttoned-up' lifestyle. But her first name is also symbolic, drawing attention to the whiteness of her skin but also to the supreme value that is invested in this whiteness not only by her parents but also by the Maoris themselves. So the story by implication deals not only with Pearl's alienation from her family but with the social position of her Maori abductors, set apart from the larger, and privileged, white culture represented by Pearl's own family. (However, Pearl's name also suggests her own childish innocence of racial attitudes – an innocence which facilitates her rejection of her own family and its bourgeois [and Beauchamp] values in favour of those of the Maoris.)

Here the heroine's allegiance is undivided; bestowed upon other alienated figures who themselves give her a sense of belonging. It is not until later that Mansfield's sense of alienation and her deepest desires come, poignantly and through a deeper use of mythic structures and resonant symbolism than she has so far attained, to be invested in a single source.

Two or three years after she finally made her return journey to London, Mansfield submitted one of her 'fairy tales' to *Rhythm*, a highly professional arts magazine which had just started up in the capital. Its editor, feeling that the story was not in keeping with the house slogan 'Before art can be human again it must learn to be brutal', rejected the tale but invited the author to submit something else.

Mansfield's new offering was 'The Woman at the Store' (1911), a colonial tale set in the New Zealand outback; one which gives her complex attitude towards alienation a precise geographic and historical context. This time *Rhythm*'s editor, John Middleton Murry, was delighted. He published it in the spring of 1912, following it with two other Mansfield tales in the same manner – 'Ole Underwood' (written 1912, published January 1913), and 'Millie' (written 1913, published in *Rhythm*'s successor *Blue Review*, in June 1913).

Though they too are set in New Zealand, Mansfield's three early colonial tales have at first sight little in common with the later, and better-known, 'family' stories. The mature pieces are located in a settled and prosperous suburban bourgeois world that aspired to a partly imagined, partly recollected vision of metropolitan existence, and they reflect the social confidence and material prosperity of their milieu; the tales, two of which are set in the outback, focus on the isolation, the austerity, and the rootlessness of life in a new colony. They do however share the suburban stories' preoccupation with familial tensions.

All three colonial tales make gestures in the direction of popular, action-based fiction: each deals with the consequences of a murder already committed, then moves towards a further killing. Each also makes use of its adventure and mystery elements in order to project a deeper preoccupation with the consequences of family discord and distress.

The tales deal primarily with how behaviour, and in particular gender characteristics, are affected by life in the tough and alienating world of the colonies – how this world 'masculinises' women and leads men to deny the 'feminine', or affectionate and nurturing, aspects of their personalities. All three also treat violence between the sexes; a violence which appears to be largely a result of the psychological instability caused by this denaturing process.

'The Woman at the Store' was inspired by a camping trip its author made with friends to the volcanic wilderness in the centre of New Zealand's North Island. The journey took place in 1907, a few months before her final departure for England. The story follows three horseback riders Jo, Hin, and the unnamed Narrator on a journey across the pumice plains. They put up for the night at an isolated store owned by a friend of one of the travellers, and run in his absence by his wife. It later emerges that she and her daughter have been deserted by him.

Jo makes up to the storewoman, and the two of them spend the night together. Next morning he remains behind while Hin and the Narrator ride off, carrying away with them the disturbing memory of a picture that the Woman's daughter has drawn for them. This shows the Woman shooting a man then digging a hole for his body.

The tale opens with a description of the barren country through which the three companions are riding:

> All that day the heat was terrible. The wind blew close to the ground; it rooted among the tussock grass, slithered along the road, so that the white pumice dust swirled in our faces, settled and sifted over us and was like a dry-skin itching for growth on our bodies. The horses stumbled along, coughing and chuffing. The pack-horse was sick – with a big open sore rubbed under the belly. Now and again she stopped short, threw back her head, looked at us as though she were going to cry, and whin-nied. Hundreds of larks shrilled; the sky was slate colour, and the sound of the larks reminded me of slate pencils scraping over its surface. There was nothing to be seen but wave after wave of tussock grass, patched with purple orchids and manuka bushes covered with thick spider webs. (p. 550)

This opening swiftly dismantles any old-world Romantic illu-sions the reader may cherish about the benignity of the natural setting. Mansfield's larks in particular are counter in every respect to the single, tuneful, transfigured (and transfiguring) lark of Eng-lish Romantic poetry.[28] But the dismantling of Romantic illusion does not end there. The vulgarity of some of the Child's drawings, and the 'mad excitement' (p. 559) she displays when showing them off, suggest a related undermining of traditional notions regarding the sacredness of art and the innocence of the child: it appears that no aspect of the consoling old-world Romantic vision can be sustained in the alienating environment of the new colony.

Later in the tale, the inhospitable character of the landscape is personified in a reference to the 'savage spirit of the country [which] walked abroad and sneered at what it saw' (p. 554). It is clearly this 'savage spirit' which has ruled the life of the Woman; driven her to murder her husband; brought about her four miscarriages – and, when she finally manages a live birth, given her a 'mean, under-sized brat, with whitish hair and weak eyes' (p. 556) whom she is at first unable to nurse. In her physical difference and moral per-versity, as well as the difficulty of her entrance into the world, the Child becomes a signifier for the unnaturalness of the settlers' very presence in the colony.

The point is underlined in the way the albino nature of the Child makes specific – and ironic – reference back to the layer of pumice dust which coats the travellers. This is itself compared to a clown's makeup: 'Hin rode beside me, white as a clown' (p. 551). So the new settler's white skin is envisaged in the tale, not as a mark of inherent racial superiority but as buffoon's mask or pathological state; a source in the short term of discomfort, ridicule, or melan-choly, and a condition which renders visible the malign influence of an alien land upon its settlers.

It is hardly surprising that within the colonial world of this tale the norms of the travellers are masculine (not to say macho) ones. These are established at the outset, through Jo's and Hin's 'man's talk' and their sexist attitudes.

Appearing as she originally does in a masculine context, and apparently colluding in her companions' male camaraderie, the Narrator will almost certainly be assumed by the reader to be a man. However, hints are planted – in the careful eye with which she notes the characters' apparel, and in the implication of 'femin-ine' weakness in an episode in which she daydreams and nearly falls off her horse – that this may not be the case. There is another hint in the matter of the dream itself:

> I half fell asleep and had a sort of uneasy dream that the horses were not moving forward at all – then that I was on a rocking-horse, and my old mother was scolding me for raising such a fearful dust from the drawing-room carpet. 'You've entirely worn off the pattern of the carpet,' I heard her saying, and she gave the reins a tug. (p. 551)

The dream is clearly regressive, and appears to contain a warn-ing against sexual fantasising. This is picked up in a detail from the main story about how one of the travellers' horses had rubbed herself raw, and so needed embrocation. The warning in the dream is delivered to a youthful Narrator by her mother. In the main story the swaggering little ditty which (we are told) Jo had been singing earlier, and which he resumes as soon as he catches sight of the Woman at the Store, appears to award a similar role to the mother-figure – one of attempting to curb her daughter's sexuality:

> 'I don't care, for don't you see,
> My wife's mother was in front of me!'
> (p. 551)

Nonetheless firm evidence of the Narrator's sex is withheld until over halfway through the tale. The disclosure is eventually made by the Child when, twitted by Hin, she promises vengeance with a threat to 'expose' the sex of his companion, whom she has seen bathing naked in the creek:

> '. . . I'll draw all of you when you're gone, and your horses and the tent, and that one' – she pointed to me – 'with no clothes on in the creek. I looked at her where she couldn't see me from.' (p. 557)[29]

The story, then, sets out to build up and then subvert the reader's expectations with regard to the sex of the Narrator: just as earlier it undermined old-world belief in the superiority of the colonialist by playing with the notion of whiteness as either mask or disease, it now destabilises our certainties with regard to the perception of sexual identity, this time in order to emphasise how in a macho colonial context the feminine makes itself over, or is subsumed into, the masculine. Hints of the author's strategy are also contained in the characters' names: 'Jo' is written thus, as if it were a woman's name; 'Hin', though puzzling,[30] may simply be an idiosyncratically shortened version of the Maori girl's name Hinemoa.

The interrogation of gender in 'The Woman at the Store' is undertaken largely in relation to its title-figure. She is presented less as a character than as a construct – or presumed construct – of a series of macho fantasies. The men in the tale see her, not as the grimly self-reliant and vengeful figure she has become but in terms of two classic stereotypes of the feminine – the dollybird (she was once 'Pretty as a wax doll' [p. 556], conforming precisely to the settler culture's blonde-and-blue-eyed ideal of feminine beauty) and the provider. When Jo asks, '"What's the old bitch got in the store?"' (p. 555), he shows how when sex is regarded as a commodity the two roles become one: the Woman is as open to appropriation as

her goods; her body itself, a store. It is through the Woman that
Mansfield draws together male attitudes towards the female and
towards the land of the new colony: both are sites of appropriation
in a land of scarcity. (The store figures frequently in settler writing
as an indicator of the need to hoard known, valued, and scarce
commodities.) The Woman, described by the Narrator as 'sticks and
wire', illustrates too the way women tend to be manipulated by
others (that is, men). Her missing front teeth also suggest depriva-
tion or domestic violence; her 'red, pulpy hands', domestic servitude.

As the Child's second sketch reveals, the Woman at the Store has
in fact already repudiated her 'feminine' identity – by murdering
her husband as an act of vengeance against him for his desertion
of her. The story implies that a similar fate awaits Jo, and for similar reasons. And his red-spotted kerchief – which looks as if it has
already been spattered with blood – marks him too out as a possible
future victim. So the story indicates how mistaken conventional
stereotypes regarding the nature and capacities of woman can be
. . . and the dangers of adhering to them.

The Woman, then, has herself been made over into a kind of
personification of the sinister, alien Other – the 'savage spirit of
the country':

There is no twilight in our New Zealand days, but a curious
half-hour when everything appears grotesque – it frightens – as
though the savage spirit of the country walked abroad and sneered
at what it saw. (p. 554)

In appropriating the power of the man however – something indicated in the readiness with which she takes up the gun – the Woman
does not take on his status: her role simply changes from that of
passive Object to alien and inhuman Other.

For the male settler, part of the Woman's symbolic usefulness
resides in the fact that she allows him to distance himself from his
own feelings of alienation towards his adopted country, by permit-
ting its harsh and threatening aspects to become the distinguishing
characteristics of that portion of his own race already designated as
Other.[31] At the same time the tale implies that the settler woman
only performs 'her' role by becoming the bearer of a new otherliness
– the brutality of the macho pioneering male himself.

'The Woman at the Store', with its emphasis on the construction
of (inauthentic) gender and racial identity, also questions its own

authenticity. The landscape of the story appears only to come into existence as the travellers ride into it; a melodramatic, jokey, and slightly unreal tone is sustained throughout; and in the end the store vanishes as Hin and the Narrator depart leaving Jo to the Woman, and hence to his presumed fate: 'A bend in the road, and the whole place disappeared' (p. 562). Finally the store, the Woman, the whole tale may, it is implied, be simply an illusion; a fiction; a series of constructions, just as the killer woman herself may also be a construction of the (male) imagination.

'Ole Underwood' is Mansfield's most striking testimony to her belief in the power of the sub-rational aspect of the psyche. Like 'The Woman at the Store' it investigates how the female principle comes to be denied in the tough world of a new colony – this time through the observation, not of a 'de-gendered' woman but of a would-be macho man.

From the outset Ole Underwood is presented as a parody of the pioneer – rootless, piratical, at odds with all he meets:

> Down the windy hill stalked Ole Underwood. He carried a black umbrella in one hand, in the other a red and white spotted handkerchief knotted into a lump. He wore a black peaked cap like a pilot; gold rings gleamed in his ears and his little eyes snapped like two sparks. Like two sparks glowed in the smoulder of his bearded face. (p. 562)

Shortly afterwards we see him contending, Lear-like, with the wind:

> 'Ah-k!' shouted Ole Underwood, shaking his umbrella at the wind bearing down on him, beating him, half strangling him with his black cape. 'Ah-k!' shouted the wind a hundred times as loud, and filled his mouth and nostrils with dust. (p. 562)

This wind in part renders his own tormented and tormenting state of mind, and the extent to which he is at odds with himself: at the same time its superior force and the universality of its effects (it works upon the pine forest, the manuka bushes, the sea and the sky, as well as on the protagonist himself) suggest his powerlessness – and offer a hint that he is doomed. Most importantly, however, his relationship with the wind – which, like that he establishes with the characters he encounters later on – is one of resistance and conflict, something that again epitomises the colonist's uneasy relationship with his adopted country.

With his outward swagger and inner insecurities, his violence and vengeful puritanism, Underwood offers an unflattering portrait of the pioneer – one which makes no concession at all to the glamorous remittance-man of received white New Zealand history. Indeed his descent as the tale progresses, from jaunty self-confidence through increasing furtiveness into irrationality and violence, itself represents a kind of deconstruction of the myth of the great colonial enterprise.

Underwood's tale is set, not in the outback where he seems to belong, but in New Zealand's capital Wellington – recognisable for its maddening wind, a harbour which laps at the edge of the town, its prison on the hill. The narrative traces the hero's progress down one of Wellington's 'windy hills' opposite the prison, across town, and onto a ship berthed at the wharf. This swift journey is at the same time one into his past – he was a sailor, he killed his woman for sleeping with another man, and he did time in prison for it. But it is also a journey towards his future: the narrative breaks off as he comes upon a sailor sleeping on what he in his crazed condition imagines to be 'his' bunk, with 'his' woman's picture above it smiling down at him. And there is an important sense too in which this future is also his past – a mental re-run of his beliefs regarding 'his' woman's affair. The story also traces Underwood's journey into the depths of his being, and in this respect it becomes one of increasing madness.

The hammerblow of Underwood's heartbeat becomes the dominant image of the story – a reminder of the hard labour he no doubt served in gaol as well as of his hardness of heart:

> Something inside Ole Underwood's breast beat like a hammer. . . . One, two – one, two – like someone beating on an iron in a prison, someone in a secret place – bang – bang – bang – trying to get free. Do what he would, fumble at his coat, throw his arms about, spit, swear, he couldn't stop the noise. Stop! Stop! Stop! Stop! Ole Underwood began to shuffle and run. (pp. 562–3)

The metaphor also suggests a desperate unconscious struggle to liberate himself from his own past – and from himself.

The use of such an image of course involves a transformation in the traditional significance of the heart as the seat of romantic love to an association of it with the destructive passions. It also underlines the fact that Underwood's behaviour involves both the coldly mechanical and the instinctual, the visceral, the destructive – the terrible extremes of possibility which are left when the affective impulse, and any inclination towards co-operative behaviour, have been eliminated. Mansfield wrote other stories centring upon the weakness of the heart ('The Stranger', 'A Weak Heart', etc.): here she focuses on its murderous hardness.

As the story continues, and as his fit of madness increases, Ole Underwood becomes increasingly aggressive; increasingly the violator of those he meets. At the same time he becomes more contemptible – even something of a victim-figure reviled by his adversaries. Only a group of Chinese, themselves members in New Zealand of a minority settler group and in this respect even more 'alien' than Underwood himself, regard him with an impartial gaze; without either fear or contempt.

All Ole Underwood's adversaries are female. Having tormented a clutch of hens he is himself accosted by an old woman. Later he comes on a little girl who is hanging out the washing:

> When she saw Ole Underwood she let the clothes-prop fall and rushed screaming to the door, beating it screaming 'Mumma – Mumma!' That started the hammer in Ole Underwood's heart. Mum-ma – Mum-ma! He saw an old face with a trembling chin and grey hair nodding out of the window as they dragged him past. Mumma – Mum-ma! He looked up at the big red prison perched on the hill and he pulled a face as if he wanted to cry. (p. 563)

The increasingly demented hero appears to take the owner of the 'old face' for his own mother – once perhaps a source of comfort (for the anguish of the girl's cry has become his own) but now, as witness to his disgrace, a projection of some vestigial sense of guilt.

Underwood's next moment of madness takes place in a pub. It appears to have several triggers – the sexiness of the bar-girl (described, tellingly, only in relation to the other men: 'She kept on laughing. Ha! Ha! That was what the men liked to see, for she threw back her head and her great breasts lifted and shook to her laughter' [p. 564]) but also the provocative redness of a bunch of flowers on the counter, and offhanded references to him by the other drinkers. This time he vents his anger on the flowers, which he crushes in his hand.

The cat he comes on in a timber-yard provokes him still further.

Again the causes are several, but all are tied together in a knot
of uncontrollable feelings that involve the cat, his woman, and
himself:

> She trod delicately over to Ole Underwood and rubbed against
> his sleeve. The hammer in Ole Underwood's heart beat madly.
> It pounded up into his throat, and then it seemed to half stop
> and beat very, very faintly. 'Kit! Kit! Kit!' That was what she used
> to call the little cat he brought her off the ship – 'Kit! Kit! Kit!' –
> and stoop down with the saucer in her hands. (p. 565)

Initially the tramp appears to warm to her. But, seized by an
attack of 'the old, old lust' and muttering, ' "I will! I will! I will!" '
(p. 565), he flings the cat into a nearby sewer. The words suggest
that he is in the control of his affronting (and transgressing)
will: but the reference to 'the old, old lust', and the association of
his gesture with hyperintensity followed by release – 'The hammer
beat loud and strong. He tossed his head, he was young again' –
signal that he is governed by a deranged, and wholly uncontrolled,
sensuality. And it is this action which leads to his boarding the little
ship of his past in order to murder once more.

As with the 'Woman at the Store', then, two killings frame Ole
Underwood's tale. He has murdered once, and is about to do so
again. And as we approach both the story's ending and the second
murder the referents get grimmer, and more extreme: the sewer
into which he tosses a stray cat signifies the baseness of his passions; the devouring sea which 'sucked against the wharf-poles as
though it drank something from the land' (p. 566), the surge of
destructive energy which precedes his murderous act.

The cat too is not simply an adversary, or victim – the returned
soul of Underwood's murdered woman: like the wind at the beginning of the tale or the sewer and sea towards the end, it stands
in part for certain aspects of his own self; this time his softer and
more vulnerable, more 'feminine' side. (He himself has already been
compared [on p. 563] to a cat, one that shared with him the status
of outcast.) And it is a confrontation with these softer qualities –
combined with memories of a more affective past – that in the end
proves too much for him. In flinging 'his' cat into the sewer he
is denying – or expelling – these despised, and feminine, aspects of
himself in preparation for his new act of murder.

Mansfield's frequent use in 'Ole Underwood' of the symbolic

colour red, as well as the hero's string of female adversaries, suggests it is affective relations in particular that he cannot cope with; passion or tenderness that awakens his destructive rage. His fondling of the cat, for example, becomes an inevitable prelude to his destruction of it – as well as a hint that for him there is a close connection between intimacy and violence. His portrait suggests that he is also another colonial type – a puritan, one for whom there is a necessary link between sex and intense possessiveness, transgression and ultimate punishment, antagonism and sexual desire.

Not initiated into the social and cultural world, Underwood is not in possession of language, its medium of self-expression and communication, either. His own means of expression is uncontrolled violence; his nearest approach to language a series of monosyllabic phrases that are beaten out by the 'hammerblows' of his heart, and which culminate in the murderous possessiveness of 'His ship! Mine! Mine! Mine!' (p. 566). His speech-patterns, rigid and elemental, are counterpointed by the more flexible, and highly poeticised, rest-of-the-text with its complex inversions, repetitions, and elaborations.

Underwood's lack of any self-reflective consciousness, any ability coherently to regard and to assess his own reactions and emotions, is a further measure of the primitive and sub-rational nature of his psyche. Even his 'memories' present themselves merely as sensations. And Mansfield's refusal to admit us as readers to his consciousness – something exceptional in her works – adds to our sense that he is beyond the pale; out of reach of her, and our, compassion.

Mansfield visited the celebrated Post-Impressionist (or Expressionist) Exhibition held in London in 1910. What she saw there profoundly influenced her way of seeing the world, and her own art. In a letter to painter-friend, Dorothy Brett, she wrote:

> Wasn't that Van Gogh shown at the Goupil ten years ago? Yellow flowers, brimming with sun, in a pot? I wonder if it is the same. That picture seemed to reveal something that I hadn't realised before I saw it. It lived with me afterwards. It still does. That and another of a sea-captain in a flat cap. They taught me something about writing, which was queer, a kind of freedom – or rather, a shaking free.[32]

'Ole Underwood', written within a couple of years of her visit to the Exhibition, is Mansfield's most direct attempt to emulate the aims and ideals of the Expressionist movement – principally those which concerned the rendering of intense emotion through heightened, and distorted, recordings of external 'reality'. She signals the attempt in two ways – through her pervasive use of red, the favoured colour of the Movement,[33] to suggest murderous passion (it is one of the main triggers of Underwood's actions); and through her dedication of the tale to her friend the Expressionist painter Anne Estelle Rice. Rice later painted the wellknown portrait of Mansfield which hangs in the National Gallery in Wellington, and which also prominently features the colour red. It is tempting to see the painting as Rice's return tribute for the story.

'Millie', the third of the colonial tales, also investigates what becomes of femaleness and female identity in the outback – this time through an investigation of the emotional trajectory of the heroine, a farmer's wife, through a day in which she is left alone at home while her husband joins in the hunt for a young Englishman presumed to have murdered a neighbour.

After seeing the husband off, Millie retreats to their bedroom and gazes at herself in the fly-specked mirror. Her gaze explores, not her physical image but her state of mind – the way she is feeling. However, her consciousness, like Underwood's, is unreflective, and leaves her unenlightened: 'She didn't know what was the matter with herself that afternoon. She could have a good cry – just for nothing – and then change her blouse and have a cup of tea' (p. 572).

Next her attention is caught by a couple of pictures on the walls. One is a print of a Windsor Castle (*sic*) garden party, with emerald lawns and oak trees and gracious gentlemen and ladies in the foreground, and the head of Queen Victoria superimposed; the other, a photograph of Millie herself and her husband Sid on their wedding day. Here the background is a distinctively New Zealand one (though it is just as opposed to the burning landscape of the story's opening as to that of the garden party): 'behind them were some fern trees and a waterfall, and Mount Cook in the distance, covered with snow' (p. 573).

Taken together, the pictures offer a clue to Millie's predicament. For, like a similar pair of pictures in the home of the Woman at the Store, they indicate the cultural and social gulf between New Zealand and the far-off country from which its settlers derive their origins, and which in those days they called home. There is also a marked contrast between the ceremonial 'showpiece' occasions rendered with painstaking realism in the pictures, and the emotions which the tale conveys – raw, unstable, unreasoning, unpredictable.

Millie the colonial even doubts the veracity of the garden party print: ' "I wonder if it really looked like that" ' (p. 572).

When she eventually finds a young man lying prostrate in the yard outside, her earlier feeling of unease switches abruptly to one of rage. But as she gazes intently at him she discovers what she had been unable to find in her own mirror – a figure of vulnerable and suffering, humanity. She feels his heart then offers him brandy and water. As she comforts him she experiences another change in mood – this time to tenderness. The change is rendered as a painful and unaccustomed, insemination:

> A strange dreadful feeling gripped Millie Evans' bosom – some seed that had never flourished there, unfolded and struck deep roots and burst into painful leaf. 'Are yer coming round? Feeling all right again?' (p. 574)

Millie's new-found tenderness comes about because of the stranger's youthfulness and childlike helplessness, but it is also the result of her own frustrated urge towards motherhood. This has already been highlighted – significantly, just before she sensed the presence of the young man in her yard:

> 'I wunner why we never had no kids. . . .' She shrugged her shoulders – gave it up. 'Well, *I've* never missed them. I wouldn't be surprised if Sid had, though. He's softer than me.' (p. 573)

When it eventually dawns on her that her visitor is the 'English johnny' who is wanted for murder she at first determines to stand by him. Yet late that night, when he is heard trying to make his escape and the hunting-party charges after him, her mood again switches – this time from protectiveness to the primitive elation of pursuit:

> at the sight of Harrison in the distance, and the three men hot after, a strange mad joy smothered everything else. She rushed into the road – she laughed and shrieked and danced in the dust, jigging the lantern. 'A–ah!! Arter 'im, Sid! A–a–a–h! Ketch him, Willie. Go it! Go it! A–ah, Sid! Shoot 'im down. Shoot 'im!' (p. 577)

With her night-dress flicking her legs – goading her on as it were – and shrieking a wild call of encouragement, Millie ends the tale as she began it ('My word! when they caught that young man! Well, you couldn't be sorry for a young fellow like that' [p. 572]) – by supporting the hunting-down of Harrison. Except that now her support is fuelled by the dark elation of repressed feelings and the hunting instinct.

Her final shrieks of exhilaration have as little to do with the impartiality of justice as her earlier vows in support of Harrison. And even the notion of retributive justice, an ideal though a harsh one, is broken against the force (and gleefulness) of the characters' determination to pursue.

The fact that the fugitive is a citizen of old England as well as a suspected murderer makes the tale at another level an exposition of colonial/metropolitan oppositions and tensions. The alienation of Millie from her adoptive land has already been indicated in her unexplained childlessness – a condition which stands against the typically large pioneering family of history, but which for Mansfield is evidence of her heroine's alienation. Translated to a strange land she is unable either to bond with it or to commit herself to it – something the birth of a child might have implied.

It is moreover an *English* 'child' who awakens Millie's maternal feelings – a child of the nationality any son or daughter of hers, would have had if she or her parents or grandparents had remained 'at home' in England, and thus a further indication of her displacement.

But if a future in the adoptive country is to be entertained at all then any sentimental feeling for 'home' on the part of the settlers – represented in this tale by Millie's feelings for the Englishman – must be hunted down, and ruthlessly exterminated: hence her final, dramatic resort to bloodlust. Fundamentally she, like Ole Underwood, is in pursuit of her own 'weakness'.

In 'Millie' Mansfield shows how conventional primness operates even – perhaps especially – in the colonial world to repress the primitive and the instinctual. At the same time she demonstrates the strength of these urges. Both Millie's late-flowering tender impulses and her zeal for pursuit stem partly from her childlessness. They are also linked to the frigidity of her relations with her husband. Sexual inhibition is implied in a scatter of small details – the presence of the snow-covered Mount Cook in their wedding photograph and perhaps also the image of Queen Victoria, signifier of an age of sexual restraint, in the garden-party print; Millie's 'tight screw' of hair; the spark of interest she shows in the suggestively-named Willie Cox ('Not a bad young fellow, Willie Cox, but a bit too free and easy for her taste' [p. 571]). These frustrations combine with the isolation and the masculine ethos of the colonial outback to drive Millie into apeing male behaviour – at the same time as she is seen to be playing out her most instinctual responses as a woman.

Nowhere of course does the story confirm the fugitive's guilt in the murder that his pursuers – self-appointed agents of summary justice – accuse him of: he has been convicted only by their settler animosity. In essence it is Millie and her friends who are the would-be murderers, their bloodthirsty behaviour which is under scrutiny; not his.

The colonial tales, then, reveal the complex psychological play which comes about as the settler struggles both to adapt to the new land and to develop a new psychology with which to confront it. The most significant aspect of this attempt has, in the intensely macho colonial world, to do with the debate between the sexes – or between gendered aspects of the personality. These tales are disturbing pieces which deal in discord and displacement, but also in disintegration: the conventional colonial tale of the physical struggle for survival has become in Mansfield's hands one for the survival of the reasoning and reasonable self – one in which even the prior existence of that self has been called into question.

Particularly intriguing is the case of Ole Underwood. Of the key figures in the three colonial tales he is the one who is closest to disintegration – his inability to handle language and through this to re/construct his identity and his world indicate this. But he also serves as a counter-figure to later, Romantic and somewhat senti-mentalised yarns by male New Zealand writers about what has become known as the 'man alone' type – the gruff but essentially goodhearted loner who ventures into the bush, endures, returns unscathed. Mansfield's rendering of the type exposes a darker truth – that of an incoherent and deranged figure whose eruption into the social arena, the town, triggers his final crackup.

In these early pieces Mansfield also re-visions the genre of the colonial tale itself, inscribing into it a role for woman and the feminine principle and investing its bluff, blunt, action-oriented hero with a disturbed psychology. At the same time she makes use of the tales' strong narrative line and mystery elements to render what had often in her earlier works been unacknowledged material, as an integrated part of the text.

2

Isolation

Mansfield remained alone – and lonely – for much of her adult life. When she left New Zealand to settle in London at the age of nineteen she was, apart from Ida Baker, a friend from Queen's College days, among strangers. As we have seen she felt particularly isolated during the Bavarian period. And even after she acquired a companion – later a husband – in Middleton Murry she was often on her own: especially so after 1917 when failing health forced her to spend most of her time on the Mediterranean coast or in alpine Europe.

It is hardly surprising then that many of her stories should focus upon isolation, nor that their heroines (and occasionally heroes) should be the victims of circumstances which touch upon her own – urban rootlessness, exile, deeply-felt bereavement, effective poverty. But it is notable too that some of her early 'literary' pieces – pieces which were written during her schooldays, and which therefore pre-date her lone second voyage to England – also concentrate on loneliness.

Mansfield's purchase on isolation has its roots in the Romantic aesthetic of the early nineteenth century. According to this view solitariness is a privileged condition closely allied to that of romantic love; one linked to imaginative vision and to strong and pleasurable feeling. As the century drew to a close, however, the condition of literary isolation also came to mark the subject out as a creature of some dark, and generally fatal, destiny.

But Mansfield's presentation of alone-ness also has a more modern aspect – a concern with the social conditions and causes of isolation, and a Modernist belief that loneliness is an essential aspect of the human condition. She is also concerned with the devastating effect of isolation on the personality: as we have seen in the colonial tales, the fantasies of several of her solitaries are linked either to violence or to the near-disintegration of the psyche.

One of the most striking of Mansfield's early pieces is called 'Die Einsame' – The Lonely One (1904). It too was written while the author was at Queen's College, and was first published in the school's magazine.

'Die Einsame's' heroine is a kind of cross between a Nature-spirit and a mermaid. She lives alone, and in a context which reflects this condition: 'All alone she was. All alone with her soul. She lived on the top of a solitary hill. Her house was small and bare, and alone, too.'[1] She is also a creature of contradiction, making a cult of her isolation but attempting to end it at the same time. Her inner conflict is reflected in the archetypal divisions (forest and sea, night and day) around which the piece is constructed.

The sketch is loaded with many of the conventions and extravagances of its century. It is Romantic or late romantic – *fin-de-siècle* in its celebration of unrestrained and spontaneous passion; in its affirmation of the emotional basis of the personality; in its creation of a heroine who is both doomed and ardently aspiring, passive victim and the seat of powerful, contradictory, and proactive emotions, and a pre-Raphaelitish border figure inhabiting the half-land between human and divine. It is also typicaly Romantic in the connections it draws between death, night, religious experience, creative ecstasy and sexual desire. But in its preoccupation with the complex attitudes and attachments of the adolescent personality and its implication that these may lead to problems, the sketch offers as well a hint of something new.

The heroine of 'Die Einsame' spends her days in the forest, her nights by the seashore singing songs of 'passionate longing' to God. One night a particularly abandoned rendition signals an end to her previously well-ordered and predictable pattern of existence. She finds herself stranded in the forest at night, and is overcome by fear. She is then driven, either by this fear or by some more imperious desire, towards the sea. It is in this element that she finally perishes. An epiphanic figure (God? a lover? God as lover?) approaches her in a white boat made of moonshine – the only touch in this piece of the later, more overtly subversive Mansfield. The heroine wades into the sea to meet him, crying, 'Take me!' The boat vanishes. She tries to get back to the land but strikes her foot on a hidden rock, and is drowned. 'Then a great wave came, and there was silence.'[2] The traditional tale of the fatal influence of the siren has been turned on its head: in this case it is the siren who gets lured to her death.

The story is a forerunner of later, more realistic pieces by Mansfield that deal with the adolescent heroine and the 'moment' of her maturing – 'The Garden-Party', 'The Young Girl', 'Her First Ball', the concluding episodes of 'Prelude' and 'At the Bay'. But where the later stories are on the whole preoccupied with how the heroine's developing emotions interact with her social circumstances, 'Die Einsame' charts her emotional trajectory alone. Like many of the later stories, it is particularly concerned with the shifting emotions and conflicting feelings of adolescence.[3]

The 'Die Einsame' heroine works through several abrupt changes of mood. She has a sense both of omnipotence and of helplessness. She feels peace, then fear. She longs for security but has a passionate desire for expanded awareness. She laments the discontents of isolation but also cultivates solitude. She yearns both to be free, and to be ravished. As I have suggested above, her moods are reflected in the setting: the sea, which she visits at night, is figured as an arena of longing; the forest, domain of daytime existence, as familiar, and secure. And the moods and passions which dominate her, also generate and control the narrative within which she moves. The story develops according to her shifting emotions, and its crisis is precipitated at the very point at which her singing reaches a crescendo of sexual ecstasy.

With its magical forest and creatures, its mermaid-heroine, and its preoccupation with the climactic 'moment' of maturation the tale has the flavour of fairytale. Just as significant, however, are the ways in which it departs from the classic fairytale pattern. One of these is the total absence of any reference to the heroine's family – or indeed of any social context at all. This inevitably transforms her quest from a struggle for independence to one for companionship – for a soulmate. A second point of difference is the ending, in which the traditional triumphal resolution has been replaced by one familiar both to the Romantic *Bildungsroman* (failure to mature results in death) and to the Modernist sense of the individual's tragic isolation within a hostile universe.

A third point relates to the choice of the sea as an element in the story's setting. Fairytale traditionally features the forests of Northern Europe, but no sea. In 'Die Einsame', as in other Mansfield pieces, the sea is prominent, and has a complex set of significations – as a site both of danger and desire, of liberation and of extinction. Perhaps most significantly it is a domain associated with a key character's next critical life-experience. For the young Mansfield herself of course the sea was a measure of the distance between her native New Zealand and the England in which at the time of writing 'Die Einsame' she was living. One might then expect it to become a vehicle of the strong but mixed emotions which she invested both in the country of her exile and in that exile itself: such emotions are precisely those which are sustained by the tale's heroine.

A later, more ostensibly realistic sketch entitled 'The Wind Blows' (1915?) concerns itself explicitly with the sea-voyage as passage to independence and maturity. The literal voyage is one the youthful heroine hopes to make from her home in Wellington, New Zealand, to the great world overseas. This tale does not, however, end in disaster – its conclusion remains open (or rather, self-reflexive) with the heroine and her brother on the shore gazing wistfully at a steamer that has just put to sea, but in imagination transformed into shipboard figures looking back at their own former selves.

In Modernist fashion the scene encapsulates feelings of apprehension and unsettlement as well as of anticipation. It also suggests the way the Modernist self is destabilised under the impress of time and strong emotion – here the emotions engendered by contemplation of the great journey overseas. And the sketch anticipates Mansfield's later New Zealand stories in employing fiction as a strategy to overcome separation: it was written after she had made her return voyage to England alone – without her brother, in other words – and may be regarded as a re-visioning of that situation from the perspective, not of his death (which had not occurred at the time) but of their recent reunion in England.

Almost all the mature 'woman alone' stories have an old-world setting. Here the pressures exerted on the women concern the threat of social isolation – in particular the marginalising of those who fail to conform to society's norms.

These stories are exceptional among Mansfield's works in the slightness of their subtexts. This is because their purpose is not the redemption of personal feelings but – in the tradition of Romantic humanitarianism – to give to the disregarded a voice, and to the reader a sense of the reality of the social outcast's inner life.

In a world in which woman gained status largely from having a male partner and family, women who lived their lives without were considered to be of no significance; worthy merely of ridicule or of exploitation. Mansfield is here breaking silence on behalf of the despised, and ignored, spinster – giving her a voice; asserting her right to the subject-position. She is also affirming her qualities – bleak courage in the face of hard times, adaptability, a capacity for unselfish love, innate creativity. Issues of literary decorum are involved as well: Mansfield gives a cleaning-woman, a boardinghouse-keeper, a lonely spinster, the stature and status, of heroines. And in the gap she reveals between their lack of social esteem and the richness and generosity of their inner lives lies the stories' irony.

Mansfield presents her heroines and their fates straightforwardly, refusing either to sentimentalise or to console her readers with a conventional happy ending. In this respect she is by implication taking to task the falsely romantic vision of some of her writing contemporaries – their assumption that to find a husband is to live 'happily ever after'. This attitude had become even more pernicious after the mass slaughter of young men in the Great War had increased the then customary surplus in the population of women over men. In a review of the novel *Cousin Philip* by the once-famous Mrs Humphrey Ward, Mansfield takes the view to task – and thereby sketches out her own manifesto. She is speaking of the heroines of novels like Mrs Ward's:

> Once they find the right man to look after them and be kept busy and out of mischief furnishing the little nest, modern women will be as safe as their grandmothers once they find the right partners. But suppose, we find ourselves asking as we lay the book aside, there should not be enough partners to go round? In the world of 'Cousin Philip' such questions are not asked, much less answered.[4]

'The Little Governess' (1915) is the earliest of the old-world 'woman alone' stories. Though written only a couple of years after 'Millie' it seems to belong to a different realm. The shy, naïve young heroine is on her first journey abroad. Flattered by the attentions of an elderly gentleman she meets on the train she goes off to spend the day with him, and because of this fails to meet up with her prospective employer. Fantasy, which marked for the shopgirl Rosabel a temporary escape from a pinched and humdrum reality, is here a deceiving friend – leading the heroine astray, and even cheating her of her employment.

Like Rosabel's, the Little Governess's fantasies are structured according to the motifs of fairytale, subverted in order to expose the gap between fantasy and reality. The model is again 'Cinderella'. The Little Governess regards the old man as her 'fairy grandfather' – a corruption of the customary godmother. And he does give her a magical day . . . until, that is, the critical hour of six o'clock (a time in humdrum opposition to the 'witching hour' of midnight) when she is due to meet her future employer, and the spell is finally broken. The kiss of the story is not the transforming romantic gesture of the redeemer-lover of fairytale but a lewd sexual overture delivered 'on the mouth! Where not a soul who wasn't a near relation had ever kissed her before.' And the 'fairy godfather' who delivers it is now exposed as a dirty old man with a 'hard old body' and a 'twitching knee' (p. 188).

A couple of lesser episodes reinforce the moral of the main tale – the vulnerability of an attractive but impecunious young woman travelling on her own. The Little Governess is safely installed in a carriage marked 'Dames Seules' when a porter, insulted by the smallness of the tip she offered him, inserts the 'fairy grandfather' into the carriage with her. And later on a waiter at the hotel, similarly antagonised, finally ensures she does not meet up with her prospective employer.

But the story is also about the formation of the governess's own personality and attitudes, and the way these contribute to her plight. The image which most aptly marks her vulnerability, also painfully conveys her naïveté and as-yet unstructured identity. It appears at the moment of decision in which, flattered by the old man's status and attentions, she accepts his offer to show her round town: a 'drop of sunlight fell into her hands and lay there, warm and quivering' (p. 184).

Her closeted upbringing instils fearfulness in her – and therefore the need she feels for a protector. This is signalled at the story's beginning, with the advice she is given by the lady at the Governess Bureau:

> 'You had better take an evening boat and then if you get into a compartment for "Ladies Only" in the train you will be far safer than sleeping in a foreign hotel. Don't go out of the carriage; don't walk about the corridors and *be sure* to lock the lavatory door if you go there. The train arrives at Munich at eight o'clock, and Frau Arnholdt says that the Hotel Grunewald is only one minute away. . . . I always tell my girls that it's better to mistrust people at first rather than trust them, and it's safer

to suspect people of evil intentions rather than good ones.... It sounds rather hard but we've got to be women of the world, haven't we?' (pp. 174–5)

The Little Governess interprets what she encounters in the light of this advice: the landscape appears threatening and unfamiliar, the station porter looks like a robber, any suggestion of masculinity in the men she meets is 'horrible'.

In its concern with the situation of women the story also touches on the dullness and austerity of the one 'respectable' profession open to young women like the Little Governess. Mansfield's interest in the subject may well have been sparked by her time at Queen's College, itself founded in 1848 for the education of future governesses. But governessing was also the profession of several celebrated nineteenth-century fictional heroines, Jane Eyre being the best-known. These earlier heroines' lives were transformed by the magic of romance: as in her version of the colonial tale, Mansfield on the other hand makes it clear that romance equals illusion.

Because of her situation (sex, age, class) the heroine is caught in a double bind: being on her own and therefore vulnerable she is constrained to remain alone. Even the advice which is given for her protection ensures that she is left at risk.

The double bind is written into the text as a pun. The Little Governess begins her continental train journey alone, and in a 'Ladies Only' compartment. But for females in her position even language is treacherous – the notice 'Dames Seules' could well be construed by men as an invitation rather than a deterrent:

The little governess shrank into her corner as four young men in bowler hats passed, staring through the door and window. One of them, bursting with the joke, pointed to the notice *Dames Seules* and the four bent down the better to see the one little girl in the corner. (pp. 177–8)

Most of Mansfield's 'women alone' are older than the Little Governess, their lives correspondingly more closed-in. The title-figure of 'Miss Brill' (1920), for instance, is an ageing spinster, this time one living abroad in a kind of undeclared exile. Her life is one of acute loneliness, also unacknowledged. She is shown on her weekly treat – a visit to the local park. But there are no friends to meet her there: her pleasure consists simply in 'sitting in other people's lives for just a minute while they talk[ed] round her' (p. 332).

Her attention is caught by those who mirror her own situation. She becomes fascinated by the fortunes of an 'ermine toque' who is snubbed by the man she attempts to engage in conversation but who to Miss Brill's relief – for she identifies of course with the wearer of the toque – recovers rapidly and goes in search of new distractions. She notices as well that there is 'something funny' about the other old people: 'They were odd, silent, nearly all old, and from the way they stared they looked as though they'd just come from dark little rooms or even – even cupboards!' (p. 332). She also feels that everyone she sees is on show: couples and groups parade themselves proudly, and the band plays with added *brio* now the seasonal crowds have returned.

Growing in confidence, Miss Brill moves from observation of the scene to imagined participation in it:

They were all on the stage [she reflects]. They weren't only the audience, not only looking on; they were acting. Even she had a part and came every Sunday. No doubt somebody would have noticed if she hadn't been there; she was part of the performance, after all. How strange she'd never thought of it like that before! (p. 334)

When the band starts playing a moment later the theatre company of her imagination becomes a collective creative entity – a choir, about to burst into songs of harmony and understanding.

But just as her illusion of belonging reaches its peak it is shattered – by the ridicule of a young couple who share the bench with her, and whom a moment earlier she had welcomed as the hero and heroine of her daydream. But to them she is merely as a figure of fun; an impediment to their romancing.

Central to the depiction of Miss Brill's character is her moth-eaten fur. This she treats as a companion and friend, although to the reader the relationship is even closer than this: the fur, which participates in all the key aspects of her personality – loneliness, the need to fetch a little glamour into one's life, a predisposition to melancholy, the tendency to take quite a few of life's knocks, an air of plucky bravado – is an analogue for her own self:

Miss Brill put up her hand and touched her fur. Dear little thing! It was nice to feel it again. She had taken it out of its box that afternoon, shaken out the moth-powder, given it a good brush, and rubbed the life back into the dim little eyes. 'What has been happening to me?' said the sad little eyes. Oh, how sweet it was to see them snap at her again from the red eiderdown! . . . But the nose, which was of some black composition, wasn't at all firm. It must have had a knock, somehow. Never mind – a little dab of black sealing-wax when the time came – when it was absolutely necessary. . . . Little rogue! Yes, she really felt like that about it. Little rogue biting its tail just by her left ear. She could have taken it off and laid it on her lap and stroked it. (p. 331)

So self-effacing is Miss Brill that her attribute seems finally to take over her character. It figures therefore that it should be the fur which the young lovers single out for particular ridicule: ' "It's her fu-fur which is so funny," giggled the girl. "It's exactly like a fried whiting" ' (p. 335). A break in typography marks the shock of the heroine's reception of this casual cruelty – but also her inability fully to acknowledge it. She hurries home to her own 'little dark room – her room like a cupboard' (p. 335) refusing to accept the image of herself which others have shown her; but refusing also to surrender those illusions about herself which are necessary to her survival: her lack of fortitude is a kind of courage – a way of getting by. In a sense the box she packs the fox away in might as well be her own coffin for the closing-in of her life is now complete.

In a letter to Middleton Murry's brother Richard, Mansfield indicated how important it was to her to pin down the heroine's personality in her style:

> In *Miss Brill* I chose not only the length of every sentence, but even the sound of every sentence. I chose the rise and fall of every paragraph to fit her on that day at that very moment. After I'd written it I read it aloud – numbers of times – just as one would *play over* a musical composition – trying to get it nearer and nearer to the expression of Miss Brill – until it fitted her.[5]

The style-flourishes of 'Miss Brill', its frequent repetitions, omissions, and exclamations, do indeed capture Miss Brill's personality – her lack of condfidence, her tenderness, her defiant, gushy gaiety. They also reflect her situation: the opening sentence with its subliminal suggestion of make-up, of spotlights, of celebration, and its final note of caution, is a precise indicator of the state of mind in which she herself sets out for the park:

Although it was so brilliantly fine – the blue sky powdered with gold and the great spots of light like white wine splashed over the Jardines Publiques – Miss Brill was glad that she had decided on her fur. (p. 330)

And the next sentence neatly foreshadows the story's bleak autumnal ending:

The air was motionless, but when you opened your mouth there was just a faint chill, like a chill from a glass of iced water before you sip, and now and again a leaf came drifting – from nowhere, from the sky. (pp. 330–1)

Miss Brill, then, is a sensitive, even fragile Modernist consciousness whose being, like that of Virginia Woolf's heroine Mrs Dalloway – for whom she may in part have served as a model – is on the verge of being dissolved into the world around it. Even her name, with its hint of a slightly vulgar abbreviation and flavour of jaunty bravado, suggests her character. And she is so much her story that this name is also to be found not only in its title but, like a hidden signature, in the opening lines – in the 'brilliantly fine' of the sky and the air's 'faint chill'. Indeed the two phrases themselves form an analogue to the precarious balance of her mood, poised as it is between unjustifiable hope and irredeemable despair.

Though she never wrote directly about the Great War – of which she had no personal experience – Mansfield travelled extensively in wartime France, and left a vivid record of her impressions in letters and in her Journal. She was also one of the first writers to put on record the view that the War marked a watershed in the history of the European consciousness. And she was adamant that any 'honest' writing of the post-War period had to take account of this change:

the more I read the more I feel all these novels will not do . . . I can only think in terms like 'a change of heart'. I can't imagine how after the war these men can pick up the old threads as though it had never been. Speaking to *you* I'd say we have died and live again. How can that be the same life? It doesn't mean that life is the less precious or that 'the common things of light and day' are gone. They are not gone, they are intensified, they are illumined. Now we know ourselves for what we are. In a way it's a tragic knowledge: it is as though, even while we live again, we face death. But *through Life*: that's the point.[6]

I feel in the *profoundest* sense that nothing can ever be the same – that, as artists, we are traitors if we feel otherwise; we have to take it into account and find new expressions, new moulds for new thoughts and feelings . . . We have to face our war.[7]

Mansfield's short story 'The Fly' (1922), a piece notable for its lack of lyrical 'surface', is her own most anguished attempt to 'take into account' the effects of the War. It centres on the grief of the hero – referred to throughout as the Boss – at the loss in battle of his only son, and the way repression of this grief affects him. It opens with a courtesy-visit paid by Woodifield, an ex-employee retired after a stroke, to the Boss's office. The Boss notes with satisfaction how the man, though five years younger than he, has deteriorated since he was 'put out to grass'.

Then Woodifield tells of how his own daughters, while on a recent visit to Belgium to inspect their brother's war-grave, came upon that of the Boss's son. The Boss's complacency vanishes immediately. As soon as Woodifield leaves he shuts himself up in his room and prepares to be overcome by a weeping fit.

But he falls instead to brooding about how much his son had meant to him, and about the cruelty of Fate (though he does not mention the word) in snatching him away just as he had been about to step into his shoes at the office.

He gets up to have a look at the boy's photograph. Mansfield's description of the picture is laden with hints of doom: it shows 'a grave-looking boy in uniform standing in one of those spectral photographers' parks with photographers' storm-clouds behind him' (p. 413). Then the Boss notices that a fly has fallen into the inkpot. He digs it out with his pen, shakes it onto a piece of blotting-paper, and watches fascinated as it dries itself.

Then, just as it appears 'ready for life again', he drops a blot of ink on it. This sets the fly writhing once more. The process continues until the insect finally dies. At this the Boss, seized by a 'grinding feeling of wretchedness' (p. 418), sinks into a state of senile bewilderment greater even than old Woodifield's.

The Boss is the last of Mansfield's overbearing paterfamilias figures. Like all the others this portrait is dedicated to undercutting his pretensions. But where earlier tales like 'A Birthday' focused on the hero's comic sense of self-importance, 'The Fly' lays bare the sombre insecurities which lie behind his authoritarian manner.

The episode with the fly pays tribute to the celebrated lines from Shakespeare's *King Lear*, 'As flies to wanton boys are we to the gods: they kill us for their sport.' But this quotation cannot be mapped in any simple and straightforward way onto Mansfield's story. The Boss certainly acts like a god (or for that matter like a 'wanton boy') towards the fly. He also acts like the generals of the Great War – old men who sent young men to their deaths. It is no wonder the Boy of the photograph looks stern. But far from being the omnipotent figure that he at first appeared, the Boss himself seems on the verge of falling victim to the fate which snatched away his beloved son.

Grim ambiguities in the story's diction help to drive home its point. In the early stages of his grief the Boss is convinced that his feelings will never diminish: 'Time, he had declared then, he had told everybody, could make no difference' (p. 416). The irony of course is that it *does* make a difference. The grief is no longer as sharp as it was – pretending it is has become something of a ritual: 'He wasn't feeling as he wanted to feel' (p. 416). Furthermore Time's scythe, having mown down the son, is now ready to cut down the father as well. (Reference to a scythe is made, pertinently, in the description of the fly cleaning itself.) By the end of the story 'old' Mr Woodifield, five years younger than the Boss but originally distinguished sharply from him in his doddery, childlike dotage, has become his counterpart: once again a 'false' Mansfield double has proved to be a true one.

During the course of the story the Boss's dark preoccupations shift, appropriately, from his son to himself. He had earlier claimed that 'Time . . . could make no difference' (p. 416) to his grief. This proves to be the case – though not with regard to the grief, which does change and decay. It is the Boss's own journey through time towards death which is inevitable, and only his pride and initially his vigour prevent him from acknowledging this. The story's ending, with its fine ambivalence of language, confirms his fate:

And while the old dog padded away he fell to wondering what it was he had been thinking about before. What was it? It was

...He took out his handkerchief and passed it inside his collar. *For the life of him* he could not remember. (p. 418)

(Italics mine.) It was of course his dead son he had been thinking of before the fly attracted his attention.[8]

Mansfield is thoroughly Modernist in using the Great War as a metaphor for the tragic fate of humanity. But she is also Modernist in the portrait she paints of the Boss as a self-divided figure, the most complex, and the most fundamental, of his several self-divisions being that which makes him both tormentor and victim.

Antony Alpers mentions Chekhov's story 'Small Fry' as a possible source for Mansfield's 'The Fly', though only more or less to dismiss it:[9] but in fact the Chekhov story with its 'little-man' hero in some ways offers a more appropriate text than the sublimely tragic *King Lear*. It tells of an oppressed petty civil servant who, while writing a sycophantic letter to his hated superior, notices a cockroach running across his desk. He squashes it with his hand and incinerates it in the flame of a lamp, feeling relieved after this small act of transferred vengeance of his earlier animosity.

Critics have pointed out the connections between the Boss and Mansfield's father. But his position also precisely mirrors Mansfield's own at the time she wrote the story – in the way he looks both back to a close relative's death and forward to his own. She had by then less than a year of her own life left, and reference to the timing of the Boss's son's death – we are told that it occurred a little over six years ago – confirms that she must as regards the son have had her own brother Leslie's death in mind.[10] Indeed a lesser-known, and unfinished, sketch of hers is actually called 'Six Years After'. This too focuses on the grief of a parent, a mother this time, at the death of her son in war. Its mood is gentler than that of 'The Fly' – although as if in compensation for this, the author scrawled the words, 'Oh, my *hatred*!' at the end of the manuscript.

Mansfield also uses the fly-image several times in her writings in connection with feelings of desperation, on at least one occasion applying it to herself: 'I feel like a fly who has been dropped into the milk jug and fished out again, but it's still too milky and drowned to start cleaning up'.[11] And she once used it in connection with a divine malevolence (or neglect) like that implied in 'The Fly':

Oh, the times when she had walked upside down on the ceiling, run up glittering panes, floated on a lake of light, flashed through a shining beam! And God looked upon the fly fallen into the jug of milk and saw that it was good. And the smallest Cherubim and Seraphim of all who delight in misfortune struck their silver harps and skirled: How is the fly fallen fallen.[12]

In 'The Fly', then, Mansfield constructs a model through which she is able to suggest the mental torment which befalls both the boss class – those who were responsible for the slaughter of the Great War – and the bereaved. Much of the story's dark power resides in the way she implicitly aligns the personal with the universal, and allows the complexities of one level of discourse to drain into the other. One of her last works, 'The Fly' reveals its significance through masterly use of symbolic detail and linguistic ambivalence – and of course through an evocation of the repressions which the pain of grief has brought about in the Boss's mind. In this story Mansfield not only confronted the loss of her brother: she revealed a new, more conscious understanding of the mind's workings.

'The Canary', written in July 1922, was Mansfield's last 'woman alone' story. It is also her last completed work. Like others of the late stories it challenges conventional notions of the romantic heroine by focusing on an ageing and socially disregarded figure and making her the vehicle for a meditation on art, love and death.

The Narrator and key character of 'The Canary' is a boarding-house keeper who lacks human companionship and is mocked by her lodgers. Before the coming of her Canary she had bestowed her affections on the flowers in her garden ('but they don't sympathise' [p. 415]), and on the evening star. But Venus simply reflected her own indefinable melancholy back at her: 'It seemed to understand this . . . something which is like longing, and yet is not longing. Or regret – it is more like regret' (p. 413).

Once the Canary enters her life, however, it is he who becomes the focus of her attention. And she values him not only as a friend and companion – and symbolic lover – but also as an inspired Romantic artist; the composer and singer of exquisitely fashioned songs.

Mansfield is here tilting at the traditional view of love as inspired by the charms of the beloved, by relocating its source in the needs of the lover. The heroine, herself an adept student of emotion, makes

the point: 'I loved him. How I loved him! Perhaps it does not matter
very much what it is one loves in this world. But love something
we must' (p. 413).

At the same time, by making a bird the object of her heroine's
emotions, the author allows the pathos of her portrait to dip over
into the grotesque. In this story emotional complexity resides, not in
the psychology of the key figure but in the irony of her presentation. Romantic in her emotional reach and in her association with
a songbird, the Narrator is disqualified by her sex and lack of social
status from the exalted status of the Romantic poet.

From the outset the Narrator makes play with absences – the nail
that implies a cage ('You see that big nail to the right of the front
door? I can scarcely look at it even now and yet I could not bear to
take it out' [p. 418]), and the cage that no longer contains a canary.
Her auditor stays silent, even though the narrative is laced with
pleas for a response. She too is therefore effectively absent. And
these absences all serve as pointers to a more essential lack – that
of an adequate object, indeed any object, for the heroine to focus
her feelings upon.

Mansfield had promised the piece as 'a gift to Brett (her friend
the painter Dorothy Brett),[13] and it was written while Brett was
staying with her in Switzerland. The Narrator and the Canary appear to be surrogates for writer and painter; for Mansfield and Brett
themselves. This interpretation tallies with the presence, in a them-
atic sense superfluous, of two artist-figures within the same story.
For as narrator of her own tale the heroine is of course the composer and singer of a formally accomplished song of her own. The
image of caged bird as artist Mansfield also elsewhere applies to
herself – notably in a reference to how she once felt 'so *caged* that
I know I'll *sing*'.[14] So the motif of doubling is once again present,
skilfully handled so as to emphasise the irrelevance and the confining effects of merely physical circumstances, whether it be a matter
of social situation or of bodily form, and the aspiration of art.

'The Canary', then, is Mansfield's own literary epitaph. In it she
has enshrined both her sense of devotion to her own art and, as
in 'Ole Underwood', a celebration of the sister art of painting. In it
she has also paid a subtle tribute to a friend and fellow-artist – one
whom she once referred to as a 'kindred spirit'.[15]

3

The Self

Late in 1917, when on her way to spend the weekend with the 'Bloomsberries' in Lady Ottoline Morrell's country retreat at Garsington near Oxford, Mansfield caught a chill. Her health took a dramatic turn for the worse. A doctor was called, and finding a spot on her lung – the first clear evidence that she was suffering from tuberculosis – ordered her to spend the rest of the winter abroad.

So early in the New Year she set off alone for Bandol in southern France, where two years earlier she and Murry had passed several settled – and highly productive – months. This time Mansfield was less settled. But she did manage to complete two of her most original stories, 'Je Ne Parle Pas Français' and 'Bliss'. The first was unlike anything she had produced before – a lengthy monologue delivered apparently *extempore* by its Parisian narrator, a writer and sexual procurer. Then, on her return to England a few months later she began what she described as 'another member of the *Je ne Parle pas* family'.[1] This may have been 'A Married Man's Story'.[2] Work was resumed – or perhaps begun – on 'A Married Man' in 1921, only eighteen months or so before her death; but it was never finished.

'Je Ne Parle Pas Français' and 'A Married Man's Story' are strikingly similar. Both present as confessional tales, then turn into case-studies of their narrators – writers who have suffered childhood trauma. And both investigate the nature of these traumas and the way they have governed the formation of their subjects' personalities.

Both works also interrogate long-held humanist notions of the integrity and stability of the human self. The narrator of 'Je Ne Parle Pas Français' in particular confounds the traditional view: he is morally dubious, his nature elusive, his sexual preferences confused. But as well as re-visioning the self the portraits deconstruct traditional and Romantic beliefs regarding the artist – his creative autonomy, high endeavour, lack of partisan prejudice; the universality of his work; the heroic nature of his life and personality. These artists have crippling personal problems; their work is represented as a form of predation; and the process of writing itself, though a possible 'way back' to the subject's repressed experience, is offered as a journey which has significance for that artist alone.

'Je Ne Parle Pas' and 'A Married Man's Story' also investigate the relationship between gender (or gendering) and creativity. As they are the only Mansfield stories to focus on writers it is noteworthy that both are male – this from a woman writer who was deeply concerned with the way her own artistic vision was at times hindered by her domestic, female, role;[3] another indication of her intention to subvert Romantic assumptions regarding the (male) artist's high endeavour.

The Married Man's 'dark secrets' are linked to events which took place within his own first family. So his tale is inevitably concerned with the subject of familial disharmony and its effect upon the child. 'Je Ne Parle Pas Français' also has this concern, though here the secrets remain largely undisclosed. And both stories deal as well with the effect of those events on the subjects' later ability to form satisfactory relationships.

Though they are themselves engaged with the way trauma is repressed, the tales deal overtly enough with the taboo subjects of child-abuse and child sexuality, Oedipal attachment, the abuse of sexual power, prostitution and procuration in the case of 'Je Ne Parle Pas Français'; murder, wife-battering, and child sexuality in 'A Married Man's Story' – making them unquestionably the most daring of all Mansfield's works.

This view is borne out by the reactions of her first readers: Middleton Murry compared 'Je Ne Parle Pas Français' to Dostoevsky;[4] and Harold Beauchamp, to whom his daughter had sent a copy, carried out his own form of censorship by 'chuck[ing] the thing behind the fireplace'.[5] Mansfield herself commented that it made her feel *'grown up* as a writer'.[6]

The work also met with difficulties from Constable, its mainstream publisher. The first, limited, edition of 'Je Ne Parle Pas Français' (dated 1919; appeared early 1920) was privately printed by Murry's brother Richard at Mansfield and Murry's own Heron Press, and issued unexpurgated. Where this was noticed by critics it was acclaimed: J.N. Sullivan said in *The Athenaeum*[7] that it 'possesses genius', and Edward Wagenknecht wrote in the *English Journal*[8] that Mansfield had handled her theme 'subtly and delicately'.

But before including the story in the volume *Bliss* (1920) Constable's editor, Michael Sadleir, insisted on cuts. Almost all of these deal with the narrator's childhood seduction and with the subsequent corruption of his vision. Though brief, the censored passages do play a critical role in explaining the narrator's attitude and in building up the story's ironical and slightly seedy tone.[9]

Initially Mansfield rejected Sadleir's stipulation, demanding, 'Shall I pick the eyes out of a story for £40?' (Forty pounds was then a considerable sum of money, equal to almost one-fifth of her annual allowance from her father.) She went on to explain what she considered would be the artistic effect of making the cuts: 'The *outline* would be all blurred. It must have those sharp lines.'[10] But the next day she capitulated, and the story was finally published by Constable in its censored form.

The limited edition was not reprinted, nor the suppressed sections restored to the text, until Antony Alpers's hardback edition of *The Stories of Katherine Mansfield* appeared in 1984. But the Constable/ Penguin edition, the one by which the vast majority of Mansfield's readers know her, has turned out the expurgated version to this day.

'Je Ne Parle Pas Français' is set in Paris. It opens with its narrator, Raoul Duquette, musing upon his own personality and past. He goes on to recall his friendship with a young Englishman, Dick Harmon, and the sense of desertion and humiliation he felt when Dick left him to return to England. In fact Dick returned a few months later: though when he did so he was accompanied by his lover, a young woman known only as Mouse. Shortly afterwards Dick abandoned her in order – or so we are told – to return to his mother. Raoul, who admits to feeling a perverse elation at the couple's suffering, also made a point of letting Mouse down. His confessions end with an idle and rather tasteless pronouncement on the allure of the café's proprietress.

Raoul Duquette attempts early on to establish his own identity. This he does by trying out the nineteenth-century realist's thumbnail portrait. However, the old convention will not hold: his own, more problematic Modernist personality cannot be pinned down in this way. It eludes him, disappearing into the darkness of his repressions:

> My name is Raoul Duquette. I am twenty-six years old and a Parisian, a true Parisian. About my family – it really doesn't matter.

I have no family; I don't want any. I never think about my childhood. I've forgotten it. (p. 66)

A little later he tries again, this time building repression – and irony – into his description:

> I date myself from the moment that I became tenant of a small bachelor flat on the fifth floor of a tall, not too shabby house, in a street that might or might not be discreet. Very useful, that.... There I emerged, came out into the light and put out my two horns with a study and a bedroom and a kitchen on my back. (p. 67)

But between these obfuscatory attempts to define his identity Raoul lets slip a reference to an episode from his childhood that *was* crucial to the formation of his personality – his seduction by the family's laundress:

> When I was about ten our laundress was an African woman, very big, very dark, with ... frizzy hair.... She took me into a little outhouse ..., caught me up in her arms and began kissing me. Ah, those kisses! Especially those kisses inside my ears that nearly deafened me.
> *And then with a soft growl she tore open her bodice and put me to her.* When she set me down she took from her pocket a little round fried cake covered with sugar and I reeled along the passage back to our door.[11]

(Italics mine: the italicised passage is one of those that were omitted from the Constable version.) The transgressive nature of the episode is underlined in the racial identity of the African woman – the incarnation for the white male, European narrator, of the Other.

Raoul's story makes it clear that it is this encounter, repeated once a week throughout his childhood, which has led to the warping of his personality – by, amongst other things, causing him to associate sexual adventure with reward, and confusing for him woman's roles as lover and as mother. The relationship is, it is implied, responsible for his later self-regard, his shiftiness, his activities as gigolo and sexual procurer, his disposition to humiliate women. The tale has him cast frequent glances at the mirror – a reflection, so to speak, of his narcissistic fascination with himself. And, appropriately for such a bankrupt and deceiving personality, neither of his mirrors is paid for.

His attitude towards women is highlighted from the beginning, in his references to life as 'an old hag', an 'old bitch' he might take 'by the throat', and a 'rag-picker on the American cinema shuffling along wrapped in a filthy shawl with her old claws crooked over a stick' (p. 62). And it becomes the focus of the closing episode of the story, when he contributes to an abandoned woman's distress by offering help . . . then calculatedly letting her down.

The closest literary model for Mansfield's hero is the narrator of Dostoevsky's *Notes from Underground*, another first-person confessional tale.[12] Mansfield no doubt got to know the work while Murry was preparing his book on Dostoevsky. This he did during the time they spent together in Bandol, when Mansfield herself was working on an early version of 'Prelude'. Both Dostoevsky's hero and Mansfield's are socially isolated, and acutely introspective. Both are intended to represent 'modern' urban humanity. Both seem fixated on the psychology of humiliation and revenge, and some of the more perverse aspects of sexual power. And both challenge as just another vanity the kind of self-congratulatory 'truth-telling' which Rousseau makes so much of in the *Confessions* – itself an early attempt to expose Romantic notions regarding the veracity of the first-person subject.

Most strikingly perhaps, Mansfield has taken over Dostoevsky's metaphor of the 'under-ground' and applied it to her own hero's social situation and psychical formation. But in so doing she gives it the explicit referent of psychological repression – something it did not have in the original. The clue to the steal is planted in a passage in which Raoul makes a point of distinguishing himself from the prickly, intense, and pretentiously philosophical Underground Man – and at the same time aligning his preoccupations with those of Freud – by determining to make a name for himself 'as a writer about the *submerged world*. [My italics.] But not as others have done before [him]. Oh, no! Very naïvely, with a sort of tender humour and from the inside, as though it were all quite simple, quite natural' (p. 67).

So Raoul distances himself from the old, high Romantic conception of the self. But although for him personality seems defined according to what was to become the classic Modernist model – fluid and experiential – the cut-and-dried imagery he uses undercuts the Modernist vision. People, he asserts, are 'like portmanteaux – packed with certain things' (p. 60); and the waiter at his favourite café is 'a sort of cross between a coffee-pot and a wine-bottle' (p. 61).

He also declares against any Christian–dualist conception of the mind:

> I don't believe in the human soul. I never have. I believe that people are like portmanteaux – packed with certain things, started going, thrown about, tossed away, dumped down, lost and found, half emptied suddenly, or squeezed fatter than ever, until finally the Ultimate Porter swings them on to the Ultimate Train and away they rattle. . . .
>
> Not but what these portmanteaux can be very fascinating. Oh, but very! I see myself standing in front of them, don't you know, like a Customs official.
>
> 'Have you anything to declare? Any wines, spirits, cigars, perfumes, silks?'
>
> And the moment of hesitation as to whether I am going to be fooled just before I chalk that squiggle, and then the other moment of hesitation just after, as to whether I have been, are perhaps the two most thrilling instants in life. (pp. 60–1)

This anti-dualist declaration is again undercut in Raoul's preoccupation with 'contents' and 'packaging'. And it is tellingly at odds with the picture he paints of himself in his tale as a whole, as a maimed and fractured personality; and in other distinctions he sets up between the 'submerged' and 'daylit' aspects of the self, and between the self that acts and lives and the self that observes. It is also challenged in the several references he makes to photographs, which play off photography's necessarily two-dimensional revelations against hints of some more elusive, and more complex, notion of identity. And it directly opposes the dualism that is hinted at in his surname 'Du-quette' (my hyphen). (The name also has overtones of 'coquette' and '*quéquette*', a French slang term for the penis.) His mirror-glances are relevant here too – particularly as for Mansfield the look in the mirror is consistently associated with a desire, or simulated desire, for self-knowledge.

Raoul's morbid self-absorption, his position on the margins of society, his voyeurism and predatory exploitation of others, his preoccupation with intense feelings, his *maladif* tendency to look too close, all mark him out as a parody of the artist. And the titles of his works confirm his third-rateness – *Wrong Doors, False Coins,* and *Left Umbrellas* (standing presumably for botched opportunities, lack of principle, and psychic residues). As well as his treatment of Mouse, his 'night jobs' of pimp and gigolo reflect the baser aspects of his artistic role. It is also ironically appropriate that he should employ another baldly dualistic metaphor to encapsulate – or to eliminate – the complexities of the artistic process:

> All the while I wrote that last page my other self has been chasing up and down out in the dark there. It left me just when I began to analyse my grand moment, dashed off distracted, like a lost dog who thinks at last, at last, he hears the familiar step again. (p. 65)

Raoul experienced this 'grand moment' when whiling away the time in his favourite café: 'There! it had come – the moment – the *geste!* And although I was so ready, it caught me, it tumbled me over; I was simply overwhelmed' (p. 64). The 'moment' – brief, intense, overpowering – belongs to the Romantic tradition of revelatory instants. And the self-doubt which precedes it, as well as the way it is triggered by a trivial and contingent circumstance – a 'stupid, stale little phrase: *Je ne parle pas français*' (p. 64) jotted down on a writing-pad – also give it the thumbprint of the revelatory instant.

Yet this tradition too is subverted. Raoul's experience leaves him with a sense of agony rather than any feeling of inspiration, and has been set off moreover by a phrase which is associated for him with the young Englishwoman, whose catchphrase it has become. And she – alone in a foreign capital and deserted by her boyfriend in humiliating circumstances – is also let down later by Raoul himself. So the phrase which triggers Raoul's epiphany becomes linked with Mouse's vulnerability: the narrator has got his 'buzz' from a perverted sense of gratification at the way he has humiliated an apparently helpless woman. Mansfield's delineation may well owe something to the classic Modernist version of the visionary 'moment', Stephen Dedalus' strandside epiphany from Chapter 4 of Joyce's *Portrait of the Artist as a Young Man*, which more subtly undermines its hero's experience.

Raoul's partial repression of his childhood memories has led to the creation of his own 'submerged' psychical world. In logic this would seem to refer back beyond his experiences with his 'sugar-mother', the laundress, to his real mother. But the text remains dark on all aspects of his relationship with his family.

We have already seen how Mansfield uses Raoul to destabilise old certitudes regarding the fixed, and unitary, nature of the self. She also does this by lining up pairs of characters whose individual identities blur or overlap in a fashion reminiscent of Dostoevsky's in his great novels.

Much of 'Je Ne Parle Pas Français' revolves around signifiers of 'Frenchness' and 'Englishness'. At first glance these seem to be clearly differentiated – and opposed. Raoul, for example, makes frequent allusions both to his own Frenchness and to the Englishness of Dick and Mouse. And Frenchness – the Self as regards the angle of narration in the story but in moral terms the Other – is associated with corruption; Englishness with innocence. The connection is reinforced by a cutting indictment of the French and their sexual mores, inscribed by Mansfield at the head of the notebook containing the first part of the draft of 'Je Ne Parle Pas Français':

> But Lord! Lord! how I do hate the French. With them it is always rutting time. See them come dancing and sniffing round a woman's skirt.
>
> Mademoiselle complains that she has the *pieds glacés*.
>
> 'Then why do you wear such pretty stockings and shoes, Mademoiselle?' leers Monsieur.
>
> '*Eh – oh là – c'est la mode!*'
>
> And the fool grins well content with the idiot answer.[13]

However, the text's national associations – especially those which relate to Raoul and Dick – do in fact blur or overlap; a sly indication incidentally of the falseness of the narrator's wholly 'experiential' conception of the self. Raoul has an English writing-table and an English overcoat, and Dick's letter to Mouse is couched in a French that is perhaps 'a shade too French' (p. 74). They are also proficient in each other's languages, and each has a mutual interest in the literature of the other. And seeing Dick for the first time at a literary party Raoul makes enquiries about who he is. He then describes himself in a kind of echo of the response – as if the two of them were indeed *alter egos*:

> 'Who is he?'
>
> 'An Englishman. From London. A writer. And he is making a special study of modern French literature.'
>
> That was enough for me. My little book, *False Coins*, had just

been published. I was a young, serious writer who was making
a special study of modern English literature. (p. 71)

The overlap in identities does not end here. Dick's own hapless
devotion to his mother is paralleled in the way Raoul's personality
has been warped by his own relations with his 'sugar-mother' the
laundress. Mouse's declaration 'Je ne parle pas français', which gives
both title and *leitmotif* to the story, consists of the first words she
speaks to Raoul. As has already been mentioned, it is on account
of them that he experiences his ironically named 'grand moment' –
itself a semantically exact but imprecise translation of the (inauthentic) French *'le grand moment'*: something which itself illustrates
the perils of literary interchange. They also turn out to be her final
words to Raoul, made after Dick's desertion of her. However, the
claim of ignorance in the tag-phrase – which is itself a kind of self-
contradiction anyway – is denied by her lover:

> she said, wringing my hand (I'm sure she didn't know it was
> mine), *je ne parle pas Français.*
> 'But I'm sure you do,' I answered, so tender, so reassuring, I
> might have been a dentist about to draw her first little milk tooth.
> 'Of course she does,' Dick swerved back to us. (p. 78)

And there must be at least a presumption that when Mouse speaks
to the *garçon* at the hotel she does so in French.

So the phrase which at first seems to encapsulate Mouse's vulnerability may in fact be evidence of her wary shrewdness – and of her
wish to dissociate herself from those attitudes which are signified in
the story by 'Frenchness'. Certainly there is little objective evidence
for her helplessness: here as elsewhere it is Raoul's assumptions
which govern the reader's view.

Just as there is a blending and blurring of Raoul's *national* identity with that of his friend Dick, so there is a corresponding overlap
of his sexual and gender characteristics with those of Mouse.[13] His
description of himself is laced with indications of femininity:

> I am little and light with an olive skin, black eyes with long
> lashes, black silky hair cut short, tiny square teeth that show
> when I smile. My hands are small and supple. A woman in a
> bread shop once said to me: 'You have the hands for making fine
> pastries.' I confess, without my clothes I am rather charming.

Plump, almost like a girl, with smooth shoulders, and I wear a
thin gold bracelet above my left elbow. (p. 68)

He identifies on occasion with the way he assumes a woman might
feel (see e.g. page 73). And he shows a marked sexual attraction
towards Dick. Conversely Mouse is associated with boyishness
(pp. 78, 90). The link between the two characters is suggested in
the image of the butterfly which Raoul connects, first with himself – in a context which invokes notions of role-play and drag-
dressing, and which therefore points again to the notion of gender
as a social artificial construct – and then with Mouse. The image
suggests innocence and vulnerability, but also a transformation of
identity that is akin to metamorphosis – at one and the same time
more natural, and more mysterious, than any Raoul himself could
have conceived of:

> I wore a blue kimono embroidered with white birds and my hair
> was still wet; it lay on my forehead, wet and gleaming.
>   'Portrait of Madame Butterfly,' said I, 'on hearing of the arrival
> of *ce cher Pinkerton.*' (p. 74)

> Mouse . . . came upon you with the same kind of shock that you
> feel when you have been drinking out of a thin innocent cup and
> suddenly, at the bottom, you see a tiny creature, half butterfly,
> half woman. . . . (p. 80)

This overlapping of identities serves to emphasise Raoul's complex role in the story: like Mouse he is (or fancies himself to have
been) deserted, and hence humiliated, by Dick. Here rests one of
the burdens of the Madame Butterfly image. And like Dick too,
Raoul humiliates Mouse – or at least imagines himself to have
humiliated her. So he becomes an *alter ego* of both the other key
participants in the drama.

This blurring of identities serves the story's concern to render the
modern condition as one of exile: to this end, the literal exile of
Mouse and Dick blends with the metaphoric exiles of Raoul (the
artist's and the citydweller's alienation, and the individual's trau-
matic severance from his own first family) to suggest the multiple
estrangements of the modern self.

The tale itself must, however, remain suspect because of doubts
over Raoul's veracity . . . as well of course as his judgement. And
even its medium remains uncertain: are we to regard this as English,

the language both of its author and of the apparently innocent Mouse, or the corrupting French of the narrator Raoul? We have already seen that there are doubts regarding Mouse's own protestations of linguistic incompetence: even she may not be as innocent as she appears.

One further doubt resides, disconcertingly, in the possibility that Raoul himself may be neither as corrupted nor as dangerous as he wishes to believe. There is even evidence both at the beginning of the story and in a lyrical fantasy-passage towards the end, where he finally does perhaps speak candidly, that he himself hankers over Mouse . . . despite (or possibly because of) his own spurning of her. Teasingly the story also entertains the possibility that his deception of Mouse occupied a far larger place in his own unconfident mind than it did in the undisclosed thoughts and preoccupations of Mouse herself; indeed that she is less vulnerable than Raoul believes. Though distressed at Dick's flight, for example, she remains reasonably composed in the face of it. And Raoul is also very far from being able to pin her down as a character: in this respect as well she remains undefeated.

'A Married Man's Story', begun shortly after 'Je Ne Parle Pas Français', reads like a re-visioning of the earlier work but one which attempts to go beyond the barrier of the central character's repressions. It too offers a portrait of a man whose personality has been warped by a childhood trauma he has undergone, and its subsequent repression. In this case the trauma is a youthful memory – or just possibly an imagined memory, or dream – of the Married Man's mother telling him just before she died that his father had poisoned her. This has affected the man's own family life to the extent that he has become unable to relate to his own wife and child.

But there is a signal difference between the two tales. Where Raoul Duquette attempted to 'bury' his childhood (p. 67) the Married Man, confessing to a fondness for 'débris' (p. 426), burrows resolutely back into his past in the hope of discovering his own buried self – in particular the reason for his present behaviour towards his wife and son:

But really to explain what happened then I should have to go back and back – I should have to dwindle until my two hands clutched the banisters, the stair-rail was higher than my head, and I peered through to watch my father padding softly up and down. (p. 430)

In keeping with Mansfield's developing conception of character as consciousness, the story privileges memory and its contents: as the narrator himself asks, 'Who am I, in fact, as I sit here at this table, but my own past?' (p. 434). The task for him of course is to reach that aspect of his past which has been repressed, and in so doing to get at the truth about himself and his psychological complexities – the implication presumably being that these may then be able to be healed. The tale shows him dedicating himself to this task: where Raoul repeatedly faces us with the darkness of his own repressions the Married Man is resolute in his determination to uncover his past. And as Mansfield is in these tales affirming a relationship between the moral integrity of a writer and the quality of his (or her) work it is entirely appropriate that the Married Man with his dedication should not be subject to the same imputation of third-rateness as Raoul.

Outwardly at least the Married Man also belongs to a more orthodox set-up than his predecessor. In place of Raoul's roving street-life and undisclosed family background we now have someone whose family is 'known', who is a 'family man' himself, and who in the opening scene of his story is placed within a setting of apparently idyllic familial contentment.

Yet, as so often in Mansfield, this appearance of normality is an illusion. The hero, younger at the time of his trauma than Raoul and therefore perhaps more deeply affected by it, is soon shown to be someone apparently without the capacity for feeling; critically unable to relate either to his wife or to their child – of whom he admits, ' "I've never accepted him as ours" ' (p. 422). Images of dehumanisation and imprisonment thread through his story, contributing to the portrait of him as an emotionally embattled figure. In a haunting image of personal alienation, he compares himself for instance to the 'children who are suckled by wolves and accepted by the tribe, and [who afterwards] move freely among their fleet, grey brothers' (p. 428). Images of imprisonment also figure prominently: he dreams that his family 'were living inside one of [his] father's big coloured bottles' (p. 430) (his father was a chemist), and he confesses to feeling that he himself spent most of his childhood 'like a plant in a cupboard' (p. 432). A fourth image combines hints of dehumanisation and entrapment with an indication that he occupies the victim-position. When he finds a dead bird that his schoolmates have planted in his pocket he identifies it with himself: 'I looked at the dead bird again. . . . And that is the first time that I remember singing – rather . . . listening to a silent voice inside a little cage that was me' (p. 433). (As I noted in my comments on 'The Canary', a story written shortly afterwards, Mansfield frequently applies the 'caged bird' image to herself.)

At school the narrator is nicknamed Gregory Powder. This is a reference to a popular contemporary remedy for constipation – hence of course to the narrator's own emotional blockage. And at his mother's funeral he himself sees his father as a bottle of poison:

'That tall hat so gleaming black and round was like a cork covered with black sealing-wax, and the rest of my father was awfully like a bottle, with his face for the label – *Deadly Poison*. It flashed into my mind as I stood opposite him in the hall. And Deadly Poison, or old D.P., was my private name for him from that day.' (p. 435)

G.P. is of course son of D.P. – a further, ominous indication that in the absence of self-understanding the son is doomed to follow in his father's footsteps.

When his story opens the Narrator is settled at his writing-table – strategically placed so as to enable him to look out over 'his' domain of the sitting-room. Soon, however, sense-impressions trigger his writer's imagination: it is raining outside, and the sound of the rain leads him out-of-doors as it were and through a series of imagined romantic landscapes. His description of this journey, with its eightfold repetition of the Cartesian 'I am' ('I am here, I am there', 'I am arriving', 'I am conscious of' [p. 423, etc.]) is a Modernist attempt to represent the consciousness, not as some Cartesian prison but as a creative interaction between the mind and the external world. At the same time the Man's efforts to guess at the feelings of his wife and son illustrate a belief in the basically self-enclosed, and self-regarding, nature of the human consciousness. He himself, however – like Mansfield in a famous Journal passage envisaging the self as a dual entity composed of multiple superficial sense-impressions and a unified spiritual aspect[14] – soon disregards his own sense-impressions in favour of more inward, and more inspiriting, evidence of his creative powers:

Aren't those just the signs, the traces of my feeling? The bright
green streaks made by someone who walks over the dewy grass?
Not the feeling itself. And as I think that a mournful, glorious
voice begins to sing in my bosom. Yes, perhaps that is nearer
what I mean. What a voice! What power! What velvety softness!
Marvellous! (p. 424)

Locked inside the narrator's mind is another formative childhood
memory – that of a night-time embrace from one of his father's
'fancy women'. Her sensuous charm triggers a later dream – figured
as the bringing to the surface of buried psychical material – in
which she is both a focus for his desire and the censurer of it:

I dreamed she came again – again she drew me to her, something
soft, scented, warm and merry hung over me like a cloud. But
when I tried to see, her eyes only mocked me, her red lips opened
and she hissed, 'Little sneak! Little sneak!' But not as if she were
angry, – as if she understood, and her smile somehow was like
a rat – hateful! (p. 436)

Even more disturbingly this dream, which is related in the text
to the circumstances of the narrator's mother's death, appears to
trigger in him a kind of spiritual rejuvenation – pointed up by
suggestions of germination and of renewed vision:

the shrivelled case of the bud split and fell, the plant in the
cupboard came into flower. 'Who am I?' I thought. 'What is all
this?' And I looked at my room, at the broken bust of the man
called Hahnemann on top of the cupboard, at my little bed with
the pillow like an envelope. I saw it all, but not as I had seen
before. . . . Everything lived, everything. (p. 437)

Hahnemann was the founder of homoeopathic medicine, and therefore an approriate figure to find commemorated (or rejected) in the
house of a chemist. But it may also be relevant that a literal translation of the name 'Hahnemann' is 'Cocksman'[15] – something which
recalls the Duquette–*quéquette* association made in 'Je Ne Parle Pas
Français', and which appears to imply that the narrator's earlier
feelings of sexual inadequacy are at issue here as well.
The text as we have it ends, however, not with any visionary
insight but with a reference – enigmatic but unmistakably ominous

– to the narrator turning towards his 'silent brothers' (p. 437). His final return to the human community appears to remain in doubt. The implication in the story as we have it must be that he will himself follow in his father's footsteps. The structure of his own family (father, mother, small son) replicates the one in which he grew up. He himself contributed by his taxing birth to his mother's death. He even confesses to having wished he were his father; to having copied his father's sneer and having lain in the foetal position staring at his father until his image 'remained solid in [his] memory' (p. 431). (It should be noted that the father is to the son's gaze habitually bisected by the shop-counter – another ironic hint at the duality of consciousness.) Even more incriminating, in view of the fact that the death was caused by poisoning, the narrator confesses to knowing the 'mixture'. And it is perhaps prophetic that his wife's and son's present existence should be invaded by an image of instability: he watches from his table as 'her shadow – an immense *Mother and Child* – is here and gone again upon the wall . . .' (p. 423). But as the story was never finished we do not know for sure whether the Married Man's interrogation of himself would have enabled him to break with the destiny which appears to be his.

What is certain is that 'Je Ne Parle Pas Français' and 'A Married Man's Story' – experimental in form; radical, even dangerous, in content – marked a new and exciting departure in Mansfield's writing. Yet she wrote nothing else like them, going on instead to cultivate a double discourse which would allow her to cloak the taboo, or repressed, aspects of human character beneath an impeccable surface lyricism. However, the experience she gained in moving from the repressions of a figure like the semi-fictionalised *German Pension* Narrator to those of her key characters – which she was able to confront directly – undoubtedly contributed to the skill and sympathetic understanding with which she worked the subtexts of her later family stories.

4

Couples

Many of Mansfield's 'coupling' stories were written in the last five years of her life. Most draw upon her relationship with Middleton Murry. Typically they centre on the supposed high points of a lover's life – engagements, honeymoons, reunions, sexual bliss. But any jubilation or passionate intensity that they convey is compromised by undercurrents of discontent and distress. These generally concern violence and victimisation (almost always of the woman), or the unworthiness of one of the partners (usually the man).

The 'coupling' stories were conceived according to the traditional notion that relations between the sexes are, and ought to be, ones of binary opposition. Men and women, lovers or spouses, are characterised – even defined – in terms of male/female distinctions and attributes, speech and gesture, behaviour and sensibility. It is also made clear that sexual attraction is based on this binary opposition; and the opposition helps to account for the intensities as well as the fragilities of passion.

Yet while appearing to celebrate sharply defined gender differences many of these stories actually engage in subverting them. Characters who at first present as models of masculinity or femininity are shown to bear the qualities normally ascribed to their gender opposites: women turn out to be stronger than their partners, men are devoured by a terrible inner weakness.

Some of the stories also investigate conventional notions of sexual orientation. Female sexuality in particular is shown to be multidirectional, and more complex than any simple scheme of attraction between binary opposites would allow. As an adolescent Mansfield herself had several affairs with women, and Alison Laurie[1] has argued convincingly that Mansfield's lifelong friendship with her 'wife'[2] Ida Constance Baker took the form of a lesbian relationship.

'Les Deux Étrangères' (1906), an unpublished fantasy, belongs to Mansfield's Queen's College period. Like others of her juvenile pieces it shows how early she turned to the interrogation of subversive topics – questions of sexual identity and orientation, and issues relating to child sexuality and incestuous desire. It shows a familiarity with Freudian concepts which predates by several years her friendship with A.R. Orage and the *New Age* circle.

The heroine's name, Fifi, has about it an aura of foreign flightiness and sexual licence. While sick in bed – generally a sign of maladjustment in Mansfield's works – Fifi has a dreamlike visitation from two figures. One is tall and dark, the other small and pale. The tall figure wears a cloak, and carries a 'grass cutter' in his hand. He asks her to make room in her bed so that one of them can sleep with her. Fifi tells him he is too big, and offers to take the little one instead. But the tall figure persists:

> 'I would carry you in my strong arms – and show you wondrous things' cried the tall figure, advancing nearer. 'But you might hurt me with your grass cutter', and her tears fell fast. 'I am so sorry to be nasty', she sobbed, 'but please, dear dark man, go away – I would like the little baby one.'[3]

After she has rejected him three times he strides from the room.

This startling little piece deals in the taboo subjects of child sexual awareness and, by way of an early association between the heroine's father and the 'grass cutter' (she 'knew it was a grass cutter because Daddy had one in the summer',[4] paternal desire. It also shows Fifi torn between a wish to keep faith with herself and a desire to retain parental approval, as well as between desire to receive the intruder and fear of him.

This complex of feelings suggests that she has as yet no clearly defined sense of her own sexual identity. Her fear of the tall figure finds expression in a kind of castration-anxiety: she feels she may be injured in bed by his 'grass cutter'. But in preferring the baby she also seems to cleave to an aspect of the feminine – her own mothering instinct. (These details also mark her out as an early version of Sabina from the *German Pension* tale 'At Lehmann's' – caught in passion's snare.)

The piece underlines the importance of the father-figure in the formation of the girl's sexual identity. Fifi shows acute anxiety both about offending and about upsetting her father. But as well as fear of him, the tale also hints at forbidden desire. It implies too something of the difficulty she may later have in attaining her mature, female gender identity; in breaking free, that is, of his influence in order fully to realise her own self.

So it is implied that the formation of the child's sexuality is not wholly automatic; that it depends on a series of testing – though perhaps finally inevitable – choices. When Fifi says, 'Jesus was that Father mild, Mary was his little child',[5] thus substituting 'father' for 'mother', she is illustrating something of her own confusion. (The title of the piece, in which 'the two strangers' are assigned to the female gender, may be either a simple grammatical slip or else a hint that the smaller of the two figures, the one preferred by Fifi, is, like her, a girl-child.)

The tale also sets up an association between the tall figure with the 'grass cutter', and Father Time and his scythe. The sickly Fifi's fear of this figure, her repeated rejection of him, and her plea – eventually granted – to be allowed to receive the baby instead, thus point to a positive choice of life over death, of the future over the past; but in addition an early preoccupation on Mansfield's part with – and fear of – death itself.

'Summer Idylle' (1906) was also written while its author was still at Queen's College. Its self-consciously New Zealand background makes it her earliest nostalgic – recollective piece – recollective no doubt of family summers at the beach but also of her friendship with a Maori schoolfriend, Maata Mahupuku. The two heroines Hinemoa and Marina are adolescent girls, both apparently Maori. The 'idylle' of the title concerns an early-morning swim they take to an offshore island. Subliminally the piece is about the sexual awakening of one girl by the other.

Hinemoa is celebrated in Maori legend as the heroine who swam out to an island to be united with the lover she was forbidden to marry. The theme of youthful revolt in the name of passion would have appealed to Mansfield, and in her version of the tale she reinforces the element of rebellion by making Hinemoa's beloved a girl.

The strong sense of rapture in the sketch is for the most part expressed indirectly, by means of a close association between the girls and the vital natural world through which they move – a counter to traditional renderings of (female) Nature as passive. (Both girls incidentally do seem to be literal children of Nature for here as in other early Mansfield pieces the parents are 'written out' of the text: the legend's blocking agent has been internalised, as the youthful inhibition of Hinemoa herself.)

As you might expect of someone with her associations in legend, Hinemoa is in complete bodily and emotional harmony with the sea:

> a great breath from the sea that skimmed through the window and kissed her laughingly – and her awakening was complete. She slipped out of bed and ran over to the window and looked out. The sea shone with such an intense splendour, danced, leapt up, cried aloud, ran along the line of white beach so daintily, drew back so shyly, and then flung itself onto the warm whiteness with so complete an abandon that she clapped her hands like a child. . . .[6]

However, Marina's name also connects her with the sea – one of several hints that the two girls may, like the twin heroes of Mallarmé's dramatic poem 'L'Après-midi d'un faune', be regarded as different aspects, the shy and the more promiscuous, of the sexual self.

Hinemoa in particular appears to be in a condition of adolescent self-preoccupation. At the beginning this causes her momentarily to overlook her friend. Remembering, she goes to Marina's room to wake her up. The desire she now feels is evoked by means of stock Decadent imagery – a reminder of one of the young Mansfield's literary enthusiasms – that sorts oddly with the earlier emphasis on Nature and naturalness:

> Hinemoa bent over her with a curious feeling of pleasure, intermingled with a sensation which she did not analyse. It came upon her if she had used too much perfume, if she had drunk wine that was too heavy and sweet, laid her hand on velvet that was too soft and smooth. Marina was wrapped in the darkness of her hair. Hinemoa took it up in her hands and drew it away from her brow and face and shoulders.[7]

Awakening, Marina responds by crowning Hinemoa with white blossom. The colour is appropriate to Hinemoa's virginal hesitancy, a point underlined when the more precocious Marina later calls her 'the Snow Maiden'. As they swim out to the island, Marina tries to educate her friend in the play of sexual difference – and of sexual attraction: 'I like not congruity. Is it because you are so utterly the foreign element . . . you see?'[8]

Hinemoa contents herself with drawing attention to 'the hanging beautiful arms of the fern trees'. But the precocious Marina has a more ardent vision – that of the rata's[9] 'tongues of flame' and the 'beautiful green hair' of the fern trees. She offers a come-on:

> '. . . See, Hinemoa, it is hair, and, know you not, should a warrior venture through the bush in the night, they seize him and wrap him round in their hair and in the morning he is dead. They are cruel even as I might wish to be to thee, little Hinemoa.' She looked at Hinemoa with half-shut eyes, her upper lip drawn back, showing her teeth, but Hinemoa caught her hand. 'Don't be the same' she pleaded.[10]

The passage picks up on received colonial stereotypes of the Maori as both warrior and savage (noble or otherwise), and uses these to reinforce the dominating, 'masculinist' attitude she adopts towards her friend – and to which the still childlike Hinemoa appears to react with distress. However, her response is ambiguous – it could just as well be taken as a plea either for the maintenance of difference within a homosexual relationship ('Don't be the same as me') or else for its abolition ('Don't be like men').

Marina takes her pupil for a diving-lesson, instructing her to 'sink as deeply as [she] can . . . with the eyes open, and then [she] will learn';[11] a hint that here, as in 'Die Einsame', acquaintance with the sea is a prelude to new experience – in this case, because of the emphasis on 'sinking deep', presumably one of profound mystery.

Details of Hinemoa's descent are not given. However, we do learn that the experience terrifies her and that afterwards she swims straight back to the shore without waiting for Marina. In the safety of her room she comforts herself by kissing her own mirror-reflection, and observing to it in a social (and truth-denying) manner adopted by several later Mansfield characters, '"What a fright you had, dear."' Then she dresses up in a white gown 'just like a child wears' – one perfectly appropriate to a Snow Maiden.

'Summer Idylle' is a study in the complexities of adolescent psychology; an early indication of the author's insight, half-a-century ahead of its time, that this is a critical stage in the development of the individual. It also conveys that the psychic structure of adolescence is comparatively open – one in which those concerned cross accepted social boundaries or break taboos[12] with relative ease. Marina in particular is ready to experiment.

Like many Mansfield heroines Hinemoa is associated with the

mirror-glance, something which again signifies not merely vanity but a search – often fruitless – for self-knowledge. Typically, Hinemoa ends up fleeing the knowledge that her friend offers.

The lack of differentiation between characters and setting in the sketch serves also as a reminder of the girls' state of mind – a condition of sensuous self-absorption in which the world of the Other becomes a mere extension of the self. Later stories will render the confrontation of the adolescent girl with the world: 'Summer Idylle' simply abolishes that world.

Others of Mansfield's early sketches present a more explicit challenge to conventional sexual behaviour. 'Leves Amores' (1907), for instance, is a fairly frank record of a lesbian encounter between the narrator and an older woman. Claire Tomalin[13] speculates that it may have been this sketch which caused Harold Beauchamp to delay his consent to Kathleen's returning to England after her time at Queen's College.

'Juliet', the early novel-fragment I referred to in Chapter 1, is located not in the Pacific paradise of 'Summer Idylle' but within the confines of a family which upholds, and demands obedience to, a strict set of bourgeois codes and values.

The story also offers a sharper insight into the self-absorption, the contradictions and confusion, of the adolescent personality. Juliet herself acknowledges at one point: ' "I say I am independent – I am utterly dependent. I say I am masculine – no-one could be more feminine. I say I am complete – I am hopelessly incomplete." '[14] And when asked earlier if she wanted to leave New Zealand for Europe she admitted, ' "Yes – and no. I long for fresh experiences, new places – but I shall miss the things that I love here." '[15]

This sense of inner contradiction is projected in an externalised opposition between metropolitan London and colonial New Zealand, as well as one between the heroine's conventional boyfriend David and her rakish lover Rudolf. These oppositions present themselves to her as choices – or rather, stark alternatives – for action:

On the one hand lay the mode bohème, alluring, knowledge-bringing, full of work and sensation, full of impulse, pulsating with the cry of Youth Youth Youth. . . . On the other hand lay the Suitable Appropriate Existence, the days full of perpetual Society functions, the hours full of clothes discussions, the waste of life. 'The stifling atmosphere would kill me' she thought. The days, weeks, months, years of it all.[16]

But Juliet, in spite of her lifestyle and her resentment of the 'silken cords of parental authority', also shows a hankering after the conventional values she claims to reject. Her lover Rudolf tells it to her straight:

> 'Ah Mademoiselle' he said, raising his voice. 'You do not understand me. . . . We can never be friends, I fear. There are too many obstacles – you are too conventional. . . . It is the heritage from your parents. . . . You have fought against it but voilà there it is, always conquering you.'[17]

So the unhappy heroine ends up being criticised both for rebellion and for conventionality.

As previously suggested, Juliet is something of a self-portrait. She is much the same age, and represented in much the same position, as Mansfield herself while writing it. Both are caught between the conformist attitudes of their well-off and conventionally respectable families and the desire for a more independent life-style; between past and future; between New Zealand and England. And, like Juliet, her author was also at the time hesitating about her own sexual orientation. Juliet's relationships both with her girlfriend Pearl and with David are based on Mansfield's own life – the former on a college girlfriend, Vere Bartrick-Baker,[18] the latter on an unreciprocated early attachment to Arnold Trowell, twin brother of Garnet, her fiancé-to-be.

Unsurprisingly perhaps, the fictional Juliet cannot sustain the contradictions of her situation. She becomes Mansfield's first, and most dramatic, tragic young heroine; losing her beloved David to her friend Pearl then dying shortly afterwards apparently – the text is unclear at this point – while giving birth to Rudolf's child.

'Something Childish But Very Natural' (1914), Mansfield's longest completed work so far, also deals with failure to make the crucial transition from childhood to the adult world. Unlike 'Juliet', however, it locates the causes of this failure primarily within the individual's psyche rather than in the social pressures to which she is subjected.

At face value the tale reads like a sentimental love-idyll-turned-tragedy after the Victorian manner. Two young office-workers, Edna and Henry, meet on a commuter-train, and fall in love. Though they are at first blissfully happy the relationship eventually collapses because of their inability to 'cross over' from childhood into the harsher world of adult reality. Henry's Gothick dream of how they might set up house together conveys his lack of purchase on economic (or domestic) reality:

> 'perhaps if I disguised myself as an old man we could get a job as caretakers in some large house – that would be rather fun. I'd make up a terrific history of the house if anyone came to look over it, and you could dress up and be the ghost moaning and wringing your hands in the deserted picture gallery, to frighten them off. Don't you ever feel that money is more or less accidental – that if one really wants things it's either there or it doesn't matter?'
> She did not answer that – she looked up at the sky and said, 'Oh dear, I don't want to go home.' (p. 610)

And Edna rejects all Henry's attempts at sexual intimacy:

> 'Somehow I feel if once we did that – you know – held each other's hands and kissed, it would all be changed – and I feel we wouldn't be free like we are – we'd be doing something secret. We wouldn't be children any more ... silly, isn't it?' (p. 607)

Her determination not to enter the adult world is indicated in the cameo-scene of self-enclosed virginity which frames her as she and Henry emerge from a concert. Significantly this comes just after she has refused his gesture of intimacy:

> She turned and looked at him, pressing her hands to her cheeks in the way he knew so well, and behind her as if in a dream he saw the sky and half a white moon and the trees of the square with their unbroken buds. (p. 608)

Though upset by her rejection Henry still offers, appropriately, to 'bury the bogy' (p. 608) of her fears in the virgin-square.

Crisis is triggered at a moment of apparent resolution. While on an outing in the country the couple discover their dream-cottage. They rent it, Henry returns to wait for Edna. But Edna never turns up and the story's ending is one of darkness and despair.

For the alert reader hints of this outcome were present from the start. In the opening episode, for instance, Henry, discovering that his hat no longer fits him, puts it on one side. But the too-small hat,

from an earlier stage of life as it were, has nevertheless left its mark
– something which of course pleases the backward-looking Edna.
Similarly Edna's own flowing golden hair is more than a mere des-
criptive detail. Her refusal to put it up inevitably becomes emblematic of her refusal to *grow* up. But it also suggests both a desire
to attract and the need for a screen behind which to hide. When at
their second meeting Henry begs her to take her hat off and show
her hair she only does so under protest. And, though flattered by
his compliments, she at some deep level regards the request as an
intrusion: 'She leaned her elbows on her knees and cupped her chin
in her hands. "That's how I sit when I'm angry and then I feel it
burning me up. . . . Silly?" ' (p. 603).

The title of the story is taken straight from that of a poem by
Coleridge. The piece was composed in Germany, and sent home
to the poet's wife as a consolation – highly ambivalent – for his
absence from her:

> Had I but two little wings,
> And were a little feathery bird,
> To you I'd fly, my dear,
> But thoughts like these are idle things,
> And I stay here.
>
> But in my sleep to you I fly,
> I'm always with you in my sleep,
> The world is all one's own,
> But then one wakes and where am I?
> All, all alone.
>
> Sleep stays not though a monarch bids,
> So I love to wake at break of day,
> For though my sleep be gone,
> Yet while 'tis dark one shuts one's lids,
> And so, dreams on.

The poem is itself an enigmatic piece – superficially romantic and
lyrical, but with undertones of unease. These are particularly strong
in the hint that the narrator is prepared to bury himself in his
dream. Mansfield's story in effect spells out the implied terms of
the poem, making Henry's and Edna's failure to confront adult
life and their own adult selves the source of tragedy.

Coleridge's poem is discovered by Henry in an anthology on a station bookstall. No depth-reader, he is struck only by its surface charm. And, portentously, it is his discovery of it which leads to his first meeting with Edna: delayed, he dashes back on board just as the train draws out, and clambers into her compartment instead of his own.

The narrative becomes more dreamlike as it proceeds. Temporal connections between the later sections are not spelt out, and the relationship – if any – between the village and dream-house of the fifth section, and those of the sixth and seventh, are not disclosed. When visiting the house of Section V and fantasising with Edna about the idyllic life they might have there, Henry suddenly beats a panicky retreat from his own vision. At the same time he confers a kind of paradoxical reality on it by prophesying that, ' "It's going to turn into a dream" ' (p. 610).

At the beginning of the sixth section dream and reality get still further confused. Crisis is heralded by a direct allusion to Coleridge's poem – and by a hint that Henry is about to be overwhelmed by the dream:

> Ever since waking he had felt so strangely that he was not really awake at all, but just dreaming. The time before Edna was a dream, and now he and she were dreaming together and somewhere in some dark place another dream waited for him. (p. 611)

His repressed feelings find expression in images of *fin-de-siècle* vampirism – perhaps a portent of the dark vision that awaits him. But Henry himself ignores these sombre images:

> Edna with the marigold hair and the strange, dreamy smile filled him up to the brim. He breathed her; he ate and drank her. . . . He wanted to kiss Edna, and to put his arms round her and press her to him and feel her cheek hot against his kiss, and kiss her until he'd no breath left and so stifle the dream. (p. 612)

The final extract of the story has the hero waiting for his beloved in their new cottage. Ambiguities and sombre allusions become more frequent, finally coming to disturb the placid surface of the prose – even though Henry's own mood remains one of joyful anticipation. First he takes off his watch and leaves it in a china jar on the mantelpiece, thus symbolically abolishing time. His observation that he and Edna will have 'all to-morrow and to-morrow and to-morrow night' (p. 616), a darkly familiar phrase, only points up the ambivalence of the gesture. He then goes out and sits on the doorstep. Here the last boundaries between waking and sleeping are dismantled: 'He could hardly keep his eyes open, not that he was sleepy, but . . . for some reason . . . [both sets of suspension-marks are Mansfield's] and a long time passed' (p. 616).

The myth of the biblical Fall enters the story as Henry's Eden of bliss finally becomes the wilderness of this world – filled with shadows, and accommodating the 'serpent' of Edna's telegram: 'The garden became full of shadows – they spun a web of darkness over the cottage and the trees and Henry and the telegram. But Henry did not move' (p. 616). The dream which governed his and Edna's life together has come at last to engulf him; and in a finely ambivalent ending Edna has refused both the state of maturity and Henry himself.

'Something Childish' is a deceiving piece. It appears at first to be an insipid little tale of a childwoman and man in the Victorian mould. Claire Tomalin,[19] for example, calls it 'one of [Mansfield's] most vapid stories'.

However, to the extent that its pastiche of Romantic/Victorian sentimental attitudes fronts fundamental criticism of them it becomes a disturbing (even if not fully coherent) fable on the perils of clinging to the condition of childhood. The hero and heroine interpret the title of Coleridge's poem – and hence that of their own story – in a superficial and saccharine way: ' "That's all life is – something childish and very natural. Isn't it?" "Yes – yes, " she said eagerly. "That's what I've always thought" ' (p. 604). But the title is grimly ironical: childishness and its perpetuation, though a favourite literary conceit of the nineteenth century, are in fact anything but 'natural'.

In subverting the title of a Romantic poem in this way Mansfield has drawn particular attention to the logical consequence of the Romantic/Victorian obsession with children and childhood. And the gap she opens up between the hero's perspective and her own marks a significant stage in her efforts to give coherent expression in fiction to her own complex attitudes towards childhood and romance. It is in keeping with this vein of ironic criticism that – as in 'The Tiredness of Rosabel' – she set the private, and untenable, dreamworld of her hero and heroine against a 'modern' urban setting of commuter trains and office work, of telegrams and Polytechnics – an unromantic but indisputably 'real' world.

Though the hero and heroine of 'Something Childish' bear little superficial resemblance to Murry and Mansfield the story does appear to deal in the dissatisfactions Mansfield expressed at the time with their relationship. She once spoke critically of it as a 'child love', and a year later – admittedly when seriously ill – confided to herself in her Journal, 'You are important to him [i.e. Murry] as a dream. Not as a living reality.'[20] In particular, Edna's anguished cry of, '"But, Henry, – money! You see we haven't any money"' (p. 610), has the ring of a real-life complaint about it – especially as the practical streak it reveals in the heroine has no necessary connection with the sexual inhibition which largely governs her behaviour in the story. Indeed 'Something Childish' as we have it, with all its undercurrents, gaps and ambiguities, reads like the disrupted surface of another, untellable story – that of a young woman's fortunate escape from her feckless lover.

More generally the story offers a disillusioned comment on the first, haphazard year or two of Mansfield's and Murry's life together. In April 1912 Murry became Mansfield's lodger, and a little later her lover. In September the pair moved from London to Runcton, a village near Chichester, returning to the metropolis after only a couple of months. The enterprise was planned as a rural idyll. But it was marred by shortage of cash and fears about Mansfield's sterility as well as by the appearance of an unwelcome house-guest, a former lover of Mansfield's.

The following year Murry, the victim of a dishonest printer, was himself served with a bankruptcy order. Pursued by his – or his printer's – creditors, and themselves threatened with bankruptcy, Mansfield and Murry slipped away to Paris in December 1913. It was while they were there, and with renewed financial worries and the Runcton interlude very much in mind, that Mansfield wrote 'Something Childish' – an elegy for a broken dream.

'His Sister's Keeper', which has up to now remained unpublished, and appears to be unknown even to Mansfield scholars,[21] records an episode out of that dangerous world of sexuality which Edna refused. Its young heroine is, like the Little Governess, travelling alone on the Continent. The opening image makes use of the medieval figure of the mouth of hell to deliver a gloomy modern-day prophecy of sexual devouring and damnation: 'The girl came up on deck to find Dieppe like the mouth of some giant monster.'[22] The dramatic and dangerous events that the story records take place indirectly, however: they occurred only in its past, and nominally happened not to our heroine but to her Fellow Passenger on the train in which she is travelling. The heart of the piece is a nightmarish episode in which the companion recounts how on a visit to London she was led into a strange house, and locked in the bedroom. An intruder entered and attempted to assault her. He was finally revealed to be her brother. The heroine is deeply affected by the story: but the Fellow Passenger, having told her tale, seems simply to shrug it off.

It is hardly surprising that a narrative concerned with the taboo subjects of incestuous desire, attempted rape, and the relationship of desire to sexual violence should engage in strategies of evasion and displacement. Apart from the fact that the episode purports not to have happened to the heroine but to her double, and to have taken place in the story's past rather than its present, the whole thing hovers on the edge of fantasy: though the attack is reported as if it were an actual incident it is interpreted by the heroine merely as a 'strange, terrible dream'.

Before the telling of the tale the larger narrative had already set the two girls up as doubles, even though the Fellow Passenger has an air of greater confidence and experience than the heroine. Most notably both of them have brothers of whom they are extremely fond: the Fellow Passenger speaks the precise words about her brother that the heroine would have liked to have heard about hers. And the placing of the apostrophe in the story's title makes the brother the keeper of his *sisters* (plural), thus confirming the doubling relationship. That the heroine herself is in truth the intended victim of the incident, and the Fellow Passenger merely a device, is borne out by their different reactions to the relating of it.

Yet despite Mansfield's strategies of displacement the content of the story remains plainly dangerous, and it may well be partly because of this that it, unlike many of the other early writings, has remained unpublished and unknown even to this day.

Two later stories, 'A Dill Pickle' (1917) and 'Psychology' (1919?), both published by Mansfield in her second collection, *Bliss*, also investigate the element of power in sexual relationships. Here, however, the issue is the socially sanctioned one of mental control, and there is a corresponding emphasis on psychological complexity.

'Psychology' (1919?) is the more interesting of the two. It records a meeting between two lovers who claim to have found an answer to the kind of violence that governs 'His Sisters' Keeper'. They are a fashionably 'modern' couple, both writers, who attempt to live up to the rationalist ideal of a love-relationship based on 'pure' friendship.[23]

The story deals in the gap between the couple's tranquil Platonist ideal and their disturbingly passionate and complex feelings for each other. Though issues like domination, exploitation and passion are brushed aside by Mansfield's lovers, a deep-seated attachment to them remains, unsettling both their behaviour and their image of themselves.

The extent to which they are self-deceived is indicated in the ambivalence and inconsistency of their assertions. Here, for instance, is the woman rhapsodising to herself about the nature of their relationship:

> the special thrilling quality of their friendship was in their complete surrender. Like two open cities in the midst of some vast plain their two minds lay open to each other. And it wasn't as if he rode into hers like a conqueror, armed to the eyebrows and seeing nothing but a gay silken flutter – nor did she enter his like a queen walking soft on petals. No, they were eager, serious travellers, absorbed in understanding what was to be seen and discovering what was hidden – making the most of this extraordinary absolute chance which made it possible for him to be utterly truthful to her and for her to be utterly sincere with him. (pp. 112–13)

The image of the lovers' minds as 'two open cities in the midst of some vast plain' clearly conveys the aloofness and aridity of 'rational' friendship; and though rejected, the old romantic stereotypes (man as conqueror, woman as 'a queen walking on soft petals') remain seductive: what is more, they even suggest a solution to the lovers' dilemma – that of *mutual* conquest.

Later on, the man describes how he is entranced by the bust of a sleeping boy he has admired in the woman's studio:

> 'Often when I am away from here I revisit it in spirit – wander about among your red chairs, stare at the bowl of fruit on the black table – and just touch, very lightly, that marvel of a sleeping boy's head.'
>
> He looked at it as he spoke. It stood on the corner of the mantelpiece; the head to one side down-drooping, the lips parted, as though in sleep the little boy listened to some sweet sound. . . .

'I love that little boy,' he murmured. And then they both were
silent. (p. 114)

The man's admission of an attachment to the statue – a hint either
of homosexuality or of a devotion to high aestheticism, or most
likely, in a shaft at Bloomsbury, both – suggests deeper feelings.
But these are again suppressed in the name of Platonic friendship.

Then the man, speaking with what sets itself up as the voice of
propriety but which may well be a submission to more irrational
or more complex feelings, abruptly declares his intention to leave.
The woman is deeply hurt by this apparent rejection. But then an
adoring friend – an 'elderly virgin' – makes a chance call, offering
a bunch of violets and a boost to her confidence. Having no deep
emotional commitment the heroine finds it easy in this case both
to demonstrate affection and to retain control. Moreover the meeting leads to her writing a warmly conciliatory letter to her lover: by
increasing her – the woman lover's – self-esteem the 'elderly virgin'
has enabled her to take the initiative with her man. In other words,
the complexities of the relationship are not limited to the couple's
own behaviour: an apparently uninvolved a third party – presumably based on Mansfield's friend Ida Constance Baker – has also had
a critical effect.

The connection between the two episodes is signalled in the fact
that the heroine addresses both man and woman in the same way:
'"Good night, my friend. Come again soon."' (pp. 118–19). More
importantly, there is also a link-passage – a scene that invades the
heroine's consciousness as the man is taking his leave of her, and
which returns as the 'elderly virgin' offers her gift:

> For a moment she did not take the violets. But while she stood
> just inside, holding the door, a strange thing happened. . . . Again
> she saw the beautiful fall of the steps, the dark garden ringed
> with glittering ivy, the willows, the big bright sky. Again she
> felt the silence that was like a question. But this time she did not
> hesitate. She moved forward. Very softly and gently, as though
> fearful of making a ripple in that boundless pool of quiet, she put
> her arms round her friend. (p. 118)

The setting itself however, another Eden scene with its references
to a fall and a dark garden, to (poison) ivy and a (weeping) willow
– the Book of Genesis was mentioned earlier in the sketch – does

not augur well for the future course of the lovers' relationship. An earlier description of their misunderstandings has already made ironical reference to the labours of Adam and Eve:

'What a spectacle we have made of ourselves,' thought she. And she saw him laboriously – oh, laboriously – laying out the grounds and herself running after, putting here a tree and there a flowery shrub and here a handful of glittering fish in a pool. They were silent this time from sheer dismay. (p. 116)

And the pool-image recalls the description of the statue:

That silence could be contained in the circle of warm, delightful fire and lamplight. How many times hadn't they flung something into it just for the fun of watching the ripples break on the easy shores. But into this unfamiliar pool the head of the little boy sleeping his timeless sleep dropped – and the ripples flowed away, away – boundlessly far – into deep glittering darkness. (p. 114)

Here the striking thing is how the 'circle of warm, delightful fire and lamplight' (p. 114) modulates into the depth-image of the pool – an analogue for the shift from the conscious to the unconscious mind; from the light of perception to the dark springs of action.

In an earlier conversation the lovers had touched upon the then avant-garde subject of 'psycho-analysis' – the only direct indication in any of Mansfield's writings that she was aware of Freud's work. The man praises the habit amongst his generation of writers of 'going into its symptoms – making an exhaustive study of them – tracking them down – trying to get at the root of the trouble' (p. 115), on the ground that it is 'just wise enough to know that it is sick and to realise that [this is] its only chance of recovery' (p. 115). The woman declares herself against such a view. But in a letter written at the story's end – that is, after her meeting with the 'elderly virgin' has transformed her attitude towards her lover – she seems to cede to his point of view: '"I have been thinking over our talk about the psychological novel . . . it really is intensely interesting . . ."' (pp. 118–19).

The story does indeed underline the way in which the mind's depths work against its conscious intentions – something which the then revolutionary practice of 'psycho-analysis' was intended to reveal. The rational relationship to which the hero and heroine aspire is represented as a living lie – hindering access to disturbing but deeper and more 'genuine' feelings, and in contrast to one of its stated objectives forcing the woman to make all the concessions. (In a touch of black comedy – which draws again on the sex–food analogy – the man observes that he looks on food as something just 'to be devoured': when asked if that shocks her the woman replies, ' "To the bone" ' [p. 113].) The story's real joke is that the subject of the would-be rationalist lovers' one item of intellectual discussion concerns recent insights into the mind's irrationality.

'Bliss' (1918) engages in a more expansive manner – though still in-directly – with lesbian desire. This it does as part of a more extended investigation of the nature of female sexuality and the degree to which it is governed by social and cultural context – an agenda Mansfield's story shares with other key Modernist works.

Attempts had of course been made in the English fiction of the nineteenth century to convey the distinctive nature of woman's sexual desire – usually as part of an effort to render female aspiration in general: the most notable of these attempts are to be found in the novels of Charlotte Brontë. But with the relative liberalising of sexual attitudes after the Victorian period[24] and the Modernists' new faith in the supremacy of inner experience, there was renewed interest in conveying the nature of desire itself. In particular, a number of early twentieth-century writers devoted themselves to suggesting, and rendering, the nature of distinctively female sexuality. (Relevant here too is the general Modernist tendency to associate the human consciousness with qualities which our culture has traditionally de-fined as female, or feminine – passivity, fluidity, receptivity, acute sensitivity, irrationality.) Molly Bloom's soliloquy at the end of Joyce's *Ulysses* is the most celebrated of these attempts; Mansfield's 'Bliss', one of the first and in some ways the most radical.

Bertha Young, the heroine and perceiving consciousness of the story, is a married woman who has reached the age of thirty with-out ever feeling sexual desire for her husband. Yet when the nar-rative opens she is in the grip of near-hysterical ecstasy. The mood appears to be causeless:

Although Bertha Young was thirty she still had moments like this when she wanted to run instead of walk, to take dancing

steps on and off the pavement, to bowl a hoop, to throw something up in the air and catch it again, or to stand still and laugh
at – nothing – at nothing, simply. (p. 91)

This passage is followed by a mirror-glimpse in which Bertha
catches sight of herself 'waiting for something . . . divine to happen'
(p. 92, suspension-marks Mansfield's) – a sign that she may be on
the verge of some personal discovery. The story goes on to trace the
trajectory of her blissful feelings both before and during a dinner-
party she and her husband Harry are hosting for their friends. These
feelings are mobile and outward-directed: they focus first on some
fruit she arranges, next on her baby daughter Little B, then on a
pear-tree in her garden. They are also directed at her friend Pearl
Fulton, and finally at Harry himself.

Bertha's emotions fill her with an energy that clearly demands
release. But she is uncertain how to express it without offending
against the constraints of 'civilisation'. And although she is nervous
of her mood and attempts to escape from it she also tries to precipitate an increase in its power:

in her bosom there was still that bright glowing place – that
shower of little sparks coming from it. It was almost unbearable.
She hardly dared breathe for fear of fanning it higher, and yet
she breathed deeply, deeply. (p. 92)

When Bertha arranges a dish and a bowl of fruit for the dinner-
party she builds it into two pyramidal shapes. These shapes appear
to float in the air, lustrous and dematerialised – like symbols of
some abstract and archetypal beauty. She interprets the vision as
a confirmation of what she herself half-jokingly dismisses as her
'hysterical' condition. This reflects not only her extravagance of feeling but also the excesses of the contemporary aesthetic movement,
with its preoccupation with perceptual intensity and the detachment
of the art-object from 'real life'.

Obtaining no release from her 'ecstasy' through this act of artistic devotion, Bertha rushes off to see her baby daughter. But it is
supper-time in the nursery, and Little B is in the clutches of her
nanny. Like the 'poor little girl in front of the rich little girl with
the doll' (p. 93) Bertha feels excluded – though she does manage to
snatch up the baby and feed her while Nanny is out of the room.
The action only renews her charge of ecstasy.

If as C.A. Hankin suggests[25] the pyramidal shapes of the previous episode are supposed to symbolise breasts then the implication is clear. Bertha has followed upper-middle-class fashion and delivered her daughter up to the care of a nanny instead of nursing and looking after her herself. She now harbours a suppressed longing to do just this. And it is, the narrative implies, this unconscious desire to nurture Little B which expressed itself through the shapes into which she arranges the fruit – and which then sent her dashing off to the nursery. The breast-shapes also of course suggest another aspect of her self which she denies – her sexuality.

Moving from the nursery to the drawing-room, Bertha finds her attention caught by the view from the windows:

> At the far end, against the wall, there was a tall, slender pear tree in fullest, richest bloom; it stood perfect, as though becalmed against the jade-green sky. Bertha couldn't help feeling, even from this distance, that it had not a single bud or a faded petal. Down below, in the garden beds, the red and yellow tulips, heavy with flowers, seemed to lean upon the dusk. A grey cat, dragging its belly, crept across the lawn, and a black one, its shadow, trailed after. The sight of them, so intent and so quick, gave Bertha a curious shiver. (p. 96)

The heroine's reaction to this scene is divided. She feels deeply moved by the beauty of the pear tree, and indeed lays claim to it as 'a symbol of her own life' (p. 96). On the other hand, she withdraws instinctively from the sight of the cats – slinky, and sexually engaged. She also sees the tree as 'tall' and 'slender' – like herself perhaps. And indeed when she dresses for dinner it is in white, green and jade; colours that mimic the colours of the tree and the sky. Her explicit denial here of any connection with the tree ('She had thought of this scheme hours before she stood at the drawing-room window' [p. 97]) should be read as a sign of unconscious intent: as earlier critics have noted, Bertha's language throughout is self-deceivingly double.

Three of the guests at the Youngs' dinner-party turn out to be members of a smart 'arty' set whose superficial chatter serves to counterpoint Bertha's 'moments' of flaring intensity. The fourth guest is Pearl Fulton, an enigmatic young woman described in the story as a 'find' of the hostess's. Where Bertha identifies with the pear-tree to the extent of dressing herself in its colours, Pearl's silver signals her lunar affinity.

After dinner the two women go together to gaze out of the draw-ing-room windows, as the heroine had earlier done on her own. The moon is now up. As they stand side-by-side contemplating the scene Bertha envisages the tree in the shape of a flame that stretches ardently upwards – this detail is repeated several times – towards the rim of the moon. This she takes as a sign that she is experienc-ing a moment of perfect communion with her friend:

> And the two women stood side by side looking at the slender, flowering tree. Although it was so still it seemed, like the flame of a candle, to stretch up, to point, to quiver in the bright air, to grow taller and taller as they gazed – almost to touch the rim of the round, silver moon. (p. 102)

So the tree, taking on the aspiring quality of flame, and striving to reach (and presumably to penetrate) the virginal moon, both expresses and encodes the sexual attraction Bertha feels for her friend. (Most critics now accept that the episode centres upon les-bian desire.) In the next paragraph, however, Bertha reverts abruptly to the female position, seeing both herself and Pearl Fulton 'caught in that circle of unearthly light' (p. 102); and envisaging the two of them being showered with silver flowers.

Our heroine, then, permits herself to believe she has enjoyed a moment of true intimacy with Miss Fulton. Yet there are again indications that this belief is false: the flame representing her ar-dour only 'almost' touches the moon's rim, and both women are described as 'creatures of another world ... *wondering what they were to do in this one*' (p. 102, my italics). A second later Bertha herself admits that she may simply have imagined Miss Fulton's murmur of affirmation.

Finally – though only by way of a reference to her 'moment' of communion with Pearl – Bertha trains her emotional intensities on her husband. Believing Harry to dislike Pearl, she rehearses the pleading of her friend's case with him:

> 'Oh, Harry, don't dislike her. You are quite wrong about her. She's wonderful, wonderful. And, besides, how can you feel so differently about someone who means so much to me. I shall try to tell you when we are in bed to-night what has been happen-ing. What she and I have shared.'

At those last words something strange and almost terrifying
darted into Bertha's mind. And this something blind and smiling
whispered to her: 'Soon these people will go. The house will be
quiet – quiet. The lights will be out. And you and he will be alone
together in the dark room – the warm bed. . . .'
 She jumped up from her chair and ran over to the piano.
 'What a pity someone does not play!' she cried. 'What a pity
somebody does not play.'
 For the first time in her life Bertha Young desired her husband.
(p. 103)

So that which was identified at the beginning of the story as
'bliss' is finally revealed as repressed sexual desire fervently (and,
as the Cupid-figure indicates, blindly) seeking its own satisfaction.
The association with fear is also strong: though only partially articulated, Bertha's evocation of a 'strange and . . . terrifying' Cupid-figure
suggests the anticipation of a communion with Harry far more mysterious, and more disturbing, than any that may already have taken
place with Miss Fulton. The qualifier 'almost', as in 'almost terrifying' (p. 103), simply acts as an intensifier.
 It is, then, through her dimly-acknowledged passion for the apparently virginal Miss Fulton that Bertha at last becomes able to contemplate a fully-committed sexual relationship with Harry[26] – just as
the heroine's brief encounter with her adoring 'elderly virgin' friend
towards the end of 'Psychology' served to unblock her passion for
her heterosexual lover. The break in the text of the extract quoted
above indicates, as do similar gaps in other Mansfield stories, a
perceived connection between the two subjects.
 Bertha's shift of focus from Miss Fulton to her husband marks the
final stage in that sequence of events which traces her unfolding desire. There is a final, brutal twist, however, when she realises moments
later that her husband and her friend are lovers; and that she, far
from having achieved an intimate understanding with each of them,
is being excluded by them from their relationship with each other.
 The story ends with a brief return to that other couple – Bertha
and her pear tree. The topic of the pear tree is broached once more
in Miss Fulton's cynical farewell to her hostess: ' "Your lovely pear
tree!" ' (p. 105); words which were originally Bertha's own. With
Miss Fulton's farewell ringing in her ears the heroine rushes over
to the windows again – only to find that 'the pear tree was as lovely
as ever and as full of flower and as still' (p. 105).

To register the full significance of this conclusion we must turn once more to Bertha's initial vision of her garden. The diagrammatic nature of this vision, coupled with the emphatic and intensely personal way Bertha reacts to at least one element of it, hints that it may be a kind of objective correlative for her state of mind.

The lone pear tree seen in 'fullest, richest bloom' (p. 96) is unquestionably the dominant element in the scene. It is also the one aspect with which Bertha herself identifies. Why does she do so? The tree's lovely white flowers – 'not a single bud or a faded petal' (p. 96) – may at first suggest a kind of bridal openness. But as self-pollination does not normally take place in the case of the pear, and as Bertha's garden has only a single tree, a different (and opposed) interpretation, that of sterility, may well be the crucial one.[27]

The other features of this scene – the tulips 'heavy with flowers, [that] seemed to lean upon the dusk' (p. 96), and the cats, to which the departing Pearl Fulton and her pursuer Eddie are compared – appear to represent, respectively, generative fulfilment and a crudely instinctual sexuality. But, though both elements appear to have a certain relevance to the heroine's own psyche, neither compels her attention in the way the tree has. She does, however, bestow a passing shudder on the cats – something which in the story's complex psychical organisation suggests a deepseated fascination with them.

The garden, then, forms an emblem of Bertha's sexual proclivities.[28] However, mediated as it is by Bertha herself, it represents these proclivities not in a neutral manner but subtly influenced by her own idealised view of herself. The tree, beautiful and inviolate, stands for her own desired self-image; the tulips (presumably) for that aspect of procreative fulfilment which she has in some sense realised, but largely ignored, in Little B; the cats for an instinctual sexuality which she herself perceives as bestial, and emphatically rejects.

One might add that this emblematic vision marks the transition in the text from (or break between) the fruit and child scenes, in which sex is not directly involved, to the two later encounters, in which sexual engagement with another – with all its attendant risks and complexities – is the subject at issue. The emblem, and those aspects of the narrative on either side of it, emphasise the full extent of the split in the heroine's sexual identity between that which is approved and acknowledged, and that which is repressed. It also gives some indication of the consequences of this repression.

Unable to engage in a fulfilling sexual relationship with her husband, Bertha is overcome by feelings of frustrated desire. She does not realise, or else refuses to acknowledge, the nature and source of these feelings. But they are imperious, dictating her responses to those objects and persons she encounters during the evening – and eventually even guiding her towards Harry, their apparent ultimate object.

Mansfield's description of the manner in which the heroine comes to focus attention first on the fruit-arrangement, then on her daughter, then on Pearl Fulton and finally on Harry himself, does appear to suggest a dedicated and reasonably consistent – if subconscious – attempt on Bertha's part to find an outlet for these feelings.

This is not, however, the case. Any desire on Bertha's part for a renewed sexual engagement with Harry is mingled both with fear and with a sense of potential disillusion: 'Was this what that feeling of bliss had been leading up to? But then, then –' (p. 104). The prospect of a climax (in both senses) has been held out, yet none has been realised. We are presented in 'Bliss' neither with the conventional happy ending of romance nor with the sense of illumination which ought to conclude an 'education' story.

The story's plot, then, fails to resolve itself into a conventional narrative progression. Yet its subversion of conventional expectations does not, as some critics have suggested,[29] indicate incompetence on the part of its author: rather, it is a reflection of her attempt to convey both the non-goal-directed nature of Bertha's sexuality and the way the social climate in which she lives causes her to repress her own desires.

The heroine's anxieties and repressions, then, are no merely personal malaise. They have their origin within a social context closely defined in the story as that of the arty metropolitan upper middle class, represented by the Youngs' dinner-guests, together with Harry himself – although their real-life origin lies in the pretensions of the Garsington set: Mansfield herself described the would-be poet Eddie as 'a fish out of the Garsington pond'.[30]

Though Mansfield's manner of narration excludes us from these characters' inner lives, their social chatter, threaded through as it is with images of rape, mutilation, and sexual predation, reveals their obsessions. Some of the characters are also fixated on food – Mansfield's most frequent indicator of an aggressive and overbearing attitude towards sex. And as Hanson and Gurr point out[31] Bertha has considerable natural sexual vitality. Her inhibitions, far from being innate, are a reaction to the sadistic and salacious attitudes that characterise her milieu.

Sex, then, has become for the heroine critically divided – on the one hand a matter of innocence and spirituality in which bodily impulses play no part; on the other an affair of crude lust that denies the 'higher' aspects of the personality.[32]

Divided attitudes towards sexuality are also signified in the story's opposing metaphors of stillness (associated with the pear tree) and extravagant motion, with its attendant implications of a fast lifestyle. The latter finds its most striking, and comic, expression in Eddie Warren's nightmare taxi ride:

> 'I have had such a *dreadful* experience with a taxi-man; he was *most* sinister. I couldn't get him to *stop*. The *more* I knocked and called the *faster* he went. And *in* the moonlight this *bizarre* figure with the *flattened* head *crouching* over the *lit-tle* wheel ... saw myself *driving* through Eternity in a *timeless* taxi.' (p. 98)

And indeed in what becomes a sort of in-joke, taxi-riding is throughout associated with basic, physical sex – perhaps a reference back to a similar, and memorable, scene towards the end of *Madame Bovary*.[33] Harry, Eddie Warren, and Pearl all arrive in taxis, and when Bertha observes that her friend ' "lives in" ' them Harry outrageously replies, ' "She'll run to fat if she does. . . . Frightful danger for blonde women" ' (p. 99).

The consequences of this double attitude towards sex bear of course most heavily on women. The most glaring example of this is the way Mrs Norman Knight advertises her degradation through her 'monkey' dress. The only way for a woman to keep her self-possession in such a culture may be to dissimulate, like the enigmatic Pearl – acting publicly as a devotee of the goddess of chastity; carrying on an assignation in secret.

In 'Bliss', then, Mansfield presents what amounts to an anatomy of female sexual desire. This she renders, not as goal-directed but as fluid and tentative; giving the appearance of randomness yet conveying a strong sense of inner compulsion in the way it moves from artistic arrangement to child, from woman to man. She has also depicted in her heroine a sexual passion that gains in strength and richness through its association with artistic sensitivity and maternal affection; and one that connects heightened emotion with a wider range of experience than sexual gratification alone.

Desire and sexuality come then to relate to the whole field of (female) experience – in contrast to the single focus and goal-directed pursuit of the (male) lover. In transferring woman from object to subject position, and in focusing upon this subject rather than on the single, unifying object of Petrarchan tradition, Mansfield implicitly subverts key aspects of that tradition.

Bertha's impassioned awareness of Miss Fulton also works in terms of touch and a kind of symbolic or emotional apprehension rather than the visual cataloguing common to courtly-love poetry. Similarly we are told that Miss Fulton appears to live 'by listening rather than seeing' (p. 99). And in presenting us with a subject who aims to dissolve the conventional division between Self and Other by seeking to identify herself with the Other rather than being absorbed or conquered by it Mansfield is questioning the conventional Self–Other duality as well.

Bertha's several references to herself as 'hysterical' are clearly popular uses of the word. But the references, more apposite than the speaker would acknowledge, do serve as a clue to the story's subtextual engagement with hysteria in its clinical sense – as an involuntary expression of the subject's sexual desire.

The story also questions conventional assumptions regarding the normative nature of heterosexuality. By encouraging her readers to identify with Bertha and her 'polymorphous and perverse' sexuality Mansfield implicitly criticises the rigidity of conventional views on sexual behaviour. At the same time she makes clear the differing character of the woman/woman relationship (hesitant, 'mystical', beautiful) from the woman/man (mysterious, terrifying, 'sublime').

The story has from the beginning received a great deal of adverse criticism.[34] Much of this, however, is the result of a failure to comprehend its radicalism both in content and in form – in particular the way its narrative subverts any tendency towards logical sequence, climax, resolution – both in order to reflect Bertha's sexual trajectory and as an indication that for her there *is* no conventional happy ending, just as there is no climax in the sexual sense. Despite the early mirror-glimpse, nothing, in the end, 'happens' . . . because Bertha has still not made contact with her deeper self.

'Bliss' is an ambitious work: its investigation into the nature of female desire and its attendant experiments with the nature of narrative form give it a radical feel even today. And its overt juxtaposing of the lyrical–sentimental with a satirical vision marks a significant stage in the evolution of Mansfield's 'doubling' technique . . . though she later presents similar elements vertically, with a subversive underlying meaning subtly disturbing the lyrical surface.

However, the very starkness of the opposition in 'Bliss' between the lyrical and the satirical modes makes for stridency, and some of its symbolism is over-complex: it lacks the understated power of Mansfield's later, greater stories.

'The Stranger' (November 1920) is also concerned with the stereotypes of 'feminine' and 'masculine'. Its apparent initial acceptance of them gives way to a corrosive investigation that ends by thoroughly compromising any conventional notion of gender identity.

The story is, on the face of it, a touching if somewhat pointless evocation of a quayside reunion between a husband and wife after the woman's return from a visit to Europe. (It was apparently based on Annie Beauchamp's homecoming after her own trip to England in 1909 to 'sort out' her errant daughter.)

Mansfield begins, as she often does, by drawing superficial distinctions between male/female apparel and attributes, speech and gesture. These distinctions are then used to unlock underlying divergences of behaviour and sensibility. The reader's initial impression (obtained partly from the man himself) is of the husband as a strong and dominant, even overbearing, figure; the wife as small and vulnerable. But as the story unfolds, his extreme emotional dependence upon her is revealed.

'The Stranger' begins by presenting the husband Hammond as he sees himself – in terms of a series of attributes and associations that are conventionally linked to maleness and to masculinity:

> In front of the crowd a strong-looking, middle-aged man, dressed very well, very snugly in a grey overcoat, grey silk scarf, thick gloves and dark felt hat, marched up and down twirling his folded umbrella. He seemed to be the leader of the little crowd on the wharf and at the same time to keep them together. He was something between the sheep-dog and the shepherd. (p. 350)

And Janey Hammond is first seen – also through the husband's own eyes – as 'a white glove shaking a handkerchief' (p. 354). The sight of these feminine attributes triggers an outburst of protective feeling on Hammond's part:

> how small she looked on that huge ship. His heart was wrung with such a spasm that he could have cried out. How little she looked to have come all that long way and back by herself! (p. 354)

This second view is clearly not an 'objective' one: the husband's impression of Janey's smallness, like the story's opening vision of the people on board ship as 'flies walking up and down the dish on the grey wrinkled tablecloth' (p. 350), is a function of distance. But it is also the result of his need to believe that he has a vulnerable wife, in order to bolster his uncertain sense of his own masculinity. His possessiveness – another indicator of insecurity – leads him to make unreasonable demands upon Janey's independence. It also leads him to set their children up as his rivals for her attention.

Hammond fears, however irrationally, that his wife's heart has been stolen from him by a young man who died in her arms shortly before the ship arrived in port. The shock of this is rendered in terms of a metaphorical seizure of the heart, which causes him loss of strength; heart-spasms and a 'slow, deep flush' (p. 361); feelings of extreme cold, of acute disorientation, of mutilation and even death.

This symbolic coronary links Hammond with the 'stranger' whom Janey comforted, and who did in 'fact' die of a heart attack. For Janey has also been a stranger to Hammond himself. By the end of the story the 'little woman' proves to have been not only the strong partner in the marriage but – to Hammond's chagrin – a pillar of support to 'the whole first-class' (p. 356) as well. The ship she travelled on, depicted at the beginning of the story as a kind of great female principle, host to all the tiny figures who parade her decks, proves in the end to be the appropriate image for Janey herself:

> It seemed to the little crowd on the wharf that she was never going to move again. There she lay, immense, motionless on the grey crinkled water, a loop of smoke above her, an immense flock of gulls screaming and diving after the galley droppings at the stern. You could just see little couples parading – little flies walking up and down the dish on the grey crinkled tablecloth. (p. 350)

It is after all Hammond who is the vulnerable one. (The ironies are compounded when we remember that it was Mansfield's mother, the original of Janey, who in fact died of a heart attack, two years before the story was written.)

'Mr. and Mrs. Dove' (July 1921) also interrogates conventional notions of gender identity. It was panned by the critics when it appeared – in the *Sphere* – and the author herself expressed disquiet about its contrived quality.[35] Yet it is worth reading for its gentle wit, for its subtle deconstruction of romantic love, and for its audacious rendering of passion and sexual threat – as well as for its investigation of gender stereotypes.

The story begins by tracing the progress of the shy young suitor Reggie as he sets off to propose to his beloved. Reggie is inexperienced, goodnatured, unassuming . . . and just a little absurd. His callowness is suggested in the bright green aura – in fact a reflection from the tree outside – that confronts him as he peers, anxious (and womanlike), into his mirror:

> He was still fearfully pale – worse even than usual this afternoon, he thought, bending forward and peering into the mirror. Good heavens! What had happened? His hair looked bright green. Dash it all, he hadn't green hair, at all events. That was a bit too steep. And then the green light trembled in the glass; it was the shadow from the tree outside. (p. 286)

Before leaving the house he also muses on the nature of his feelings for his beloved:

> was this queer, timid longing to have the chance of looking after her, of making it his job to see that she had everything she wanted, and that nothing came near her that wasn't perfect – just love? How he loved her! (p. 286)

Then he indulges a fantasy which both infantilises his Anne and places her in a situation of security-within-danger – asleep in a train in the Southern African jungle . . . watched over of course by himself.

This pleasing fantasy is tested only moments later, when Reggie's vision of a vulnerable and docile Anne gives way to the real-life spectacle of his 'mater' in the garden dead-heading the flowers. She is flanked by her lieutenants, a couple of 'ancient' Pekes who function as miniature signifiers of her own ferocity.

The mater herself makes clear her competing claim upon her son's affections: '"I should have thought you could have spared your mother your last afternoon ..."' (p. 288). And her hold over him is indicated through a jokey reference to a popular song:

> whenever Reggie was homesick out there, sitting on his dark veranda by starlight, while the gramophone cried, 'Dear, what is Life but Love?' his only vision was of the mater, tall and stout, rustling down the garden path, with Chinny and Biddy at her heels. . . . (p. 287)

The threat to Reggie's manhood which the mater poses is suggested literally and, though the suggestion is again decked out as a joke, the joke is an uneasy one:

> The mater, with her scissors outspread to snap the head of a dead something or other, stopped at the sight of Reggie.
> 'You are not going out, Reginald?' she asked, seeing that he was.
> 'I'll be back for tea, mater,' said Reggie weakly, plunging his hands into his jacket pockets.
> Snip. Off came a head. Reggie almost jumped. (pp. 287–8)

Subliminally conscious of the threat, Reggie eventually manages to unhook himself from it by turning his attention to the flowers, present victims of the mater's attentions: 'Snip went the scissors again. Poor little beggars; they were getting it!' (p. 288).

Finally liberated from his mother he sets off for Anne's home. He is now also free to appreciate the beauties of the afternoon – and indeed to become a sexual being. As so often in Mansfield the landscape becomes an indicator of the state of mind of the character who passes through it: this one is filled with signs of fertility. The sun has broken out after rain, the flowers are large and brilliant, droplets of water splash down on Reggie, petals and pollen scatter over the sleeve of his coat. And the speed and urgency of his quest, as well as his final entry, reckless but overawed, into Anne's family's shadowy drawing-room, all suggest the conquering hero's entry into the beloved.

With the appearance of Anne herself, however, the story's mood changes. Reggie's romantic dreams and sexual urgency give way abruptly to her clearsighted, ironical, and slightly disparaging vision

of their future together. She 'fixes' this vision of humdrum domesticity in a deadly comparison of the two of them to her pet doves:

> 'You see,' explained Anne, 'the one in front, she's Mrs. Dove. She
> looks at Mr. Dove and gives that little laugh and runs forward,
> and he follows her, bowing and bowing. And that makes her
> laugh again. Away she runs, and after her,' cried Anne, and she
> sat back on her heels, 'comes poor Mr. Dove, bowing and
> bowing . . . and that's their whole life. They never do anything
> else, you know.' (p. 291)

Other details – the blue-and-cream (i.e. dove-coloured) tie which
Reggie is wearing, and the cooing which echoes his declamations –
have already prepared the way for the comparison.

The parallel is a typically (for Mansfield) ambivalent one. On the
one hand it diminishes Reggie's and Anne's relationship – Reggie's
slavish devotion in particular. On the other hand by drawing upon
the dove's classical significance as an emblem of peace and love it
signals that the marriage will be one of loving harmony.

Just as Reggie's mater is to be supplanted in his life by Anne, her
guardian pekes are in the narrative substituted for the doves. The
substitution indicates, amongst other things, that Anne will make
him a more amiable companion than the mater. So the story concludes with Anne calling her retreating lover back to her – where
the mother had precipitated his retreat:

> '*Roo-coo-coo-coo! Roo-coo-coo-coo!*' sounded from the veranda,
> 'Reggie, Reggie,' from the garden.
> He stopped, he turned. But when she saw his timid, puzzled
> look, she gave a little laugh.
> 'Come back, Mr. Dove,' said Anne. And Reginald came slowly
> across the lawn. (p. 294)

Yet the two women also bear comparison. Just as the mater now
dominates her son, so will Anne have authority over her husband.
Reggie's alluring dream of protecting the beloved, and hers of a
romantically masterful lover, both collapse before the reality of her
more forceful personality. And the uneasy sense the reader may
have that the Anne–Reggie match, though triumphing over a false
romanticism, is not ideal, is confirmed by the author's own gloss:
I mean to imply that those two may not be happy together – that
that is the kind of reason for which a young girl marries.'[36]

'The Doves' Nest' (January 1922) also employs the dove metaphor, drawing on a different aspect of that bird's cultural significance – its inability to defend itself. Though unfinished and relatively
unknown it is one of Mansfield's most brilliant pieces, powerfully
conveying its luminous setting ('the whole Mediterranean swung
before the windows' [p. 442]) and linking it to the heroine's anticipation, almost certainly not to be realised, of sexual rapture.

The piece is ostensibly lighthearted – the story of how an eligible
bachelor becomes romantically drawn to the young heroine while
lunching at her mother's villa. But it also functions as a cautionary
tale with tragic undertones; a warning to innocent young women to
beware the marriage trap.

Again Mansfield subverts the stereotypes of female and male. Presumed 'feminine' traits like timidity and scattiness are treated with
gentle ridicule while what these days is known as 'trophy-hunting'
is unmasked by the figuring of a glamorous middle-aged bachelor
as a sinister predator about to snatch a fledgling from the nest.

This nest, that of the title, is a smart Mediterranean villa in which
an English widow Mrs Fawcett, her nubile daughter Milly, and their
companion Miss Anderson have taken up residence after the death
of Mrs Fawcett's husband. Like several others of Mansfield's loca-
tions the villa is a female enclave: not only the residents but also its
servants – Marie the disturbingly insightful maid, and Yvonne the
earthy kitchen-hand – are female, and males do not as a rule ven-
ture over its threshhold. The one man to have done so was absent-
mindedly ridiculed by Mrs Fawcett, and has not returned. (As a
clergyman – and a married one – he was more or less emasculated
anyway.)

However, the women have a double attitude towards their seclu-
sion. They see the villa as a haven – ' "I could live for years without
going outside the garden gate," ' (p. 441) Mother observes – but
they also feel its lack of men as a critical deficiency:

> why should the fact of their having a man with them make
> such a difference? It did; it made all the difference. Why should
> they feel so stirred at the sight of that large hand outspread, mov-
> ing among the wine glasses? Why should the sound of that loud,
> confident 'Ah-hm!' change the very look of that dining-room?
> (p. 451)

So, when an eligible bachelor on a visit from the States pays a call,
he is made welcome – even fêted.

Milly, another Mansfield adolescent hovering on the verge of womanhood, is more circumspect than the older women. But her boisterousness at the prospect of his appearance, her explicitly-stated 'yearning to fly' the nest, her embarrassments and hesitations, her Gothicky fears and fantasies, all indicate her interest. However, the child in her indignantly rejects Miss Anderson's little Homage to Men:

> 'It will make quite a little change in our little party,' said the much-too-pleasant voice. 'I confess I miss very much the society of men. I have had such a great deal of it in my life. I think that ladies by themselves are apt to get a little – h'm – h'm . . .'. And helping herself to cherry jam, she spilt it on the cloth.
> Milly took a large, childish bite out of her roll. There was nothing to reply to this. But how young Miss Anderson made her feel! She made her want to be naughty, to pour milk over her head or make a noise with a spoon.
> 'Ladies by themselves,' went on Miss Anderson, who realised none of this, 'are very apt to find their interests limited.'
> 'Why?' said Milly, goaded to reply. (pp. 447–8)

Food is used throughout as a signifier of sexual experience. Much of the time Milly herself is the target of this innuendo, figuring as a sort of sacrificial lamb to be set before the honoured guest. The parallel is spelled out for us by Mrs Fawcett – who not unnaturally declines to grasp its significance herself:

> 'I think a leg of lamb would be nice, don't you, dear?' said Mother. 'The lamb is so very small and delicate just now. And men like nothing so much as plain roast meat. Yvonne prepares it so nicely, too, with that little frill of paper lace round the top of the leg. It always reminds me of something – I can't think what. But it certainly makes it look very attractive indeed.' (p. 444)

And the story as we have it ends with Milly herself nibbling at a sugar-lump that she has apparently been offered by Mr Prodger – a clear portent of the giving (or receiving) of sexual favours.

As the story proceeds, all the women in turn offer up a tributary gift to their guest. From the cook there is, appropriately, more food – a gorgonzola fit for a prince; from Miss Anderson the chance of some manly political discussion. Milly's gift, that of her own self, of course marks the ultimate sacrifice.

But it is the maid's present that is the most intriguing. Well before Mr Prodger's visit Marie had dreamed of arranging the oval flower-dish on the dining-table as a series of funeral wreaths appropriate to the situation and sexual identity of each of the ladies in turn. These floral creations become a kind of female, and domestic, equivalent to the 'Tomb' poems of the French poet Mallarmé. The first of them, *Tomb of Mademoiselle Anderson*, is made up of black pansies (for deathly piety), lily-of-the-valley (for chastity), and heliotrope (Miss Anderson more than any of the other women follows male attitudes, turns towards male authority). Mother's tomb, though it suggests cheerfulness and jollity, is dubbed *coeur saignant* by Marie (for the 'bleeding heart' of the widow). Milly's arrangement is 'all white' (for virginity) with just a sprig or two of dark, funereal edging (presumably for Father).

However, it is the luncheon for Mr Prodger that gives Marie her greatest opportunity – to make up a floral 'funeral creation' for the honoured guest. This mock-heroic enterprise is attended by hints of proscription and of broken command, and by trepidation on the part of Marie herself – none of which is surprising when the linguistic derivation of the word 'orchid' (Greek for 'testicle') is brought to mind. It is also marked by danger, as the jokey tone suggests:

> But to-day – the glory of her opportunity made Marie feel quite faint as she seized her flower scissors. *Tombeau d'un beau Monsieur.* She was foridden to cut the orchids that grew round the fountain basin. But what were orchids for if not for such an occasion? Her fingers trembled as the scissors snipped away. (p. 446)

In her flower-arranging the unnervingly insightful Marie becomes another of Mansfield's domestic artists – women who are both ironised and celebrated for raising everyday household chores to the level of high cultural activity. Clad in a heart-shaped apron, and hinting as she does at the prospect of marriage between Milly and Mr Prodger, she is also a sort of domestic Cupid. And it is she as well who makes the traditional connection, hinted at elsewhere in the story, between sexual union and mortality.

As well as Mr Prodger another, less material male presence hovers over the villa – the ghost of Father. (At one point a butterfly, traditional emblem of the soul, is also mentioned in connection with him.) Mother feels she has been guided by Father's ghost in issuing her fateful luncheon invitation to his old friend:

'I suddenly seemed to hear Father say to me "Ask him to lunch."
And then there was some – warning. . . . I think it was about the
wine. But that I didn't catch – very unfortunately,' she added
mournfully. (p. 443)

And in another conversation with Milly she confesses to misgivings
about having bought her brimless hat (the 'jampot', as Milly calls it)
– presumably because 'jampots', unlike the safer 'mushrooms', project a flirtatious image. Their shape also suggests female sexuality.
Mrs Fawcett, though clearly unaware of these connotations, muses
over whether she ought to remodel the 'jampot' as a workbag, thus
transforming her image from woman-as-temptress to woman-as-
provider; turning it symbolically as well as literally upside down.
Again it is the memory, or ghost, of Father which guides her:

'. . . I am still not quite certain whether I was wise in buying a
jampot. I cannot help the feeling that if I were to meet Father
in it he would be a little too surprised. More than once lately,'
went on Mother quickly, 'I have thought of taking off the trimming, turning it upside down and making it into a nice little
workbag. . . .' (pp. 448–9)

More than any other of Mansfield's stories, 'The Doves' Nest'
deals in the difference between the genders – subtle distinctions
in sensibility, in manner, in predisposition: how one presses the
'bell-push' or makes conversation; whether one notes the beauty
of the scenery (as Mother does) or enquires with Mr Prodger, ' "Is
all this antique furniture genuine, may I ask?" ' (p. 441). The repeated
metaphoric association of the women with flowers draws attention to their presumed feminine beauty but also to their fragility.
And the description of the mood of anticipation as they await Mr
Prodger's arrival suggests that passivity which is a presumed aspect
of their sexual nature: 'In that moment of hovering silence something timid, something beseeching seemed to lift, seemed to offer
itself, as the flowers in the salon, uplifted, gave themselves to the
light' (p. 450). The passage also exposes with gentle irony the deference which women habitually pay to men.
The ladies are associated with birds and butterflies as well as with
flowers, so that their field of relevance takes on something of the
charm and crowded precision of a Gothic tapestry. This is in contrast to the austere presentation of Mr Prodger, whose consciousness

remains enigmatically closed to the reader throughout – a rare thing in a Mansfield story. He is also completely without the ladies' rich penumbra of associated emblems. Like the spinsterly Miss Anderson he is endowed only with the abstract quality of coldness: he catches a heavy cold; his hand is 'so very chill . . . like a hand stretched out to you from the water' (p. 450).

Being cold, Mr Prodger gravitates naturally towards the heat. He comes to the Riviera for the sun, and when staying in hotels orders 'hot plates' (call girls?) at all hours. He also admires the supper-gong that is compared in the text to a fallen sun, and which Marie coaxes into an orgasmic burst of triumph:

> the beautiful brass gong, that burned like a fallen sun in the shadows of the hall, began to throb. First it was a low muttering, then it swelled, it quickened, it burst into a clash of triumph under Marie's sympathetic fingers. (p. 451)

Neither his natural coldness nor his pursuit of the passion he so conspicuously lacks augurs well for Milly in her future relations with him. But Marie's observation, '"*Et voilà pour les cors de Monsieur!*"' (p. 445), made as she seizes a bottle of Sauternes to take to the table, indicates that Mr Prodger will not have it all his own way.

In 'The Doves' Nest', then, Mansfield pokes fun at stereotypical feminine attitudes – the deference that women pay to men, their belief that only the presence of a man can bestow a sense of occasion, the way they need A Man to take the decisions for them . . . even when the 'man' in question is a ghost.

But there is a darker theme underlying the story's surface mood of comedy and amorous celebration. For Mr Prodger, the object in one way or another of each of the women's desires, is also a darkly sinister figure – the predator who invades the nest of gentle and compliant doves in order to snatch the fledgling from their midst. Though charming, feminine helplessness has its perils.

Yet once again there is a hidden joke. For the tale is also something of a *conte à clef*: the name of the heroine is that of a well-known writer and campaigner for women's suffrage, Dame Millicent Fawcett, after whom the present-day Fawcett Society is named. The implication here is of course a feminist one – that Milly finally gets her revenge on her forceful future husband . . . by becoming a pioneer of women's rights.

Mansfield must have known of Millicent Fawcett and may well even have met her, for she and her husband, the MP Henry Fawcett, lived in Gower Street in Bloomsbury, just up the road from a house which John Maynard Keynes once rented out to Mansfield and Murry together with their friends Dorothy Brett and Dora Carrington. The Fawcetts' home was also just a few doors away from the Bloomsbury residence of Lady Ottoline Morrell, another friend of Mansfield's. The engaged quality of 'The Doves' Nest' certainly suggests personal acquaintance on the author's part. (Henry Fawcett, the real-life Mr Prodger, was incidentally blind – another referent for the images of darkness associated with him but also a touch of bad taste on Mansfield's part that may have contributed to her abandoning the story.)

The work's underpinning of highly-charged radiance with a sense of future doom is reminiscent of the New Zealand stories of the same period: although they escape its uneasy mixture of comic innuendo, lyrical rapture, and menace.

Like 'The Doves' Nest', 'Poison' (November 1920) backs a tale of sexual passion with the brilliance of a southern landscape. Here, however, the passion is in decline: the relationship has decayed into one of obsessive jealousy on the one side, dedicated deception on the other.

The piece is sustained by only the slightest of plots. Two lovers are living together in a secluded villa. The woman can think only of a letter she is expecting from another lover. She asks the man to go and collect the afternoon's post; and he, half-aware of what is going on, sees the request as yet another drop of poison in the dose he is being administered.

Though the letter does not arrive during the course of the story a newspaper containing a report of the trial of a husband accused of poisoning his wife turns up instead. This moves Beatrice the heroine to hold forth on the frequency with which wives and husbands in general resort to poisoning each other:

'The man in the dock may be innocent enough, but the people in court are nearly all of them prisoners. Haven't you ever thought' – she was pale with excitement – 'of the amount of poisoning that goes on? It's the exception to find married people who don't poison each other – married people and lovers.' (p. 679)

There is a critical gap between the self-deceiving picture the Narrator creates of himself as the blissful lover, and the underlying anxieties and tensions he feels about the loyalty of his partner. These surface in the ambivalence of his language and behaviour – most strikingly in the image of sexual devouring which for him recalls the beginning of their relationship:

> I was twenty-four at the time. And when she lay on her back, with the pearls slipped under her chin, and sighed 'I'm thirsty, dearest. *Donnez-moi un orange,*' I would gladly, willingly, have dived for an orange into the jaws of a crocodile – if crocodiles ate oranges. (p. 676)

His being deceived is hinted at in Beatrice's quotation (or misquotation) of the first two lines of Coleridge's 'Something Childish But Very Natural'[37] – in itself a clear indication that the woman's allegiance lies elsewhere:

> Had I two little feathery wings
> And were a little feathery bird ...
> (p. 676)

In a commentary that is in some ways more illuminating and more eloquent than the sketch itself Mansfield gives an account of the nuances and subliminal tensions she had tried to convey in it. She also indicates her own feeling that she has failed:

> The story is told by (evidently) a worldly, rather cynical (not wholly cynical) man *against* himself (but not altogether) when he was so absurdly young. You know how young by his idea of what woman is. She has been up to now, only the vision, only she who passes. You realise that? And here he has put *all* his passion into this Beatrice. It's *promiscuous love*, not understood as such by him; perfectly understood as such by her. But you realise, the *vie de luxe* they are living – the very table – sweets, liqueurs, lilies, pearls. And you realise? she expects a letter from someone calling her away. *Fully* expects it? That accounts for her farewell AND her declaration. And when it doesn't come even her *commonness* peeps out – the newspaper touch of such a woman. She can't disguise her chagrin. She gives herself away. . . . He, of course, laughs at it now, and laughs at her. Take what he says about her 'sense of order' and the crocodile. But he also regrets the self who dead privately would have been young

enough to have actually wanted to *marry* such a woman. But I meant it to be light – tossed off – and yet through it – oh, subtly – the lament for youthful belief. These are the rapid confessions one receives sometimes from a glove or a cigarette or a hat.

I suppose I haven't brought it off in *Poison*. It wanted a light, light hand – and then with that newspaper a sudden . . . let me see, *lowering* of it all – just what happens in promiscuous love after passion. A glimpse of staleness. And the story is told by the man who gives himself away and hides his traces at the same moment.[38]

The fascination of this teasing little sketch lies, then, in the way its readers share in the narrator's neuroses by being forced to question whether or not the poisoning is for real. In doing this they are also obliged to question the extent of the boundary between fiction and reality – and thus of course to acknowledge the power of Mansfield's fable. By pushing her fiction to the frontiers of 'reality' she denies them the easy consolation of any escape from its truths. The references in her commentary to the light touch she had been aiming for indicates the effort she made to register deep and distorted feelings by implication only – without weighing down the tone of the whole; something which is in keeping with her overall artistic agenda.

The stories we have been looking at play on the northerner's traditional enthusiasm for the southern European landscape; 'The Man without a Temperament' (1920) reflects the discontents of the enforced expatriate in the same setting. At the same time it uses illness as a metaphor for the repressions and concealed power-politics of a sexual relationship.

The piece centres around an English couple. The wife is a chronic invalid, and they have moved abroad for the sake of her health. Of necessity their relationship becomes one of absolute dependence on her part, of total sacrifice on his. The dependence is conveyed through casual references to her light, dragging steps, her leaflike hand, her 'cobweb' of a shawl. It is the wife who unwittingly spells out the extent of the sacrifice: '"You're bread and wine, Robert, bread and wine. Oh, my darling – what am I saying?"' (p. 143).

Robert, however, makes his sacrifice in a mood of simmering resentment. Most of the time this lies half-buried beneath a façade of passivity and calm. But it breaks through in his nervous tics – like his insistent ringing of the hotel's service-bell, and his habit of turning the signet ring on his finger. The ring-turning gesture is particularly eloquent: it draws attention both to his obsession with the apparent endlessness of his present existence ('Eternity. . . . Like a great ring of pure and endless light'[39]), and to the fact that it is his marriage which has trapped him. Again it is his innocent wife Jinnie who gives the game away: ' "do you mind awfully being out here with me?" ' (p. 143) she asks as she herself revolves the ring.

Robert's one-word response is on the face of it a curious one:

> He bends down. He kisses her. He tucks her in, he smooths the pillow.
> 'Rot!' he whispers.
>
> (p. 143)

It has been suggested to me that this reply, which concludes the story, is a terse command to his wife – something in direct contradiction to his apparent gentleness. It is moreover his most straightforward expression of what he feels is happening to him: he is rotting away. But the response also reflects his northerner's attitude towards the alien south with its luxuriant vegetation – an attitude which connects ripeness with rankness, the natural (and the decaying) with decadence.

The richly suggestive setting of the story indirectly reflects other key aspects of the Salesbys' relationship as well – its damaged and dependent nature ('two crippled palms, two ancient beggars [stand] at the foot of the staircase' [p. 130]); its unreality (the plush interior of the hotel contains 'conjuror's furniture' [p. 130]); its connotations of entrapment, of threat, and of predation: the American Woman is sitting 'in the shadow of a great creeping thing with wide open purple eyes that pressed – that flattened itself against the glass, hungrily watching her' (p. 129); the hotel lift is an 'iron cage' (p. 130); and the 'coils' of knitting belonging to two of the guests are compared to snakes (p. 129).

The other hotel guests are little more than cardboard cutouts. But, like the guests of the German pension, they are cutouts charged with supranormal vitality. All are couples or caricatures of couples – the spinsterly Two Topknots, the American Woman with her lapdog Klaymongso, the weirdly vital Honeymoon Couple, the ageing and malicious General and Countess. Each makes an implicit comment both upon coupledom in general and upon the relationship between the Salesbys in particular – the Topknots on their sexlessness, the Honeymoon Couple on their listlessness, the General and Countess on their proneness to an early, and querulous, ageing.

Finally the American Woman and her pet suggest the unacknowledged imbalance of power in the Salesbys' relationship – in particular Robert's slavish yet resentful devotion. According to the
American, she and her Klaymongso (American for Clémenceau,
Prime Minister of France during the last years of the Great War
and its immediate aftermath) are '"having a feast of reason and a
flow of soul"' (p. 140) – that is, celebrating the Enlightenment values
upon which the United States and post-revolutionary France were
founded. This of course parodies the association between the two
countries – once perhaps a relationship between equals but in the
period after the Treaty of Versailles one in which France was very
much the client partner.

The Honeymoon Couple in particular have an uncanny vitality
that underlines both Jinnie's perpetual exhaustion and the edgy
self-control of her husband. They enter the story 'half-striding, half-
running' (p. 133); their laughter – 'wheeling, tumbling, swooping'
(p. 135) – can barely be contained within the artificial space of the
glass verandah; a fishing trip they have just been on acquires a
strong sexual undertone: 'She looked as though her young husband
had been dipping her in the sea and fishing her out again to dry in
the sun and then – in with her again – all day' (p. 134).

In tubs in a corner of the garden, three little girls – surely the
three children for whom the Honeymoon Couple had reserved
part of their catch – are bathing naked. But as Robert approaches
they flee in terror shrieking, '"The Englishman! The Englishman!"'
(p. 135). Jinnie is outwardly puzzled by their modesty: '"Surely
they were much too young to . . ."' (p. 136) – though inwardly she
interprets their fears as a sign of Robert's sexual magnetism, seeing him afterwards in a flattering (if slightly menacing) light: 'She
thought he looked pale – but wonderfully handsome with that
great tropical tree behind him with its long, spiked thorns' (p. 136).
However, the truth is surely that the little girls have sensed and
been disturbed by the repressed aspects of Robert's sexuality.

'The Man Without a Temperament' concludes in the couple's
bedroom. Jinnie is in bed, and bathed in moonlight – a chaste, even
sepulchral figure. In the distance lightning flutters' – flutters like a
wing – flutters like a broken bird that tries to fly and sinks again
and again struggles' (p. 142), a Mallarméan image suggesting some
distant, dying struggle which the reader finally realises with a sense
of shock, must be the heroine's.

The final episode of the story has Robert catching and killing a mosquito which has found its way inside Jinnie's mosquito-net. The episode resists any easy interpretation, but the blood-sucking insect does appear to connect with Robert's own distorted view of Jinnie; the killing with his own repressed desires.

A note in Mansfield's *Journal* for 10 January 1920 indicates the close connection between 'The Man Without a Temperament' and her relations with her own husband: 'Thought out *The Exile* [an early title for 'The Man Without a Temperament']. Appalling night of misery, deciding that J. had no more need of our love'[40] and in an earlier *Journal* entry[41] she lamented that Murry was 'not warm, ardent, eager, full of quick response, careless, spendthrift of himself, vividly alive, *high-spirited*'; that is, that he lacked 'temperament'.

Mansfield wrote the story while residing abroad – like Jinnie – for the sake of her health but, unlike Jinnie, alone. It is one of the few pieces by her that features a male centre of consciousness. The work may be interpreted both as a consolation to herself for what did *not* happen, and as a fictionalised release of her own resentment towards Murry precisely because it did not. (Murry, who had declined to accompany her, pleading pressure of work, was at the time editor of *The Athenaeum*. In the story, a doctor Robert consults before setting out asks, ' "hang it all, old man, what's to prevent you going with her? It isn't as though you've got a regular job like us wage earners" ' [p. 142]). The biographical parallel helps to explain the apparent unfairness in the portrait of the dutiful Robert, who is everywhere crucified for his suppressed resentment; nowhere given credit for the apparent generosity of his conduct.

'Widowed' (?written 1921), a late unfinished sketch, has been undeservedly ignored by Mansfield experts. Antony Alpers for instance – one of the few even to mention it – dismisses it as a joke.[42] But there is steel beneath Mansfield's humour: 'Widowed' is a provocative piece which offers a sharp comment and an original perspective on relations between the sexes.

It opens with the heroine and her new husband tripping downstairs to their honeymoon breakfast. There is a felicitous sense that the details described, banal in themselves, are poetry to lovers: the husband parts his hair with a couple of brushes; he enquires solicitously whether Geraldine has 'got enough *on*' (p. 506); when they stand together at the dining-room window watching the gardener make a bonfire of the dead leaves, Geraldine exclaims prosaically, ' "I do think there is nothing nicer than a real satisfactory fire" ' (p. 507).

Suddenly the sketch takes us back thirteen months – casting as it does so an eerie double significance on all that has just happened. On the earlier occasion Geraldine was also gazing at a garden bonfire. Her thoughts then were almost identical to those she has just voiced: '"There is nothing nicer," she thought, "than a really satisfactory fire"' (p. 508). On the former occasion she was watching alone because Jimmie, her husband of that time, had already left the house to go riding. He apparently suffered a fatal accident, for the story as we have it ends with his body being brought back home under a sheet. Geraldine, appearing not to understand what has happened, reacts with imperturbability.

The power of this sharp and unsettling tale rests on its dual nature. At first sight it appears an inconsequential sketch about a stupid and insensitive woman who has an eye for hunky men, and who remarries rather precipitately after the death of her first husband. On another level, however, it contains the traces of a fertility-myth according to which the heroine presides goddess-like over the autumnal passing of one of her partners – and appears by implication about to preside over the departure of the second as well.

Crucial to the construction of this subtext are the parallel, or repeated, details that inform the descriptions of episodes from Geraldine's two marriages. The most significant is that concerning the bonfires of burning leaves. The earlier comes at the presumed moment of Jimmie's death – when Geraldine's feeble imagination totally fails her:

> She imagined him as she stood there . . . riding. Geraldine was not very good at imagining things. But there was mist, a thud of hooves and Jimmie's moustache was damp. From the garden there sounded the creak of a gardener's barrow. An old man came into sight with a load of leaves and a broom lying across. He stopped; he began to sweep. 'What enormous tufts of irises grew in London gardens,' mused Geraldine. 'Why?' And now the smoke of a real fire ascended.
>
> 'There is nothing nicer,' she thought, 'than a really satisfactory fire.'
>
> Just at that moment the telephone rang.
>
> (pp. 507–8)

The heap of burning leaves appears to suggest a funeral pyre. Geraldine's musings as she watches the gardener build up the fire imply that, just as iris-tufts die down each autumn only to sprout again in the spring, so the demise of her first husband may signal the beginning of a new regenerative cycle. The concluding sentence of the sketch as we have it supports this interpretation. By confirming to the reader – if not to Geraldine – that Jimmie is dead, and by leaving the body in his 'gay, living, breathing dressing-room' (p. 510), it seems to lead us straight back to the sketch's opening: 'They came down to breakfast the next morning absolutely their own selves' (p. 506).

Once this mythic dimension is perceived the reader has the fun of spotting sinister undertones to even the story's most innocent-seeming details: 'They came down to breakfast the next morning *absolutely their own selves*' (p. 506 – italics mine). Although there is no direct indication that she is actually responsible for her first husband's death, Geraldine's composure when the body is brought home may suggest the victorious survival of the female principle over the male. Neither of the men is strongly characterised incidentally, and the second isn't even named: not surprising when both of them are seen merely to be transient, and clearly dispensable, manifestations of some abiding essence of Man.

Though its comic tone warns, like that of 'The Doves' Nest', against too solemn an interpretation, 'Widowed' does offer a disturbing perspective on domestic friction. And its reincarnation-theme further unsettles pre-Modernist assumptions regarding the stable, and unitary, nature of individual identity.

5

The Family

It is above all the New Zealand family pieces which have gained Mansfield her reputation for writing in the tranquil lyrical mode. Ian Gordon, for instance, describes her final achievement as the creation, 'in sharply-realistic and contemporary prose, [of] a romantic dream-world':

> New Zealand becomes an Arcadian country – 'it must', she wrote in one of her notebooks, 'be mysterious, as though floating. . . . The people (Ah the people – the people we loved there)' are idealised, happy, encapsulated in a world that never was, like the figures in one of Katherine's best-loved poems, Keats' *Ode On A Grecian Urn*.[1]

Yet the family stories, more than any others of Mansfield's pieces, are the product of a sustained double vision. There is the Turgenevian lyricism, that mood of absorbed intensity which Gordon speaks of – the result of the writer's nostalgic idealisation of her own early years combined with a Romantic vision of the child as vehicle of innocence, sensitivity and moral scruple: but there is also an undercurrent which works against the Romantic view – a twentieth-century vision which sees in the child the origin of adult fears and discontents; the causes of insecurity as deepseated and longlasting; and the family itself as a site of tension and distress.

Mansfield shows particular interest in two stages of a child's development – that at which, no longer a baby, it begins to explore its independence from its parents (and discovers for the first time the degree of its dependence), and a later time when as an adolescent she or he is on the verge of entry into the adult world. As with the stories we have already looked at, mythic traces – here of the expulsion from Eden or the entry into the underworld – disturb the chronicle realist's account.

The home itself, both literal and symbolic, is also a significant element in the family stories. Moving house, the building of an ideal home, the collapse of the dream-house, the home as symbol of ideal art – these are some of the motifs around which the author weaves her continuing preoccupation with lost security and depth-experience. And the symbol of the vanished or desecrated home reflects perhaps more than any other both her sense of exile and her experience of estrangement from family.

The troubled aspects of Mansfield's vision of childhood are most evident in the early works – before separation from her family lent enchantment to her view of it, and before it resulted also in a complex encoding of familial tensions.

The most challenging of these early pieces is 'The Little Girl' (1912), written a year or so after the author's return from Bavaria. It is effectively one of the Burnell stories although the name Burnell is not yet deployed, and the extended family of the later stories so far exists in little more than nuclear form – father, mother, grandmother, and child Kezia. But the principals of the Burnell drama are already present – remote and dictatorial father, unsympathetic mother, kindly grandmother, and a child sensitive and eager to please but ridden with anxieties (signalled here in her proneness to stuttering and to nightmares). Saralyn Daly[2] notes that in the original version this child was called Kass, Mansfield's own family nickname – an indication, borne out by the feel of the piece, that the narrative is modelled on an episode from Kathleen's own childhood.

Nominally the story records the child's punishment by her father for an unintended misdemeanour; her resentment of this; and their eventual reconciliation. More fundamentally it deals with the way her fear of her father is translated into an affection that has undertones of sexual intimacy.

Kezia sets the narrative off when she inadvertently destroys one of her father's speeches by using it to stuff a pincushion she wants to give him for his birthday. He beats her for this, and she is left full of resentment towards him. Later however, when the mother is taken ill – and conveniently removed from the scene – a reconciliation takes place between them.

Kezia, asleep in bed, has one of her recurrent nightmares – this time involving a butcher with a knife and a rope: presumably a figuring of her father. (Again an association between food – particularly meat – and sex may be noted.) On this occasion, however, her real-life father comforts her and takes her into his own bed. So the child, aware up to now only of his sternness, gets to know his kindly side. She also discovers his vulnerability: 'Tired out, he slept before the little girl. A funny feeling came over her. Poor Father! Not so big, after all – and with no one to look after him . . .' (pp. 570–1).

As well as a narrative convenience the absence of Kezia's mother during the latter part of the story is an echo of the invalidism of Mrs Beauchamp; and as such, a forerunner to the famous listnessness of Linda in the later Burnell stories. Illness, listlessness, absence – all are ways in which the Mansfield mother manages to opt out of the family drama.

'The Little Girl' is striking for its avant-garde insights into the development of the girl-child and for its comparatively forthright treatment of issues still regarded as disturbing or even taboo – child sexuality, sexual awareness between father and daughter, the critical part played by the father's conduct and personality in the formation of the girl-child's identity. Just as remarkable is the story's reliance on unconscious motivation: Kezia's destruction of the speech may be read as a (highly successful) ploy to gain the attention of a distant and dismissive father, making the father's interpretation of the behaviour as wilful, not too far from the story's own.

Father's behaviour apart, a link between the patriarch of the family and that still more distant spiritual Father, is signalled in the story when the mortal father says his prayers so loudly during service that Kezia 'was certain God heard him above the clergyman' (p. 567).

But the daughter's unconscious design involves not only gaining access to her father but also entering into the domain of sexuality through him. As might be expected with such dangerous material Mansfield resorts to indirection – here principally through an echo of the 'Little Red Riding Hood' fairytale. The 'little girl's' concluding comment gives the key: ' "What a big heart you've got, father dear" ' (p. 571) – an obvious acknowledgment of her father's late-night generosity but also, by way of the fairytale ('What big teeth you've got, grandmamma!'),[3] of his earlier aggressiveness. We have already learned about the size of his mouth – good in fairytale for devouring innocent maidens; or in Mansfield's more realistic world for delivering orders, strictures on behaviour, formal speeches to the Port Authority. . . . (Kezia's speech is by contrast marked by hesitancy – her stuttering.) The father's effective usurpation of Grandmother's place in bed with the girl underlines the relevance of the fairytale.

As a parable of adolescent disquiet Mansfield's 'Red Riding Hood' corresponds closely in its implications with the interpretation offered more recently by Bruno Bettelheim in his *Uses of Enchantment*:

> 'Little Red Cap' in symbolic form projects the girl into the dangers of her oedipal conflicts during puberty, and then saves her from them, so that she will be able to mature conflict-free. . . . [The male principle is] split into two opposite forms: the dangerous seducer, who, if given in to, turns into the destroyer of the good grandmother and the girl; and the hunter, the responsible, strong, and rescuing father figure.[4]

Bettelheim adds,

> It is as if Little Red Cap is trying to understand the contradictory nature of the male by experiencing all aspects of his personality: the selfish, asocial, violent, potentially destructive tendencies of the id (the wolf); the unselfish, social, thoughtful, and protective propensities of the ego (the hunter).[5]

The ambivalence of Mansfield's language invites us to infer that the bedding of father and daughter may be read symbolically as Kezia's sexual initiation:

> 'Here, rub your feet against my legs and get them warm' said father.
> Tired out, he slept before the little girl. A funny feeling came over her. Poor father! Not so big, after all – and with no one to look after him. . . . He was harder than the grandmother, but it was a nice hardness. . . . (pp. 570–1)

The moral aspect of Kezia's education however is equally important – the realisation that the destructive and the protective aspects of the father (or lover), Bettelheim's id and ego, may co-exist within a single figure.

So the conclusion to the story shows the accommodation that must take place as the girl matures: the man will find access to more conciliatory behaviour, and she acknowledge his sternness as an acceptable, even welcome, aspect of sexual difference. By the end of the narrative the Little Girl is a little girl no longer.

Though Kezia is initially presented as helpless victim we should not fail to recognise either the degree to which she triggers the story's action or the extent of her final victory. The distant father who only noticed her in order to chide or to give her a perfunctory kiss ends up inviting her to share his bed. The (male) rule of Law and Authority has given way to the (female) order of Love and Desire. So on a symbolic level the speech's destruction means the obliteration of the patriarchal Word; of Authority (appropriately, the speech was written as an address to the Port Authority) and the Law in all their remote and forbidding formality. Father's behaviour apart, a link between family patriarch and that still more distant and Law-obsessed heavenly Father, is signalled when the Little Girl's father says his prayers so loudly during service that she is certain 'God heard him above the prayers' (p. 567).

In addition the adult, and characteristically male, forms of expression which predominated at the story's opening – speeches, sermons, admonitions (formal and authoritative; often proscriptive, self-projecting, one-dimensional) have been displaced by one of the great narrative forms of childhood, the fairytale – oral and traditional; imaginative; subversive; and amenable like Mansfield's own story to double reading.

Though fascinating – and extremely daring – the richness of subtext in 'The Little Girl' finally breaks its back. This early story is too issue-laden to be successful.

Most of Mansfield's family pieces were written some years later – after the death of her brother Leslie, and in the shadow of her own increasingly serious illness. Leslie Beauchamp came to London in February 1915, in order to enlist in the British army. Before crossing to the Continent to fight he spent several weeks staying with Mansfield and Murry in St John's Wood. Sister and brother passed many happy hours together recalling their childhood.

Six months later, in October 1915, Leslie was dead – killed not in battle but in a training accident near the Belgian front. One measure of Mansfield's grief is the changed tenor of her references to the Great War. Before Leslie's death it seems to have made little impact on her: afterwards she alludes to it frequently, and in references touched with deep feeling but also with a kind of moral passion:

Spring, this year, is so beautiful, that watching it unfold one is filled with a sort of anguish. . . .

It has made the War so awfully real – and not only the War –
Ah Ottoline – it has made me realise so deeply and finally the
corruption of the world. . . .[6]

And in letters to Murry she sharply criticises Virginia Woolf's *Night
and Day* for failing to take into account the change in consciousness
brought about by the war. Mansfield herself sees this as a moral as
well as an artistic shortcoming:

> My private opinion is that it is a lie in the soul . . . the novel can't
> just leave the war out. There *must* have been a change of heart . . . I
> feel in the *profoundest* sense that nothing can ever be the same
> that as artists we are traitors if we feel otherwise: we have to take
> it into account and find new expressions new moulds for our
> new thoughts & feelings . . . it positively frightens me – to realise
> this *utter coldness* & indifference . . . Inwardly I despise them all
> for a set of *cowards*. We have to face our war – they won't.[7]

Shortly after Leslie's death Mansfield fled with Murry to Bandol
in the south of France, in an attempt to dull the pain she felt at his
loss. Some of the *Journal* passages from that period suggest that
his death both transformed her attitude towards her childhood, and
made her determined to re-create it (and in particular Leslie) through
her writings. It is as if his permanent separation from her made
her fully aware for the first time of her effective estrangement from
them all – and determined therefore to compensate for this loss by
re-creating them in fiction:

> Now – now – I want to write recollections of my own country.
> Yes, I want to write about my own country till I simply exhaust
> my store. Not only because it is 'a sacred debt' that I pay to my
> country because my brother and I were born there, but also be-
> cause in my thoughts I range with him over all the remembered
> places. I am never far away from them. I long to renew them in
> writing.
> Ah, the people – the people we loved there – of them, too I
> want to write. Another 'debt of love'. Oh, I want for one moment
> to make our undiscovered country leap into the eyes of the Old
> World. It must be mysterious, as though floating. It must take the
> breath. It must be 'one of those islands . . .'. I shall tell everything,
> even of how the laundry-basket squeaked at 75. But all this must

be told with a sense of mystery, a radiance, an afterglow, because you, my little sun of it, are set. You have dropped over the dazzling brim of the world. Now I must play my part.[8]

Mansfield also indicates that she is planning to end her next story with the birth of the Leslie-figure, the boy-child who will complete the family:

> *The Aloe* is right. *The Aloe* is lovely. It simply fascinates me, and I know that it is what you would wish me to write. And now I know what the last chapter is. It is your birth – your coming in the autumn. You in Grandmother's arms under the tree, your solemnity, your wonderful beauty. Your hands, your head – your helplessness, lying on the earth, and, above all, your tremendous solemnity. That chapter will end the book. The next book will be yours and mine. And you must mean the world to Linda; and before ever you are born Kezia must play with you – her little Bogey. Oh, Bogey – I must hurry. All of them must have this book. It is good, my treasure! My little brother, it is good, and it is what we really meant.[9]

('Bogey' was a nickname of Mansfield's for her brother though she also used it as a pet name for Murry.) The dedication is repeated in another *Journal* passage:

> why don't I commit suicide? Because I feel I have a duty to perform to the lovely time when we were both alive. I want to write about it, and he wanted me to. We talked it over in my little top room in London. I said: I will just put on the front page: To my brother, Leslie Heron Beauchamp. Very well: it shall be done.[10]

Mansfield's *Journal* expresses her aim, and her recollective nostalgia, with a lyricism and an intensity that are quite absent from earlier pieces like 'The Little Girl'. This intensity is replicated in the New Zealand stories that followed (as indeed it had been foreshadowed in that part of 'The Aloe', the early draft of 'Prelude', which was written after her reunion with Leslie). However, the *Journal* passages, partly perhaps because they refuse the investigation of character, remain untouched by the dark complexity of the stories.

'The Aloe' was begun in March 1915, before Leslie's death. But while staying at Bandol Mansfield began work on it again and with renewed energy, completing it in less than six months after Leslie's death. It was originally conceived as the opening to a novel but developed instead into a long story – her masterpiece, 'Prelude'.

Like the later stories 'At the Bay' and 'The Doll's House', 'Prelude' centres upon the lives of the Burnell family – father Stanley and mother Linda, children Isabel, Kezia, and Lottie, grandmother Mrs Fairfield, and Linda's sister Beryl. The family is modelled closely on the author's own, the only difference in the line-up being that the second Beauchamp sister Charlotte and the youngest, Jeanne, have been combined in the single figure of Lottie, the appealingly helpless youngest Burnell daughter. The names confirm the connection: Burnell was a surname on the author's mother's side, Stanley on the father's. 'Fairfield' is an anglicising of 'Beauchamp'. 'Kezia', pronounced to rhyme with 'desire', recalls 'Kass', Mansfield's own nickname; and Charlotte – in real life an elder sister – lends her name to the fictional youngest, Lottie. Belle, the maternal aunt who like the grandmother lived with the family, seems to have inspired the name and perhaps in part the personality of the eldest daughter Isabel as well as that of her own fictional counterpart, Aunt Beryl: the two are aligned – perhaps even implicitly compared – in the late story 'The Doll's House'.

The characters' personalities are also taken from the life. Mansfield's father is the model for Stanley Burnell – down-to-earth, ambitious, domineering, inwardly insecure. The semi-invalid mother becomes Linda – remote and dreamy, burdened by fertility. Annie's sister Belle has her fictional equivalent in Aunt Beryl – vain and self-regarding, impatient with the children, terrified of a life of impending spinsterhood. Vera, the eldest Beauchamp daughter, gives something to bossy Isabel; Charlotte becomes Lottie; and the only son Leslie, whose birth is foreshadowed in 'Prelude', finally makes his appearance in 'At the Bay'. Kezia – imaginative, highminded, sensitive – again represents the author.

'The Aloe' was revised in the summer of 1917, and re-named 'Prelude'. The revised version was finally brought out the following year, by Leonard and Virginia Woolf at the Hogarth Press: 'I threw my darling to the wolves', Mansfield observed after sending off the manuscript.[11]

The story focuses on a house-removal – inevitably an occasion of new beginnings and old regrets, and of inner uncertainties. The episode was based on the Beauchamp family's own move in 1893 from downtown Wellington to a larger house in what was then the countryside. 'Prelude' opens strikingly, with the two youngest Burnell children excluded from the buggy which is to take their mother, grandmother, and elder sister to their new home – and therefore effectively banished from the mother's lap:

> There was not an inch of room for Lottie and Kezia in the buggy. When Pat swung them on top of the luggage they wobbled; the grandmother's lap was full and Linda Burnell could not possibly have held a lump of a child on hers for any distance. Isabel, very superior, was perched beside the new handy-man on the driver's seat. Holdalls, bags and boxes were piled upon the floor. 'These are absolute necessities that I will not let out of my sight for one instant,' said Linda Burnell, her voice trembling with fatigue and excitement. . . .
> 'We shall simply have to leave them. That is all. We shall simply have to cast them off,' said Linda Burnell. A strange little laugh flew from her lips; she leaned back against the buttoned leather cushions and shut her eyes, her lips trembling with laughter. (p. 11)

The unnaturalness of what amounts to a rejection by the mother of her children is signified in Linda's reference, or near-reference, to Kezia and Lottie as cast-offs – rejected clothing – while giving pride of place in the buggy to her luggage. The same point is made in a jokey aside that relegates the children to the same order of being as the furniture:

> 'Yes, everything outside the house is supposed to go,' said Linda Burnell, and she waved a white hand at the tables and chairs standing on their heads on the front lawn. How absurd they looked! Either they ought to be the other way up, or Lottie and Kezia ought to stand on their heads, too. And she longed to say: 'Stand on your heads, children, and wait for the storeman.' (pp. 11–12)

Crisis threatens – at least until a kindly neighbour comes to the rescue by offering to look after the two 'cast-offs' until the dray arrives.

The mythic analogue to Kezia's and Lottie's plight is the banishment from Eden; and the parallel is implicitly drawn in the next episode, when the pair are initiated over tea into a new, and fallen, world – that of their neighbours' children. These children are near-savages, bellicose and unsocialised, and they tease their visitors unmercifully.

After tea Kezia wanders back to the Burnells' old house. This is now apparently deserted – but the emotions that have over the years been expended in it remain, figured in the objects she finds abandoned there – 'a hair-tidy with a heart pattern on it that had belonged to the servant girl' ('The Aloe', p. 32), and, in her parents' bedroom, a pill box the child keeps as a possible container for a bird's egg. As we see later the unfulfilled desires emblematised in these objects still haunt the characters – an amour in the case of Alice the servant-girl, the wish for a son in the case of Stanley and Linda. The grandmother, who is more or less alone in not being torn by unfulfilled desire, hasn't left anything behind: 'Kezia knew there was nothing in her grandmother's room; she had watched her pack' (p. 15). (Tellingly, in view of the implications of Mansfield's early story 'A Birthday', this section is followed in 'The Aloe' by a reference to Kezia's own birth in that very room, and 'out of a reluctant mother'.)[12]

Darkness comes on while Kezia is still in the old house. Its on-set is sudden; more sudden perhaps than a New Zealander still resident at home would have perceived it – here we have an exile's intensified perception of difference (or else a frightened child's dramatisation): 'As she stood there, the day flickered out and dark came. With the dark crept the wind snuffling and howling' (p. 15). With the dark arise also Kezia's childish fears, objectified as an IT that excludes her from the old home just as the angel with the flaming sword excluded Adam and Eve from theirs.

The ninth section of 'Prelude' also echoes the Genesis myth, with a domestic re-enactment of the entry of death into the world. Watched by the Burnell children and their cousins' handyman, Pat captures and beheads a duck for the dinnertable. Most of the children react ecstatically to the sight of the flowing blood, capering like savages and uttering cries that are reminiscent of Ole Underwood's half-crazed mutterings:

When the children saw the blood they were frightened no longer. They crowded round him and began to scream. Even Isabel leapt about crying: 'The blood! The blood!' Pip forgot all about his duck. He simply threw it away from him and shouted, 'I saw it. I saw it,' and jumped round the wood block. (p. 46)

The excitement grows still more intense as the headless duck begins to waddle off across the paddock.

Tender-hearted Kezia, however, does not join in the exultation. She rushes at Pat, butting him and demanding that he replace the head. But her distress is forgotten a few minutes later when she is distracted by his cross-gender taste in personal adornment: 'She never knew that men wore ear-rings' (p. 47).

In the beheading episode we have, not the innocent and idealised children of the early Romantics but savage and instinctual twentieth-century beings. Even Kezia, whose distress at the killing of the duck contrasts sharply with the reactions of the other children, is implicated in the general loss of innocence. Her own youthful fantasy of sexual experience has already been imaged as swelling bird and animal heads: ' "I hate rushing animals like dogs and parrots. I often dream that animals rush at me – even camels – and while they are rushing, their heads swell e-enormous" ' (p. 17), making it likely that to her the episode serves, at least subliminally, as a symbolic castration.

At dawn on the family's first night on their new home the mother Linda has a dream that is reminiscent of her daughter's fantasies:

> She was walking with her father through a green paddock sprinkled with daisies. Suddenly he bent down and parted the grasses and showed her a tiny ball of fluff just at her feet. 'Oh, papa, the darling.' She made a cup of her hands and caught the tiny bird and stroked its head with her finger. It was quite tame. But a funny thing happened. As she stroked it began to swell, it ruffled and pouched, it grew bigger and bigger and its round eyes seemed to smile knowingly at her. Now her arms were hardly wide enough to hold it and she dropped it into her apron. It had become a baby with a big naked head and a gaping bird-mouth, opening and shutting. Her father broke into a loud clattering laugh and she woke to see Burnell standing by the windows rattling the Venetian blind up to the very top. (p. 24)

In this disturbing – and audaciously explicit – passage the attractive baby bird that Linda dreams of grows swiftly into something resembling a sexual organ, and then a large and demanding baby: to her children mean sexual violation, labour pains, incessant demands. And in making the bird the gift of the father Mansfield hints again at the theme of filial desire she invoked in 'The Little Girl'.

But as Linda awakens out of her dream Stanley is substituted for her father, his rattling of the Venetian blind for the father's 'clattering' and somewhat subversive laughter – an acknowledgement of the taboo nature of her fantasy.

If we return to 'Prelude', the uncensored text, as it were, the import of Linda's dream is clear enough. And a macabre joke about a strangled baby's head, made by Mr Fairfield while he ridicules her suitor Stanley, underlines the point – lovers mean babies: 'Helping Linda to a horrible-looking pink blanc-mange which Mr. Fairfield said was made of strangled baby's head, he whispered – "the ginger whale is here. I've just spotted him blushing at a sandwich..."' ('The Aloe', p. 77).

These extracts indicate a certain confederate closeness between daughter and father. But another passage in 'The Aloe', omitted from the final version of the story, goes further, stopping just short of signalling a passionate aspect to the relationship:

> Linda, his second to youngest child, was his darling, his pet, his playfellow. She was a wild thing, always trembling on the verge of laughter, ready for anything and eager. When he put his arm round her and held her he felt her thrilling with life. He understood her so beautifully and gave her so much love for love that he became a kind of daily miracle to her and all her faith centred in him – People barely touched her, she was regarded as a cold, heartless little creature, but she seemed to have an unlimited passion for that violent sweet thing called life – just being alive and able to run and climb and swim in the sea and lie in the grass. In the evenings she and her Father would sit on the verandah – she on his knees – and 'plan'. 'When I am grown up we shall travel everywhere – we shall see the whole world – won't we Papa?'....
> 'And we shan't go as father and daughter,' she tugged at his 'piccadilly weepers' and began kissing him. 'We'll just go as a couple of boys together – Papa.'
>
> ('The Aloe', p. 73)

So Linda the listless was once a wild and vital child. She was her father's favourite, and her own youthful fantasy was not to marry but to travel the world with him.

But marry she did; and, significantly, in the year her father died. This was also the year she turned sixteen, making the wedding a double celebration – both of her marriage and of her expected entry into the adult world. But, the story indicates, she did not ever fully and finally make this transition.

Another, later passage from 'The Aloe' has Mrs Fairfield taking tea with three of her daughters – Linda, Beryl and Doady Trout, mother of Pip and Rags. This has also been omitted from 'Prelude'. It includes an account of how Beryl – ever so slightly malicious – tackles Linda about her everlasting world-weariness:

'Why do you always pretend to be so indifferent to everything,' she said. 'You pretend you don't care where you live, or if you see anybody or not, or what happens to the children or even what happens to you. You can't be sincere and yet you keep it up – you've kept it up for years – *ever since – and Beryl paused, shoved down a little pleat very carefully – ever since Father died. Oh she had such a sense of relief when she said that: she breathed freely again – Linda's cheeks went white – In fact'* – and she gave a little laugh of joy and relief to be so rid of the serpent – she felt positively delighted – 'I can't even remember when it started now – Whether it started *with* Stanley or before Stanley's time or after you'd had rheumatic fever or when Isabel was born –' 'Beryl' said Mrs. Fairfield sharply. 'That's quite enough, quite enough!' But Linda jumped up. Her cheeks were very white. 'Don't stop her, Mother' she cried, 'she's got a perfect right to say whatever she likes. Why on earth shouldn't she.' 'She has *not*' said Mrs. Fairfield. 'She has no right *what*ever.'

('The Aloe', pp. 131, 133)

Here, in a few lines which were scored out even from the manuscript of 'The Aloe', and which are rendered in the italicised passage above, Beryl 'speaks truth' – mentions the unmentionable: that there is a direct connection between Linda's constantly-worn mask of indifference and her father's death.

In the drama which follows, the reactions of all the characters are revealing – Linda's carefuly detached tolerance, the normally gentle Mrs Fairfield's feelings of outrage (she, after all, was the wife), Beryl's jubilation and sense of release (she being one of the unfavoured daughters). It is striking too that Beryl's truth-speaking should as it were have been doubly erased from 'Prelude', the final version of the story: it was not transferred to it from 'The Aloe', and was crossed out even in the original manuscript. Here, as in other places, Mansfield censored her own dangerous material.

So it may be inferred that the reason for Linda's neglect of her children lies in the nature of frustrated desire. Forbidden her father's love, she effectively rejects both her husband Stanley and the children of their union. On a day-to-day basis she copes with her situation by remaining childlike herself – refusing the adult roles of wife and mother so that both she and her children end up being mothered by Mrs Fairfield.

Some indication of the effects of Linda's attitude on these children is later given by the more caring and thoughtful grandmother. This episode has also been omitted from the final version of the story – again no doubt because of its tendentiousness:

The door handle rattled and turned. Kezia looked tragically in. 'Isn't it *ever* going to be tea time' – she asked – 'No, never!' said Linda. 'Your Mother doesn't care Kezia whether you ever set eyes upon her again. She doesn't care if you starve. You are all going to be sent to a Home for Waifs and Strays to-morrow.' 'Don't tease' said Mrs. Fairfield. 'She believes every word.' And she said to Kezia, 'I'm coming darling . . .'.

('The Aloe', p. 133)

In this way Mansfield traces Kezia's insecurities, subtly but unmistakably, to the remoteness and neglect of her mother, thus relieving the child of guilt.

Characteristically Linda remains in bed on her first morning in the new home. After Stanley has left for work she turns over – away from the sun's light, and towards the wall. This is another refusal: but out of this refusal comes affirmation. Just as she stroked the bird in her dream so she now coaxes a poppy on the wallpaper into imaginative life. The poppy, thus caressed, breaks out from the wallpaper into three-dimensional reality. But it also *gives* life, by nurturing a 'bursting' bud. We are told as well of how the things Linda has touched into life 'swell out with some mysterious important content' (p. 27) – an image suggesting both pregnancy and self-fulfilment.

Suddenly, however, these 'things' become THEY – a slily smiling set of presences that have some secret knowledge of her; make mysterious demands upon her; invade the rooms that she has just vacated. THEY are also a multiple version of the IT which was the unitary personification of Kezia's childish anxieties. In 'The Aloe' IT is described as being 'round like the sun. It had a face. It smiled, but it had no eyes. It was yellow' ('The Aloe', p. 37) – a description omitted from 'Prelude' but which, as well as suggesting the sun, also reminds us of Linda's own secretive smile and half-shut eyes.

Finally these beings become part of the scene's – and the story's – general sense of becoming: all of them, and Linda as well – now with eyes wide open – are waiting for some future event to occur, some future presence to appear.

The implication is surely that the boy-child of the Burnell family, born after the story ends but before the beginning of 'At the Bay', has now been conceived – perhaps even during that first night in the new house, when Stanley was still triumphant about his purchase and Linda submitted, willingly for once, to his embrace. Linda's dream of her 'gift' of a baby follows their night of love. And the plentiful images of natural beauty, fertility and freshness also delicately suggest new life.

'Prelude' displays no overt resentment on Kezia/Katherine Mansfield's part against the mother-figure. Yet at the exact midpoint of the story – the end of the sixth episode – Linda is identified (indeed identifies herself) with a cruel and inhospitable symbol – the aloe plant which grows in front of the Burnells' new home. The episode also marks the only moment of communion in the story between Linda and Kezia – just as it very effectively conveys the estrangement between them. Equally significantly it is the topics of pregnancy and sterility over which they commune:

'That is an aloe, Kezia,' said her mother.
'Does it ever have any flowers?'
'Yes, Kezia,' and Linda smiled down at her, and half shut her eyes. 'Once every hundred years.'

(p. 34)

The aloe is perhaps the most striking example of how Mansfield uses a Romantic Nature-symbol to signify the solitary human consciousness and its link with non-human powers and qualities. Like the pear-tree in 'Bliss' the aloe is a highly complex figure: it reflects the resentfulness – even revulsion – with which Linda bears her 'lumps' of children, and the cruelty with which she neglects them; the way she hides or represses crucially determining aspects of her earlier life; her unyielding resistance to the force of circumstance. And the blindness of its stem is reciprocated in her own typically half-shut eyes: in this story, so preoccupied with perception, shut eyes mark a refusal of experience; wide-open eyes – like those of the children in the opening episode – responsiveness to it.

The brokenness of some of the aloe's leaves correspond to Linda's vision of how her own life has been wrecked by childbearing: 'She was broken, made weak, her courage was gone, through childbearing' ('At the Bay', p. 223). The main attraction of the plant for Linda is of course its sturdy resistance to reproduction – its enviable ability to confine its flowering to once every hundred years ... but also – in a characteristically Mansfieldian paradox which conveys the way Linda's nature is turned against itself – its present blossoming.

The aloe appears again in the second-to-last section of 'Prelude', where it is once more observed by Linda – in the company now not of her daughter but of her mother, and not by daylight but under the mysterious light of the moon. And this time the once-in-a-hundred-years event appears to be about to happen: ' "I have been looking at the aloe," said Mrs Fairfield. "I believe it is going to flower this year. Look at the top there. Are those buds, or is it only an effect of the light?" ' (p. 52).

Linda agrees that they may be buds. At the same time she affirms her sense of identity with the plant: ' "I like that aloe. I like it more than anything here. And I am sure I shall remember it long after I've forgotten all the other things" ' (p. 53). And in her imagination the great aloe – no longer clinging to the earth – is transformed into a ship. She herself is caught up on this ship, and conveyed by it far away from house and family – a further indication of her desire to escape their demands. Then she becomes aware again of the thorns that edge the aloe's leaves, and her heart hardens in solidarity with them:

> She particularly liked the long sharp thorns. . . . Nobody would dare to come near the ship or to follow after.
> 'Not even my Newfoundland dog,' thought she, 'that I'm so fond of in the daytime.' (p. 53)

The passage that follows conveys both Linda's affection for her 'Newfoundland dog' – a pet-name for her husband Stanley – and her resentment of his sexual appetite. But her pregnancy, which is signified also in the budding of the aloe plant, will set her free for the time being from Stanley's nightly attentions. And if the child is the longed-for heir then an end to the whole business of sex, pregnancy and birth may be in sight.

The Burnells' first day in their new house has been a momentous one. Kezia, expelled from the primal home, has entered the world of experience; and her mother has become aware of her new pregnancy. The future prospects for Beryl, the third main character, remain unclear however, and it is perhaps for this reason – to leave things openended – that the story ends with her.

She is shown writing a letter to her girlfriend Nan. The burden of the letter is her fear that for her the Burnells' move to the country will mean social isolation, and a life of spinsterhood:

> buried, my dear. Buried isn't the word. . . .
> Such is life. It's a sad ending for poor little B. I'll get to be a most awful frump in a year or two and come and see you in a mackintosh and a sailor hat tied on with a white china silk motor veil. So pretty. (pp. 55–6)

On reading the letter over Beryl acknowledges the artificiality of her letter-writing 'voice' by commenting that it has been written by her 'false' self.[13] She criticises this other self quite harshly then, continuing the process of self-examination, takes a look in the mirror; gazes adoringly at her reflection; and ends by comparing it too with her 'false' self. The double image, mirror and self, has become an index of moral duplicity:

> Oh, God, there she was, back again, playing the same old game. False – false as ever. False as when she'd written to Nan Pym, False even when she was alone with herself, now. (pp. 57–8)

Before the mirror Beryl is both narcissistically self-absorbed and unhappily aware of her own doubleness. And this sense of duality is itself a prelude to the recognition of another – that between her own self and the autonomous Other of masculinity. She is just wondering despairingly whether there was 'ever a time when (she) did not have a false self' (p. 59) when Kezia comes in to inform her, ' "Father is home with a man and lunch is ready" ' (p. 59).

At this possible sign of an answer to her prayers Beryl hastily powders her nose and dashes downstairs. Kezia, left alone in front of the dressing table, mocks her – Beryl's – preoccupations by sitting a calico cat in front of the mirror and sticking the top of a cream jar on its ear. Kezia has none of Beryl's self-consciousness, this being for Mansfield only developed in adolescence. But the guilt with which she tiptoes out of the bedroom does hint at her future participation in Beryl's condition.[14]

In 'Prelude', as in 'The Little Girl', Kezia's childish consciousness is again the seat of suppressed anxieties and of a sense of incipient and disturbing sexual awareness. But here the unease is no longer rendered in terms of stuttering and nightmares – symptoms which suggest a neurotic disturbance that may be identified and perhaps cured: in 'The Little Girl' even Father notices the stammer, and in his brusque and unsympathetic way suggests treatment for it: ' "You d-d-don't know? If you stutter like that mother will have to take you to the doctor" ' (p. 567), though later he does of course help the little girl to cope with her nightmare. In 'Prelude' by contrast her anxieties are expressed in a fantasy which, far from even being identifiable, has become so deepseated as to have been integrated into her personality. Mansfield's artistic method, then, has changed – the later story is more subtle, less of a casebook study – but so too has her assessment of the depth of her heroine's problems.

As we have seen, the main burden of 'Prelude' is an investigation of the reasons behind Linda Burnell's neglect of her children. The story thus offers through Linda and Kezia a mother-and-daughter portrait of the formation of sexual identity – and one which underlines the relevance of the relationship with both mother (in the case of Kezia) and father (in Linda's case in particular) to the formation of the growing child's sexual identity.

Linda's sister Beryl, whose dreams and discontents conclude the narrative, occupies a position in age and situation somewhere between those of Linda and Kezia. She is a young woman not yet married – a self-absorbed and less generous-hearted Kezia; a Linda who has not yet made her life's choices, and for whom all therefore remains fluid with possibility – and with danger.

I have spoken of Kezia as the story's heroine: but, as earlier critics have noted,[15] one might rather say that 'Prelude' implicitly rejects the notion of the single heroine. The adolescent Beryl, and the wife and mother Linda – and indeed the grandmother Mrs Fairfield – are all presented as future aspects of the young girl; and the intimate, one-to-one encounters Kezia has with each of them subtly underlines the point. This conception of a single, fourfold personality enables Mansfield to set up a network of interrelationships that foretell her heroine's future development (and possible future difficulties in her sexual relationships) but also convey through an evocation of Linda's warm and intimate relationship with her own mother what she misses out on.

As well as an attempt to explain Linda's neglect of her children (and hence perhaps Annie Beauchamp's of Kathleen) with respect, not to the children themselves but to the mother's own past, the story also marks the author's attempt to rehabilitate, through Kezia, herself and her own part in the life of the Beauchamp family. In spite of her inner insecurities Kezia is in many ways the idealised child of the Romantic imagination – innocent, impressionable, highminded; the bearer of future promise. And when revising 'The Aloe' Mansfield was careful to erase the traces of any less attractive aspects of this fictional self: an episode from the earlier version, in which Kezia gets her own back on the Samuel Joseph children by tricking them into eating the hot stamens of the arum lily, has been dropped, and where in 'The Aloe' she on one occasion taunts the officious Isabel with the cry, ' "Bossy! bossy!" ', in 'Prelude' she simply, and discreetly, retreats.

Through the use of devices like mythic analogy, dream and symbol Mansfield has, then, conveyed within the framework of a single story both her nostalgic memories of her childhood and an awareness of the unsettling complexities of family life. She has also transformed her grief at her brother Leslie's death into a celebration of his coming. When her mother observed that Leslie's death 'was the means of bringing poor old Kass right into the fold again',[16] her words were true in a sense that she herself would not have dreamed of.

In 'Prelude' the child's loss of primal unity is, as I have already suggested, rendered in terms of a house-removal. The old home – so familiar in Kezia's eyes that its appearance is taken more or less for granted – is the guardian of emotions already invested in it; and the new house when first glimpsed is described in terms suggesting both the excitement and the dangers of new experience:

The soft white bulk of it lay stretched upon the green garden like a sleeping beast. And now one and now another of the windows leaped into light. Someone was walking through the empty rooms carrying a lamp. From the window downstairs the light of a fire flickered. A strange beautiful excitement seemed to stream from the house in quivering ripples. (p. 18)

In the undeservedly neglected 'Old Tar' (1913)[17] Mansfield had already made the home, or homestead, into a locus both of unattainable desire and of parental love: the hero dreams for fifty years of building his dream-home, a colonial homestead. When his father dies he is eventually able to do this. But as soon as the house is finished his dream collapses: all he can think of is his vanished father. Again the tenuous nature of the colonist's attachment to place (here the patch of New Zealand the hero's grandfather had acquired from the Maoris) is indicated – in this case by being set at odds with his lineal affections.

In the later 'Sun and Moon' (1918) Mansfield miniaturises the home so as to make still clearer its significance as a repository of desire. This story is told from the perspective of Sun, a small boy aged, according to a note of Mansfield's, 'not more than 5'.[18] Unlike his smaller sister Moon he is old enough to be entering into the mature world of separate consciousness and symbolic significance. But he is also young enough to regret the loss of an earlier, unified consciousness.

The tale tells of a dinner-party given by the title-children's parents. Before the party Sun and Moon are allowed to survey the feast. Sun glories over the ice pudding in particular:

> Oh! Oh! Oh! It was a little house. It was a little pink house with white snow on the roof and green windows and a brown door and stuck in the door there was a nut for a handle.
>
> When Sun saw the nut he felt quite tired and had to lean against Cook.
>
> (p. 155)

But afterwards, when they see the desecrated remains of the feast, he is devastated – by the spoiling of the icecream house in particular: 'And the little pink house with the snow roof and the green windows was broken – broken – half melted away in the centre of the table' (p. 160).

Beyond its apparent slightness the sketch is another rite-of-passage tale; a fable about the inevitable spoiling of perfection and of the child's primal sense of contentment. The notion of the house's ideal nature, here a figure of family happiness, has lasted only as long as the dream.

Despite the mythic overtones of the title it is 'Hansel and Gretel' which this story recalls – and here Mansfield could again be said to be re-visioning a fairytale in order to elaborate on her own theme of maturation: where both the fairytale children eat of the gingerbread cottage, in the final scene of Mansfield's story it is only the younger child Moon who partakes of the icecream house. Sun, who is more mature, refuses to eat, sobbing, ' "I think it's horrid–horrid– horrid!" ' (p. 160) and stamping off to the nursery. Such an interpretation is directly at odds with the story's surface implication of immature behaviour on his part – the presumed reason for his father's anger.

Yet here too there is a complication. Before sending his son to bed, the father plays a major role in the house's destruction by smashing its roof in. It may or may not be a consolation to Sun – who already walks like a grownup, and who is no doubt the true son (Sun) of his father after all – that he will one day be able to replace this fallen house with one of his own, with which he in turn will presumably entrance and then distress his own children. There is even a hint that he already has the potential within him to build a more material house: a friend of the family recently desisted from lifting him up, observing, ' "He's a perfect little ton of bricks!" ' (p. 154).

On New Year's Day 1921 Mansfield wrote to her brother-in-law Richard Murry: 'I have written a huge long story of a rather new kind. It's the outcome of the *Prelude* method – it just unfolds and opens – But I hope it's an advance on *Prelude*. In fact, I know it's that because the technique is stronger . . .'.[19]

She was speaking of 'The Daughters of the Late Colonel' (1920), a long short story recounting the plight of two 'old maids' who have recently lost their father.[20] Like 'Prelude' this work is organised, not around any conventionally progressive narrative but according to Modernist principles – in relation, that is, to the thoughts and impressions of the central characters. But this apparently time-bound narrative also reflects the Daughters' lack of personal development[21] and their mental confusion.

The subject of 'The Daughters' is the old one of paterfamilias tyranny. However, the characters in this story – about how a dead Colonel once ruled over (and ruined) the lives of his daughters – are distanced from any obvious connection with either the Beauhamp family or Mansfield herself. It is no doubt partly because of this, as well as the subjects' avoidance of any direct sexual pre-occupation, that there is no trace of a complex subtext like that in 'Prelude'.

The Colonel's rule is underlined both in his high military rank and in his 'thumping-stick', emblem of his authority. His tyranny has stunted his daughters' development, making them indecisive, ineffectual, and submissive; preventing them in short from reaching mature independence of mind. The opening scene, in which Josephine is almost overwhelmed by schoolgirlish giggling, makes the point:

> suddenly, for one awful moment, she nearly giggled. Not, of course, that she felt in the least like giggling. It must have been habit. Years ago, when they had stayed awake at night talking, their beds had simply heaved. And now the porter's head, disappearing, popped out, like a candle, under father's hat. . . . The giggle mounted, mounted; she clenched her hands; she fought it down; she frowned fiercely at the dark and said 'Remember' terribly sternly. (p. 262)

Even the death of the Colonel alters nothing – he has so dominated his daughters' lives and personalities that his influence persists unchecked:

> Josephine had had a moment of absolute terror at the cemetery, while the coffin was lowered, to think that she and Constantia had done this thing without asking his permission. What would father say when he found out? For he was bound to find out sooner or later. He always did. 'Buried. You two girls had me *buried*!' She heard his stick thumping. Oh, what would he say? (pp. 268–9)

Half concealed beneath the Daughters' ingenuousness and sense of guilt lies a superstitious fear that Father *will* return and berate them – for burying him without permission, and for giving him such an extravagant sendoff. Mansfield plays off Constantia's unworldliness against her fears, to great comic effect: ' "But what else could we have done?" (she) asked . . . wonderingly. We couldn't have kept him, Jug – we couldn't have kept him unburied. At any rate, not in a flat that size" ' (p. 269).

The fantastical element in the story is heightened when the sisters invade Father's room in order to 'go through his things'. The presumption involved in this transgressive act leads them to imagine he is still there – ready to jump out and reprimand them for disturbing him. It is this Gothicky superstition that leads Constantia to take her one bold decision; make her one decisive act within the story – to lock up the wardrobe and its potentially explosive contents:

> And then she did one of those amazingly bold things that she'd done about twice before in their lives: she marched over to the wardrobe, turned the key, and took it out of the lock. Took it out of the lock and held it up to Josephine, showing Josephine by her extraordinary smile that she knew what she'd done – she'd risked deliberately father being in there among his overcoats. (p. 272)

The story, then, plays off social ritual and its heroines' punctiliousness about appropriate formal responses to bereavement against their underlying fears – and their relief. The fears are displayed in the frenetic abruptness of their and others' actions: the housemaid is always bursting into the room; Father himself is 'ready to spring' (p. 271); and when they give a blind the merest touch 'it flew up and the cord flew after, rolling round the blind-stick, and the little tassel tapped as if trying to get free' (p. 271).

Josephine and Constantia also stay in subjection to two women who remain behind from the old régime – Nurse Andrews, an authority-figure by reason of her profession, and Kate, the supercilious housemaid. The maid's conduct triggers perhaps the most compelling sentence in all of Mansfield's works: 'And proud young Kate, the enchanted princess, came in to see what the old tabbies wanted now' (p. 265). The one visitor the Daughters receive during the 'present' of the story, a Mr Farolles of St John's, is himself a kind of testament to the Colonel's continuing influence – for it is later revealed that after their mother's death the young Josephine and Constantia 'never met a single man except clergymen' (p. 283).

The next few episodes of 'The Daughters' are governed by a debate about who should be given Father's watch. The first candidate is a younger version of Father himself – the Daughters' brother Benny, out in Ceylon. Eventually, however, Josephine decides to give it to the more pliant nephew Cyril instead – Cyril whose '[unmanliness] in appetite' (p. 275) and proneness to be bullied by Father exonerate him from any suspicion of intemperate masculinity . . . and also identify him as a soulmate of the Daughters themselves.

In tribute perhaps to this kinship the story, which is otherwise restricted to the Daughters' perspective, offers an insight into Cyril's consciousness as well. This is given during his 'audience' with the old man – the only episode directly to dramatise the Colonel himself. But Cyril, pleading another engagement, escapes early where Josephine and Constantia are trapped in their father's service: his position is in reality nothing like theirs.

It is entirely appropriate that the Daughters, with their lack of purpose, their vagueness about time, and their inability to control their own lives, should pass Father's watch on to Cyril without attempting to take possession of it themselves. Figurative language, as so often in this story, is overtaken by reality: the sisters are quite literally timeless. And the corset-box in which Josephine thinks of sending off the watch to Benny may have an even grimmer implication – that the watch is to be identified with the heart, the source of life itself.

'The Daughters of the Late Colonel' is structured around a series of objects which convey confinement within a restricted space. As in 'Miss Brill', some of these – the coffin of course, but also the top drawer and wardrobe in Father's room – become for Ida and Constantia reminders of the fate of the dead. Others make reference to the restricted nature of the Daughters' lives and the way these lives are themselves a kind of living death – the corset-box, the dark, stuffy, and 'tight-buttoned' cab in which they return from their father's funeral, Father's room with its tomblike sense of imprisonment and anonymity.

The final section of the story, in which street-noises and sunlight steal like intruders into the sitting-room, makes it clear that the whole flat also serves as a kind of tomb for the living dead. It is appropriate then that Constantia, lying in bed, should mimic the posture of death – or of entombment: 'Constantia lay like a statue, her hands by her sides, her feet just overlapping each other, the sheet up to her chin' (p. 262).

Not only does the dead Colonel, then, return to haunt his daughters: the Daughters themselves are in their will-less subjection to him as good as dead already. Where in the first part of the story traces of Gothic comedy convey how even after his death the father terrorises Josephine and Constantia, towards the end the tone darkens as the waste of their lives is stressed. Mansfield confirms the point in a letter to William Gerhardi: 'All was meant, of course, to lead up to that last paragraph, when my two flowerless ones turned with

that timid gesture, to the sun. "Perhaps *now* ..." And after that, it
seemed to me, they died as surely as Father was dead.'[22]

It is entirely appropriate then that the last section of the story
should dwell in the manner of an epitaph on the Daughters' lives
and personalities. Now, even they are rendered symbolically: the
dreamy and romantic Constantia is associated with the moon;
Josephine, the elder and more assertive of the pair, with the sun.
Unable to 'realise' their own identities in their everyday lives, the
two women finally receive them in figurative representation. Though
the Daughters' failure to attain full individuality has meant that
they have not become fully differentiated one from the other, they
are more differentiated – and more highly individualised – in the
final section than in any other.

It is in this section too that they reflect upon their past lives
and dreams. Josephine, the more down-to-earth, ponders why she
has never married. The guilty party is of course Father: he used to
quarrel with everyone, leaving her and Constantia with nobody to
meet, let alone marry, and then after Mother's death he himself had
to be looked after. Contemplating her own unfulfilled life, Josephine
comes close to despair – though, like Miss Brill in a similar position,
she manages to disown her grief by displacing it onto creatures
even more vulnerable than herself:

> Some little sparrows, young sparrows they sounded, chirped
> on the window-ledge. *Yeep – eyeep – yeep.* But Josephine felt they
> were not sparrows, not on the window-ledge. It was inside her,
> that queer little crying noise. *Yeep – eyeep – yeep.* Ah, what was it
> crying, so weak and forlorn? (p. 283)

But the final section is really Constantia's. Earlier episodes have
hinted at her repressed antipathy to men – recently, and with an
uncharacteristically callous smile, she locked the 'spirit' of Father
up in the wardrobe, and when young she pushed brother Benny
into the local pond. Certainly her half-articulated desires, unlike
Josephine's, contain no hint of a wish to marry nor of any relationship past or present with a man. But a disposition towards martyrdom is suggested in the way she used to feel drawn by the moon
to get out of bed and adopt the crucifixion-position. The character's
original, Ida Constance Baker, and her lifelong devotion to Mansfield,
as well as Mansfield's own more ambivalent feelings about her,
may well be relevant here.

This inclination towards martyrdom is confirmed in the affinity the solitary and reflective Constantia feels for the Buddha-figure on the mantelpiece – a 'stone and gilt image, whose smile always gave her such a queer feeling, almost a pain and yet a pleasant pain' (p. 282). For her the essential quality of life has indeed been pain – and it may well be that she takes a masochistic pleasure in that.

Now, however, the figure seems to be teasing her with a secret. Though never revealed within the story, this secret appears to be the fourth and final Truth of Buddhist enlightenment – the Way which leads to Nirvana, and hence to the cessation of all pain. This must surely be the 'frightfully important' thing about the future (p. 284) that Constantia, turning away from the Buddha, wishes to communicate to Josephine . . . and which she promptly forgets before she can do so. This forgetting is in itself a kind of symbolic death – just as the obscuring of the sun will be for Josephine a moment later. The story, nominally about the aftermath of the Colonel's death, turns out to be obsessed with that of his daughters.

In June 1921 Mansfield moved to Montana-sur-Sierre in the Swiss Alps. She went for the sake of her health, as she was by then terminally ill: but the eight months she spent there turned out to be the most productive of her writing life. It was particularly fruitful where the subject of the family was concerned. 'At the Bay' (August–September 1921), a sequel to 'Prelude', was written there, as were several shorter stories of childhood and family life – 'The Voyage' (August), 'The Garden-Party' (October), which is about the Sheridans, and 'The Doll's House' (also October), another Burnell piece. In all except one of these works the world of childhood, already invaded by familial tensions, becomes increasingly disturbed by apprehensions of death. Also written at Montana were the sketch 'Honeymoon', 'Her First Ball' (another Sheridan story), 'Mr. and Mrs. Dove', 'The Dove's Nest', 'Widowed', and part of the long fragment 'A Married Man's Story', amongst others.

'At the Bay' continues the story of the Burnell family. But the tensions and antagonisms that gave 'Prelude' its subtextual power are less in evidence: such stresses as there are have become less deepseated; closer to the surface of the characters' minds, and therefore more amenable to solution. In particular there is the hint that, with Linda's final, glad acceptance of the son whose conception was celebrated in 'Prelude', some of those tensions will be resolved.

In place of the psychological preoccupations of 'Prelude', 'At the Bay' is more concerned with the 'universal' aspects of the characters' lives – including death. Hanson and Gurr point out[23] that it is structured around a single day, its twelve episodes corresponding to the twelve hours of clock-time. Jonathan Trout, one of the characters, draws attention to the symbolic significance of this summer's day:

> 'I'm like an insect that's flown into a room of its own accord. I dash against the walls, dash against the windows, flop against the ceiling. . . . And all the while I'm thinking, like that moth, or that butterfly, or whatever it is, "The shortness of life! The shortness of life!" I've only one night or day, and there's this vast dangerous garden, waiting out there, undiscovered, unexplored.'
> (p. 237)

Hanson and Gurr also point out[24] that the structuring metaphor of 'life-as-a-single-day' is a characteristically Modernist one, citing Virginia Woolf's *Waves* as an example. I have argued in my Preface that 'At the Bay' was a major influence on *The Waves*, as it and other Mansfield works were on *Mrs Dalloway* and *To the Lighthouse*,[25] others of Woolf's novels that are more or less universally claimed as leading works in the Modernist canon. The conspicuously Modernist framework of 'At the Bay' has perhaps also led some critics to rate it, despite several stylistic and conceptual flaws, above 'Prelude'.

The first section of 'At the Bay' takes place at dawn. It introduces us to the setting before any of the 'speaking' characters has emerged. Indeed, as Antony Alpers observes,[26] the story's opening takes the form of a stage-direction. This slides only gradually into the narrative mode:

> Very early morning. The sun was not yet risen, and the whole of Crescent Bay was hidden under a white sea-mist. The big bush-covered hills at the back were smothered. You could not see where they ended and the paddocks and bungalows began. (p. 205)

The work, then, opens in an atmosphere of profound silence. Both this and the pastoral figures who first enter on the stage – a flock of sheep, a sheepdog, and a shepherd – again suggest the innocence of the unfallen world.

In a letter to Dorothy Brett written just after Leslie's death, and from which I have already quoted, Mansfield draws an association between water, the New Zealand dawn, and a sense of renewal that verges on rebirth:

> You know, if the truth were known I have a perfect passion for the island where I was born. . . . Well, in the early morning there I always remember feeling that this little island has dipped back into the dark blue sea during the night only to rise again at beam of day, all hung with bright spangles and glittering drops. . . .[27]

There is an allusion here to the Maori myth of origin according to which the fisherman-hero Maui raises one of the islands of New Zealand – generally taken to be the North Island; a tribute to its vaguely fishlike shape – from the sea in his net, an account remarkably close to recent geological revelations that the country, volcanic in origin, did indeed rise from the sea, and that the North is the more recently formed of the two largest islands.

In her letter Mansfield goes on to associate the mists of a New Zealand morning with the writer's art:

> just as on those mornings white milky mists rise and uncover some beauty, then smother it again and then again disclose it, I tried to lift that mist from my people and let them be seen and then to hide them again. . . .[28]

To employ such a figure is to hint at a Romantic theory of artistic creation as both revelation and recollection – and to translate such a theory to a southern setting. The metaphor has itself been renewed in order to reinforce the point: first the sea conceals/discloses the island-setting, then the mist does the same for the characters. In both cases the eventual disclosure has the air of revelation. Writing elsewhere about the composition of 'At the Bay', Mansfield again conveys the intensity of the recollective act and the mysteries of the process of 'recovery':

> It is so strange to bring the dead to life again. There's my Grandmother, back in her chair with her pink knitting, there stalks my uncle over the grass; I feel as I write, 'You are not dead, my darlings. All is remembered. I bow down to you. I efface myself

so that you may live again through me in your richness and beauty.' And one feels *possessed*. And then the place where it all happens. I have tried to make it as familiar to 'you' as it is to me. You know the marigolds? You know those pools in the rocks, you know the mouse trap on the washhouse windowsill?[29]

Absences (through exile, and through death) and presences (through memory) dominate 'Prelude' and 'At the Bay' – their subjects as well as the circumstances of their composition. In particular the birth of the boy-child, the fictional equivalent of Leslie, is an event seminal to both stories: yet it takes place after the end of the first, and before the opening of the second – in the space between the two, as it were. In this way its sacredness is preserved even as the event itself is celebrated.

'At the Bay' is also a story of borderlines. It is set at the seaside in summer, at a place where the four elements meet. It also opens at the margin between darkness and the day. Furthermore when it introduces its characters (still unnamed) they turn out to be themselves on the border between sleep and wakefulness: we are told that as a flock of sheep passed by the settlement at dawn 'their cry sounded in the dreams of little children . . . who lifted their arms to drag down, to cuddle the darling little woolly lambs of sleep' (p. 207). (In spite of its nursery-rhyme sentimentality – reminiscent of a certain vein of nineteenth-century writing – this passage is complex in its associations. It also has a touch of linguistic sorcery in the sheep/sleep juxtaposition.) The marginal nature of the scene, then, is a kind of metaphor for the characters' states of mind, poised between sleep and wakefulness – just as they will be later between life and death.

It is out of such marginality that consciousness eventually emerges. Indeed the initial sections of the story, in their preoccupation with the basic elements of sky, sea and land; of night, day and sun, seem to owe a general debt to the creation-myths of pre-literate culture. The opening pages deal in the invasion of earth by the element of water . . . and hence by implication with the imminent fertilisation of the land:

A heavy dew had fallen. The grass was blue. Big drops hung on the bushes and just did not fall; the silvery, fluffy toi-toi was limp on its long stalks, and all the marigolds and the pinks in the bungalow gardens were bowed to the earth with wetness.

Drenched were the cold fuchsias, round pearls of dew lay on the
flat nasturtium leaves. It looked as though the sea had beaten up
softly in the darkness, as though one immense wave had come
rippling, rippling – how far? Perhaps if you had waked up in the
middle of the night you might have seen a big fish flicking in at
the window and gone again. . . . (p. 205)

The last, magical detail of the fish 'flicking in at the window' underlines the point.

Other passages from the beginning of 'At the Bay' also suggest
either the mixing of the elements ('the smell of leaves and wet
black earth mingled with the sharp smell of the sea' [p. 207]) or the
reflection of one upon the other: 'The far-away sky – a bright, pure
blue – was reflected in the puddles, and the drops, swimming along
the telegraph poles, flashed into points of light' (p. 206). And indeed
towards the end of the first section, with the description of the comic
antagonism between Florrie the cat and Wag the dog, we get a hint
of the primordial division into sexes and species (and also perhaps
of that between settled and nomadic peoples).

The reference towards the end of the section to how the flock of
sheep is now heading out of Crescent Bay and towards Daylight
Cove further emphasises the scene's symbolic organisation: the journey is from the domain of the moon (which re-establishes itself in
the final section of the story) to that of the day. The name 'Daylight
Cove' is a symbolised rendering of 'Day's Bay', a cove near Wellington where the Beauchamp family had a bach or holiday cottage, and
which was the original setting for the events described in the story.

The second section switches from the elemental world to the everyday. It offers a close-up of Stanley Burnell and his brother-in-law
Jonathan having an early-morning bathe. Stanley is his usual self –
competitive, territorial, peevish, pressed for time. Jonathan appears
at first sight to be quite different – sensitive and self-effacing. Yet
by the time he emerges from the water he too feels tense and somehow cheated: the two of them are now united in dissatisfaction.

Jonathan had greeted Stanley ironically: '"Hail, brother! All hail,
Thou Mighty One!"' (p. 208). But in the third section of the story
we see Stanley behaving as if he were just such a Mighty One –
expecting to be waited on, bewailing the loss of the walking-stick,
that is – like the Colonel's thumping-stick – the emblem of his
male authority, and bemoaning the 'heartlessness of women'. When
he finally dashes off to catch the bus the women all heave a sigh of

relief: the house is now theirs. And with his departure the story finds its true subject – the domestic domain of the women and children. But there is disunity here too. Bossy Isabel has no time for baby Lottie (although kindly Kezia does come to her aid), and the natural antagonism of the Samuel Josephs children has to be channelled into organised competition.

One of the most intriguing sections of the story is the fifth. This is devoted to an encounter between Linda's unmarried sister Beryl and her friend – or associate – Mrs Harry Kember. To the Bay community Mrs Kember and her husband Harry are sinister outsiders, and Beryl's friendship with them serves to illustrate her dilemma. Trapped within a small social circle and desperate for new or stimulating company, she is driven inevitably into the arms of the Kembers.

The couple's 'offences' are many. Mrs Kember smokes (the only person at the Bay to do so), plays bridge, uses slang. She is a sluttish housekeeper, and much – too much – at home in the company of men. She has a familiar attitude towards her servant, is (or seems) considerably older than her husband, and appears sexually shameless. By the end of the episode she is also associated with a repulsive and corrupting unnaturalness:

> 'I believe in pretty girls having a good time,' said Mrs. Harry Kember. 'Why not? Don't you make a mistake, my dear. Enjoy yourself.' And suddenly she turned turtle, disappeared, and swam away quickly, quickly, like a rat. Then she flicked round and began swimming back. She was going to say something else. Beryl felt that she was being poisoned by this cold woman, but she longed to hear. But oh, how strange, how horrible! As Mrs. Harry Kember came up close she looked, in her black waterproof bathing-cap, with her sleepy face lifted above the water, just her chin touching, like a horrible caricature of her husband. (p. 220)

Harry Kember is rumoured to sleep with other women, and there is a popular belief that he will one day commit a murder – with his wife as victim. The fantasy seems to stem in part from the general feeling that violent death would be an appropriate fate for the flashy Mrs Kember. It is rendered in a suitably sensational cinematic image:

> Some of the women at the Bay privately thought he'd commit a murder one day. Yes, even while they talked to Mrs. Kember

and took in the awful concoction she was wearing, they saw her
stretched as she lay on the beach; but cold, bloody, and still with
a cigarette stuck in the corner of her mouth. (p. 219)

The Kembers are exceptional amongst Mansfield's characters in
that they are externally conceived, and to some extent melodramatic,
figures – a mark of their being the creations of other characters'
fantasies rather than of the writer's own. But the main problem
here is that the text itself appears to come close to 'judging' them
– again a rarity in Mansfield – and thus to aligning itself with the
narrow-minded 'chorus' of the local community; further, that in so
doing it fails to acknowledge any material distinction between an
apparently trivial flouting of social convention and some deeper,
only partly articulated, unnaturalness. Indeed Mansfield even manages to imply that the two are intrinsically related, so that the rules
of the small-time social code help to define – and even to shape –
the story's conception of unnaturalness. This is very different from
the situation in (for instance) the earlier story 'Bliss', in which the
similarly conceived Norman Knights and their friends stand for
qualities that are clearly negative.

As 'outsiders' the Kembers point up not only the difficulties
of Beryl's position but also the solidarity of the Burnell family, and
the stability – but also the narrowness – of their values and way of
life. It would appear that in Mrs Harry Kember Mansfield located
many of her own characteristics – just as she had done with the
cure-guests in the *German Pension* sketches. This woman, alienated
from other members of her sex both in her childlessness and in her
unconventional behaviour, and whose husband is closely associated
with other women (as Murry had been a few months before 'At the
Bay' was written) has telling connections with the author herself.
Moreover, Mansfield knew she was dying while writing 'At the
Bay', and the marks of this knowledge are in the episode: quite
apart from the gossipy speculation about Mrs Kember's murder the
story grotesquely emphasises her lifelessness as she lies in the sun:
'Parched, withered, cold, she lay stretched on the stones like a piece
of tossed-up driftwood' (p. 218).

That Mansfield should have lodged so many aspects of her own
behaviour and situation in the character of Mrs Kember and then
depicted her as she did, have to do both with her own place in the
Beauchamp family and with the way she has integrated Kezia (once
again her own fictional counterpart) into *her* family. The Kembers

are, as it were, the price that has to be paid both for this reinte-
gration and for the atmosphere of serenity and brilliance that here
pervades the Burnell family and all its doings. At the same time the
couple still manage to stand in some sense as an implicit comment
on the narrow values of the Burnell/Beauchamp family and the
larger community that has excluded them. But there are traces here
too of a deep despair and bitterness in the writing about the pariah
couple, that may be set against the story's overtly lyrical mood and
its hints of a more gentle melancholy.

However, the unflattering rendering of Mrs Kember also suggests
a rejection on Mansfield's part of her own earlier and more freely
directed sexuality. Here gender polarity is no mere social convention but, as the opening scene suggests, a primal division. To blur
its boundaries is to offend against nature.[30]

In the sixth section of the story, and as the sun rises to its height,
we witness the sudden flowering of Linda's feelings for her baby
son. The baby, who has been lying asleep in front of her, suddenly
wakes up and smiles. This is not one of Linda's own mysterious
inward gleams but 'a perfect beam, no less' (p. 223). And it bowls
Linda over.

Just before this she had been dreaming her old dream – of hearing her father promise, '"As soon as you and I are old enough,
Linny, we'll cut off somewhere, we'll escape. Two boys together. I
have a fancy I'd like to sail up a river in China"' (p. 221). No trace
here of the distaste which at the end of the previous episode coloured the characterisation of Mrs Kember as 'a horrible caricature
of her husband' (p. 220). Then, in the dream, Linda's suitor Stanley
Burnell passes by the house, causing Mr Fairfield to interrupt his
fantasising. Similarly Linda's own reverie turns from a reminiscence
about her father to a shrewd and tolerant assessment of her feelings
for Stanley and their life together.

So Linda's early obsession with her father, eliminated from 'Prelude' (although it did figure in its draft version 'The Aloe'), is here
released onto the surface of the page; confronted; and finally accepted.

Linda goes on to contemplate her 'real grudge against life'
(p. 222) – her obligation to bear children. This she feels is aggrav-
ated by the fact that she does not love them: 'it was as though a
cold breath had chilled her through and through on each of those
awful journeys; she had no warmth left to give them' (p. 223). But
a moment later, when the boy 'warms' her with the 'perfect beam'
of his smile, she appears to melt.

The resolution, however, turns out to be a typically Modernist one – intuitional and ecstatic, but also tentative and temporary.
The boy, having received the gift for which his sisters long – their
mother's love – turns immediately from it to another, still more
primal, object of desire:

> But by now the boy had forgotten his mother. He was serious
> again. Something pink, something soft waved in front of him. He
> made a grab at it and it immediately disappeared. But when he
> lay back, another, like the first, appeared. This time he deter-
> mined to catch it. He made a tremendous effort and rolled right
> over. (p. 224)

The Linda of 'At the Bay' has yet another, and still deeper, cause
for anguish – the ancient mutability of all things. Where in 'Prelude' she was linked with the tough and durable aloe plant – itself
practically an emblem of eternity in its once-in-a-hundred-years
flowering – in 'At the Bay' she is associated with the tiny flowers
of the manuka tree. The minute here becomes as it often was for
the Romantics an example of perfection; the intensity with which
it is regarded, an indicator of supreme value:

> Pretty – yes, if you held one of those flowers on the palm of your
> hand and looked at it closely, it was an exquisite small thing.
> Each pale yellow petal shone as if each was the careful work of a
> loving hand. The tiny tongue in the centre gave it the shape of a
> bell. And when you turned it over the outside was a deep bronze
> colour. But as soon as they flowered, they fell and were scattered.
> You brushed them off your frock as you talked; the horrid little
> things got caught in one's hair. Why, then, flower at all? Who
> takes the trouble – or the joy – to make all these things that are
> wasted, wasted.... It was uncanny. (p. 221)

But we pass swiftly from object to beholder. In a passage of fine
ambivalence Mansfield moves from the notion of life sweeping Linda
away with its bustle as she pauses to examine the underside of a
leaf, to the idea of the subject herself as a leaf – with all that image's
traditional undertones of impermanence and decay:

> as soon as one paused to part the petals, to discover the under-
> side of the leaf, along came Life and one was swept away. And,

lying in her cane chair, Linda felt so light; she felt like a leaf. Along came Life like a wind and she was seized and shaken; she had to go. Oh dear, would it always be so? Was there no escape? (p. 221)

The 'solution' that is offered to the trauma of transience, of personal loss and decay, is of course also traditional – the coming of new life. Here the 'new life' is the child Linda is learning to love. But this solution is unavailable in the next section, when Kezia questions her beloved grandmother: ' "Why did Uncle William have to die? He wasn't old" ' (p. 226); and the grandmother, drawing a thread from her ball of wool as if she were one of the classical Fates, reveals her continuing sadness at the loss – even though on a conscious level she accepts it:

'Does it make you sad to think about him, grandma?' She hated her grandma to be sad.

It was the old woman's turn to consider. Did it make her sad? To look back, back. To stare down the years, as Kezia had seen her doing. To look after *them* as a woman does, long after *they* were out of sight. Did it make her sad? No, life was like that. (p. 226)

Linda's triumph of life in the sixth episode has been succeeded by the further education of the child Kezia in the inevitability of death.

We move eventually to the washhouse, where the children are playing Happy Families. Each of them takes the part of an animal – one that is emblematic of their personalities. The bossy eldest of each family, Isabel and Pip, are rooster and bull; the foolish youngest, Lottie and Rags, become donkey and sheep. The proto-artist Kezia, given to imaginative flights and transformations, wants to be a 'ninseck'.

Abruptly, as the children play at their game of chance, the day fades; and with the coming of the dark – a potent emblem, for if the day represents life then the dark must be for death – the children become nervous. Then a bearded face appears at the window terrifying them still more.

But it is only Uncle Jonathan, come to fetch Pip and Rags home. The next episode loops back a little in time – a kind of victory in itself – to show two kindred spirits, the unworldly Linda and

Jonathan, in conversation. Jonathan, bewailing his imminent return to work, compares himself to an insect (Kezia's 'animal') that finds itself a prisoner in a room it has voluntarily flown into – and out of which, despite the absence of impediments, it cannot bring itself to fly. This leads him to reflect on the shortness of life. The sunset sky is seen both as Romantic spectacle and also, more traditionally, as a reminder of the power and majesty of a jealous God. Linda, however, less remote and happier here than in any previous scene, prefers to see 'something infinitely joyful and loving in those silver beams' (p. 239). But the obvious discontinuity between Linda's vision of love and joy, and the passage which immediately preceded it, undermines the possibility of consolation.

The entrance of Florrie the cat – in the opening section the first member of the Burnell family to appear – alerts us to the fact that the story is drawing to its close. So too does the return of Stanley, now desperate to be forgiven for his ill-tempered departure that morning. The spirit of domestic comedy has a final, brief reign when we learn that, feeling ashamed of having slighted Linda, he brings home a peace-offering . . . for himself.

The concluding episode of 'At the Bay', like that of 'Prelude', is given over to the out-standing character Beryl. Her scene takes place by moonlight – for romance-minded Beryl a time of potential enchantment. Now, however, she is less prone than she had been to romantic self-deception. In a moment of reflective melancholy she tells herself, 'It is true that when you are by yourself and you think about life, it is always sad' (p. 242). Then for the first time the truth of her situation is acknowledged – baldly, and with an undertone of desperation: 'She wants a lover' (p. 242) – though her reversion to the third person indicates a lingering reluctance to admit. Then, ' "how do you know he is coming at all?" ' mocked a small voice within her' (p. 243). This is too much for even the new, reflective Beryl, who promptly dismisses the idea: the earlier voice of moral duplicity has become one which threatens to unmask her – to strip away her protective self-deception.

Even her fantasies are undercut when Harry Kember appears at the window and tries to persuade her to come out with him. Beryl hesitates but finally joins him in the garden. There however she has a horrifying vision of him and his 'bright, blind, terrifying smile' (p. 244) – a description reminiscent of Bertha's feelings of sexual terror towards the end of 'Bliss'. Now convinced of Harry Kember's 'vileness', Beryl flees back to the house. So a story which began in comic sexual discord – with Florrie the cat sparring with her old enemy the sheepdog – ends in real friction.

The coda turns back, like the prologue, to the natural scene:

> A cloud, small, serene, floated across the moon. In that moment of darkness the sea sounded deep, troubled. Then the cloud sailed away, and the sound of the sea was a vague murmur, as though it waked out of a dark dream. All was still. (p. 245)

Human disquiets are here mapped onto to the natural world; diminished; and then stilled. But even the stilling of them implies tragedy. For next to stillness is death, and death – mentioned only rarely – is a constant presence in the story, offsetting the sense of familial wellbeing that has on the whole overcome the discontents of 'Prelude'.

'The Garden-Party' (October 1921) is one of Mansfield's best-known stories and a favourite anthology-piece, largely thanks no doubt to its dazzling evocation of the party itself. But it is also a complex and difficult work which has generated more critical articles – many offering conflicting interpretations – than any other Mansfield story apart from 'The Fly'.

The party of the title is thrown by the Sheridan family – a wealthier and slightly older version of the Burnells, with the parents' personalities somewhat modified: Mr Sheridan is milder and more retiring, Mrs Sheridan pushier and more social than their Burnell counterparts. The story is thought to have been based on an actual party given by the Beauchamps at the imposing, colonial-style home at 75 Tinakori Road to which they moved after the 'Prelude' house.

'The Garden-Party' is one of several Mansfield stories that trace the young heroine's journey towards adulthood. The ritual of passage here is the party itself, and the opportunity it offers the heroine to assume adult responsibility. The point is underlined by Mrs Sheridan herself: ' "... I'm determined to leave everything to you children this year. Forget I am your mother. Treat me as an honoured guest" ' (p. 245).

The concern in the story is whether the daughter Laura will in maturing grow into a replica of her superficial and insensitive mother, or whether her own better nature – evident in her less prejudiced (though sentimental) attitude towards the workmen who come to put up the marquee – will prevail. The point is first made in terms of register: will Laura find a language of her own, or will she simply follow her sisters in adopting their mother's affected and artificial tone? When she first 'tries on' her mother's voice she is uneasy, and regresses (like Kezia in 'The Little Girl') to a stammer:

> 'Good morning,' she said, copying her mother's voice. But that sounded so fearfully affected that she was ashamed, and stammered like a little girl, 'Oh – er – have you come – is it about the marquee?' (p. 246)

Shortly afterwards, however, she is able to adopt Mrs Sheridan's voice unthinkingly. Mansfield underlines the point by having her repeat her mother's words:

> The telephone. 'Yes, yes; oh yes. Kitty? Good morning, dear. Come to lunch? Do, dear. Delighted, of course. It will only be a very scratch meal – just the sandwich crusts and broken meringue-shells and what's left over. Yes, isn't it a perfect morning? Your white? Oh, I certainly should. One moment – hold the line. Mother's calling.' And Laura sat back. 'What, mother? Can't hear.'
> Mrs. Sheridan's voice floated down the stairs. 'Tell her to wear that sweet hat she had on last Sunday.'
> 'Mother says you're to wear that *sweet* hat you had on last Sunday. Good. One o'clock. Bye-bye.'
>
> (p. 248)

At issue here is the question of whether Laura is to model herself on the attitudes and behaviour of her silly and insensitive mother; or to throw in her lot with her family, their attitudes and privileged lifestyle. This lifestyle is displayed in all its confident splendour *and* its self-absorbed triviality on the occasion of the garden party. The story's opening, with its suggestion that good weather is as much a matter of purchasing power as a grocery order, sets the tone: 'And after all the weather was ideal. They could not have had a more perfect day for a garden-party if they had ordered it' (p. 245). Mrs Sheridan even uses the family's wealth – and the occasion of the party – in an attempt to eliminate desire itself. When Laura, coming upon a tray full of canna lilies ('wide open, radiant, almost frighteningly alive' [p. 249]) she protests that nobody could have

ordered so many. But Mrs Sheridan has: '"... I suddenly thought
for once in my life I shall have enough canna lilies ..."' (p. 249).

Yet money is merely the crudest of the means by which the privileged are able to obtain their heart's desire. The opening to the
story has the roses in the garden – even perhaps the celestial arch-
angels as well – eager to acclaim, and to play their part in, the
Sheridans' festivities:

> As for the roses, you could not help feeling they understood that
> roses are the only flowers that impress people at garden-parties;
> the only flowers that everybody is certain of knowing. Hundreds,
> yes, literally hundreds, had come out in a single night; the green
> bushes bowed down as though they had been visited by archangels.
> (p. 245)

Before the party has even begun, however, an incident occurs
which divides Laura's loyalties. A workman living in a cottage down
the road from the Sheridans is killed in an accident. Out of respect
for him and his family Laura tries to get the party cancelled. But the
other women dismiss her attitude as 'extravagant' and Mrs Sheridan,
whose main concern is that the man should not have been killed
in their garden, promptly sets about distracting her with the gift of
a hat.

This is the black hat which features in several others of Mansfield's
stories, and which always serves to point up some symbolic connection between the characters with whom it is associated. The hat
in 'The Garden-Party' belongs to Laura's mother. In handing it on
to her daughter Mrs Sheridan not only distracts her from her concern for the dead man's family: she symbolically hands on her own
values and lifestyle – and at the critical moment of Laura's passing
into adulthood. The passionate and adoring gaze her daughter gives
her own reflection while trying on the hat indicates that Mrs Sheridan
has been at least for the moment successful. Even more significantly this mirror-image promptly obscures the girl's mental vision
of – that is, her concern for – the dead man's family:

> the first thing she saw was this charming girl in the mirror, in her
> black hat trimmed with gold daisies and a long black velvet rib-
> bon. Never had she imagined she could look like that. Is mother
> right? she thought. And now she hoped her mother was right.
> Am I being extravagant? Perhaps it was extravagant. Just for a

moment she had another glimpse of that poor woman and those little children and the body being carried into the house. But it all seemed blurred, unreal, like a picture in the newspaper. (p. 256)

Laura's conduct after the party also supports this reading. She agrees to her mother's suggestion that she make the charitable gesture of taking some leftovers down to the dead man's family. And when she sees the dead man she is overcome by feelings of illumination.

Again, however, this is a typically Modernist enlightenment, for the manner in which the girl responds to the corpse is inappropriately aesthetic and sentimental: 'He was wonderful, beautiful. While they were laughing and while the band was playing, this marvel had come to the lane' (p. 261). Inevitably perhaps, her reaction has been less a matter of her own finer feelings than of her mother's artificiality. (It is worth noting here that Mansfield's elder sister Vera, the unsympathetic Isabel of the Burnell stories, was, according to her own perhaps guileless admission, 'the one who went down with the things!'[31] – that is, the food left over from the garden party.)

The party itself is thrown by the Sheridans as a kind of affirmation of their wealth and social standing. But for Mansfield it has another significance. As in 'At the Bay', the narrative, and indeed the party itself, follow the course of a metaphor-burdened summer's day from dawn to darkness. And as before, the progress of this day stands, in all its brevity and splendour, for that of a human life. So when Laura moves at day's end from the brightness and plenty of her own home to a mean little cottage with shadowy inhabitants – one of whom is of course the dead man – she is prefiguring her own eventual passage from the courts of life to the land of the dead. No wonder at her unease as she makes the journey.

And the apology she blurts out before the dead man for the inappropriateness of the party hat she is wearing is highly ironical. For it is the black hat alone that marks her in spite of her youthful flowering as one of death's future victims. (Even her youth is indicated, in the hat's trimming of flowers.) In confronting the dead man she is, then, in a sense confronting her own future self.

In view of all this it is appropriate that the description of the great day should be pervaded by an underlying melancholy. The note is struck right at the beginning: 'Windless, warm, the sky without a cloud. *Only* [my italics] the blue was veiled with a haze of light gold, as it is sometimes in early summer' (p. 245). ('Only', which may read at first as relating to the blue, in fact qualifies the fineness of the day.) And the afternoon's ending is encapsulated in the fading of a flower, a traditional image for the impermanence of beauty: 'And the perfect afternoon slowly ripened, slowly faded, slowly its petals closed' (p. 257). When she gives a rather self-conscious rendering of the popular song 'This Life is Weary' Laura's sister Jose unknowingly sums up this underlying mood.

The true subject of the story, presented in a sustained subtext, exists, then, in striking opposition to its radiant surface. Overtly 'The Garden-Party' focuses on Laura's development, inviting the reader to speculate on whether she will mature into a typical member of her family – superficial and slightly callous, preoccupied with the conspicuous display that the party with such triumphant irony represents – or whether she will remain more natural and sympathetic. But at a deeper, more mythic level it deals in a sombre confrontation with death. What must have been Mansfield's anguished concern with her own death – at the time of writing only fifteen months away – is relegated to the subtext; controlled by the universality of myth, leaving the surface of the story free for an ironically lyrical evocation of the garden party . . . which in a tribute to the subtext becomes itself symbolic of life's brevity and beauty.

In August of 1921 Mansfield put aside 'At the Bay' in order to give form to an idea which was obsessing her. This she described in a letter to William Gerhardi: 'It wasn't the memory of a real experience. It was a kind of *possession*.'[32] In fact the story probably does make use of childhood memories – in particular trips across Cook Strait to Picton in the South Island of New Zealand, to visit Mansfield's paternal grandparents. But, like 'The Garden-Party', it has strong mythical undertones.

'The Voyage' centres on a young girl whose mother has just died. She and her grandmother bid farewell to her father on the wharf at Wellington (in the south of New Zealand's North Island) and take the night ferry to Picton, at the head of the South Island. There Fenella is to begin a new life with her grandparents. The story ends with the early-morning arrival at the new home, and the welcome Fenella receives from her grandfather.

The narrative translates Fenella from the atmosphere of sorrow and anxiety surrounding the mother's death to the hopes and expectations of a new life. Her progression is reinforced by the contrast between the Wellington wharf-scene with its large, alien

shapes and hastening, preoccupied figures and the lightness, whiteness, and magical miniaturism of the Picton morning. There is a
telling contrast too between Fenella's tense and preoccupied father
and her relaxed and welcoming grandfather. The child herself comes
over as barely old enough to mourn – barely old enough even to
comprehend her mother's death: her grief is registered at second
hand, through the feelings of others.

Once again, then, Mansfield has dramatised the child's loss of her
mother and of the parental home. But the losses are here associated,
not with maternal neglect but with the death of the mother: human
failure has been overtaken by fate. At the same time she takes care
to anaesthetise her heroine against the pain of grief . . . and to make
good her losses with the acquisition of a substitute home that, in
terms of emotional sustenance, proves the true one.

Once Fenella's journey gets under way the sombre realism of
the story's opening modulates into myth. The myth is that of the
rebirth of the soul; the journey, one from darkness to light. The
characters are associated, as in 'Prelude' though more overtly, with
birds – traditionally symbolic of otherworldly translation: the family name is Crane, the father is compared to a bird, Mrs Crane has
an umbrella with a swan's-head crook that pecks at Fenella during
the voyage, as if urging her to hurry. The title also hints at mythic
translation: a voyage generally signifies a lengthy journey whereas
Fenella's 'real' trip lasted only a night. The implication is that she
has moved, not merely to a new foster home but to the Home of
Homes – compensation enough for her earlier loss.

Typically, however, Mansfield concludes by casting a shadow
of doubt over her story's message. This shadow is contained in a
reference to a black-framed text that was painted by Grandmother,
and which (literally) hangs over Grandfather's head:

> Lost! One Golden Hour
> Set with Sixty Diamond Minutes.
> No Reward Is Offered
> For It Is GONE FOR EVER!
>   (p. 330)

This teasing little verse brings up the critical issue – that of time
and its passing. The motto's theme, its black frame, its critical position above the old man's head, all serve to undermine the mythical

implications of the story; to suggest that Fenella has not after all been transferred to some golden realm but to a place of comparative contentment on this earth, in which the moral wisdom of accepting time's passing prevails – a wisdom which will perhaps become important to Fenella later. Grandpa's wink at Fenella suggests that he acknowledges this truth.

But then of course she only 'almost' thinks he winks.

'The Doll's House' is Mansfield's last major family story, and the other staple Mansfield anthology-piece. It too is about the Burnell family. This one centres on a splendid doll's house that the children have been given. The house becomes a touchstone which exposes the characters' personalities through the way they react to it. The unsympathetic – and undomesticated – Beryl notices only its paint-smell ('quite enough to make anyone seriously ill, in Aunt Beryl's opinion' [p. 383]). The equally unsympathetic Isabel acts the part of Lady Bountiful in issuing invitations to the Burnells' schoolfriends to come and see it. But when they do come she reveals her lack of imagination by concentrating on its more functional aspects – carpet, beds and stove, and the way these mimic material reality: the 'beds with real bedclothes, and the stove with an oven door' (p. 387). Kezia alone notices and appreciates the 'exquisite little amber lamp' (p. 384) – an object of great beauty which does not even pretend to practical use: 'you couldn't light it'.

It is also the kindhearted Kezia who goes against her mother's express instructions in inviting the Kelvey children, daughters of a washerwoman and of a reputed gaolbird, to view the little house. As it turns out they are shooed away by the vigilant (and vindictive) Aunt Beryl – although not before Else, the younger of the two, has confirmed Kezia's perception of the rare beauty of the lamp. Once out of sight of the Burnells she confides in her sister: ' "I seen the little lamp." ' (p. 391) – a moment of affirmation and illumination which apparently constituted the 'germ' of the story. A preliminary note in Mansfield's *Journal* reads, 'N.Z. *At Karori*:. "The little lamp. I seen it." And then they were silent.'[33]

Kezia, then, is once again portrayed as the ideal child – endowed both with a kind heart and with a gift for appreciating beauty. The connection, Romantic in origin, between these qualities holds good for all the story's major characters: besides Else's sense of the lamp's 'exquisiteness' the Kelveys are a model of co-operation and understanding with the elder, Lil, always attentive to the wishes of the younger – where Kezia's own elder sister Isabel is sensible only of 'the powers that went with being eldest' (p. 384). And neither Isabel nor Beryl either appreciates the lamp or shows any compassion for the Kelveys.

More thoroughly in 'The Doll's House' than in any other of the Burnell stories Mansfield 'writes up' Kezia – making her into a character of whom the reader cannot fail to approve. Brushed off by a terse and dismissive mother (who is again more or less written out of the story) and reprimanded by an Aunt Beryl filled with gnawing anxieties over a threatening letter from a suitor, Kezia herself shows only consideration and sensibility.

As C.A. Hankin suggests[34] the young Kathleen Beauchamp's sense of rejection from her own family has been displaced in this story onto the dispossessed and inheritance-less young Kelveys. Thus, familial rejection is at last both distanced from Mansfield herself (the Kezia-figure) and transformed from a personal context to the less immediate one of class.

The doll's house itself is the last of Mansfield's miniature symbols of the idealised home. It is perceived as 'much more exciting' (p. 383) than a 'real' home, and its tiny features – particularly of course the lamp – are lovingly detailed by the narrator. And the 'real' house, apart from the back door out of which Aunt Beryl emerges, has been 'written out' of the story: with the doll's house as its miniature symbol it has become superfluous. It may be for this reason too that the inmates of the tiny house are too big really to be at home there. They also appear to have been anaesthetised:

> The father and mother dolls, who sprawled very stiff as though they had fainted in the drawing-room, and their two little children asleep upstairs, were really too big for the doll's house. They didn't look as though they belonged. (p. 384)

These figures – father, mother, and two children – correspond to the members of the Burnell family . . . minus of course Kezia/Kathleen herself, whose privilege as artist or would-be artist it is to observe the scene from outside, just as the children are able to observe the doll's house.

In her last story, then, Mansfield has replaced the idea of the home as material reality and centre of the child's emotional security, with the home as symbol of beauty and shrine for the little lamp – itself a symbol for artistic illumination. When Kezia affirms that for her the lamp is 'real' she is unknowingly using the word in its old, idealistic sense – in direct opposition to the reality of the miniature beds with the 'real' bedclothes adored by Isabel.

In this way Mansfield came finally to express through Kezia the precedence for her of her artistic vocation above the family home which seemed in some crucial way to have failed her. At the same time she locates her symbol of art and of illumination within that home, thus paying tribute to the central place which her original home and family occupied in her life and art. Yet this family, while it is immortalised – made the objects of that art – is also symbolically deprived of life. As artist at least (and 'The Doll's House' is very much about art) Mansfield was in control; no longer subject to that terrible power which parents – giants to their children[35] – wield over them.

Mansfield's last word on the family involves, not negation or suppression but transcendence. The artist has cast her spell.

Appendix 1
Katherine Mansfield:
Life and Literary Events

14 October 1888	Kathleen Mansfield Beauchamp born in Wellington, New Zealand, to Harold and Annie Beauchamp, the third child in what was to become a family of four daughters and one son.
1903	With her two elder sisters, becomes a pupil at Queen's College, London.
1906	Returns to New Zealand with the family.
1907	First story published, in *Native Companion*, Melbourne. Camping trip to centre of New Zealand's North Island.
July 1908	Leaves New Zealand for London, to make her name as a writer.
1908–9	Affair with fellow New Zealander Garnet Trowell.
March 1909	Married to George Bowden: deserts him the same day.
May 1909	Annie Beauchamp arrives in London, takes Kathleen to Bad Wörishofen (Bavaria) with her, leaves shortly afterwards for the return voyage to New Zealand.
June 1909	Kathleen moves to the Pension Müller, Bad Wörishofen: has a miscarriage shortly afterwards.
1910	Her Bavarian Sketches published in the *New Age*.
1911	Sends short stories to *Rhythm*; meets its editor, John Middleton Murry.
December 1911	*In a German Pension* published by Stephen Swift (who was also *Rhythm*'s printer).
1912	'The Woman at the Store' published by *Rhythm*. Murry becomes Mansfield's lodger and, later, her lover. The pair spend a couple of months in a village near Chichester, Sussex. Stephen Swift flees the country, leaving Murry responsible for *Rhythm*'s debts.
1913–14	Mansfield and Murry spend two months in Paris, partly to escape creditors.
February 1915	Mansfield's brother Leslie Beauchamp arrives in London on his way to fight in the Great War: stays with Murry and Mansfield.

1915	Murry and D.H. Lawrence set up new magazine *Signature*, which publishes some of Mansfield's works.
October 1915	Leslie Beauchamp killed in a training accident.
Nov 1915 to April 1916	Mansfield in the South of France, mostly at Bandol, and most of the time with Murry. Mansfield makes major revisions to her long story 'The Aloe', begun the year before.
1917	'The Aloe' refashioned to become 'Prelude'.
December 1917	Spot found on Mansfield's lung, the first clear evidence that she has tuberculosis: doctor advises her to winter abroad.
Jan to Mar 1918	Mansfield at Bandol again: writes 'Je Ne Parle Pas Français' and 'Bliss'
May 1918	Mansfield and Murry finally married, Mansfield having obtained a divorce from Bowden. Paris under bombardment as she returns through it to England with her friend Ida Baker.
July 1918	'Prelude' published by Leonard and Virginia Woolf at the Hogarth Press.
1919	Murry appointed editor of *The Athenaeum*: Mansfield becomes a regular reviewer. Mansfield advised to enter a sanatorium: she goes to the Mediterranean instead.
February 1920	'Je Ne Parle Pas Français' published privately.
December 1920	*Bliss* published by Constable.
May 1921	Mansfield, now seriously ill, leaves the Mediterranean for Switzerland.
February 1922	*The Garden-Party* published by Constable.
1922	Mansfield journeys to Paris, Switzerland, London in search of treatment.
July 1922	Last completed story 'The Canary' written.
October 1922	Mansfield ends up as a guest at the Gurdyeyev Institute in Fontainebleau.
9 January 1923	Murry travels to Fontainebleau to visit Mansfield. Death of Katherine Mansfield.

Appendix 2

His Sister's Keeper

The girl came up on deck to find Dieppe like the mouth of some giant monster and a little crowd of officials groaning a gangway on board. Then up the sanded staircase to the luggage room, where the flaring posters on the walls – Normandy – Brittany – Paris – Luxembourg – seemed like magic hands stretched out in invitation – 'See what I hold, come here.'

Her one small bag was passed without comment. There was still half an hour to spare before the train left. She was cold and tired, and went into the Buffet for a cup of coffee. Glancing at her watch she found that it was barely three o'clock. Three o'clock in the morning ... and Dieppe ... when she had only made up her mind at six o'clock the evening before, and at seven she had been at Victoria, debating still, still safe, and now ... well, anything to live. She was sick of existing. If she had spent another day of the frightful monotony it would have driven her mad, and after all so many would only have jumped at the opportunity when it was first offered. This idiotic habit of drawing back would never take her anywhere at all. She sipped her coffee slowly out of a thick, white, cup, noticed the little fern-filled dish of Hungarian peasant ware on the table, and at the table next her, a honeymoon couple – she looked half-smilingly, half-sneeringly at the blatantly new wedding-ring upon the woman's finger, their new clothes, and yellow leather handbag. They looked ridiculous – abashed, self-conscious and almost apologetic towards the waiter. Heaven preserve her!

Then out again on to the cold platform to climb into the high, padded carriage. A porter ran along smashing up the darkness with a jangling bell – shrill whistles sounded. She was settling her bag and hat and umbrella in the rack when the door was thrown open and a woman half fell, half jumped into the carriage, seizing her suit case from a porter. She threw him some money, he banged the door to, and they were off.

'That was a case of all but,' said the Fellow Passenger, panting a little, holding her handkerchief up to her lips, 'I hadn't an idea. . . .'

She tugged at the buttons of her coat collar. The girl smiled and watched her curiously. The Fellow Passenger was a woman, obviously young still, but over dressed, her childish face covered with rouge and powder, her pretty brown hair curled and puffed against her hat. She wore a scarlet blanket coat over a pale blue cloth dress, her high-heeled shoes were cut low enough to show her blue clocked stockings. She sat down in one corner, putting her feet on the opposite cushion, and began peeling off her suede gloves, a little smile still curving her red mouth; her eyes, serious. Out of the window on one side the girl saw a street of rain-washed cobble stones – on the other side the harbour full of lights – then darkness. . . .

178

She wrapped her cloak round her and took out a little copy of 'The Shropshire Lad' from an inside pocket but could not read. The Fellow Passenger was never still. She opened a red leather bag, took out a powder puff, a mirror, looked at herself critically put out her tongue, wet her finger and carefully smoothed her eyebrows, found a hairpin and put her curls in position. Then she recklessly applied the pink powder to face and throat and even the bosom of her dress.

'Gilding refined gold and painting the lily' she said, glancing up and catching the girl's eye, 'But lilies have no right to go journeying in railway carriages, my dear, even they can't be exempt from smuts. My name's Lily – a series of remarkable coincidences.'

She flung back her head, laughing like a child, and showing her little white teeth like seeds in a red fruit. Then suddenly serious 'I say that to everybody I meet travelling. It's the greatest point. Came on me like an inspiration one day when I was in the same carriage with a Salvation Army Officer. You see it puts one on such a charming footing, such a delicate, flower-like intimacy. What are you reading . . . Oh, don't tell me, it's poems. And you wanted to be alone in the carriage, to curl up and look out of the window, then read a little verse, then remember how he smiled at you in the last verse of the hymn on Sunday evening. It's a good thing I came in to chaperon you . . . you're too pretty for empty railway carriages. Are you going to stay in Paris with grandma in rooms conveniently near the Louvre. I am.'

As she spoke she laughed so much, spread out her little white hands with such a friendly gesture that the girl caught the infection.

'Do go on,' she said. 'Of course I'm going to grandma. I felt somehow you must be going to yours.'

'Oh, what a surprise,' said the Fellow Passenger, sobering a little, 'your voice isn't at all what I had hoped and expected of you – and now I see that your eyebrows too – no, not *genee* at all, my dear, you don't tell me. . . . Do you want to go to sleep?'

She suddenly stood up, stretching herself like a little kitten, yawning and rubbing her eyes 'I'm not sleepy.'

'Neither am I,' said the girl. 'I slept on the boat.'

'I am feeling queer,' said the Fellow Passenger. 'Could howl with crying or put my head out of the window and wave my hanky at nobody at all, or shoot myself or read a love poem – Hand me the book.'

The girl gave it to her in silence.

'Hallo,' said the Fellow Passenger, 'got a fit of the "tarradiddles" – your hands are on the jump.'

'I am tired,' said the girl, blushing faintly.

'I know, my dear, the heaviness that endures for a night . . . Good Lord. Now you go bye-bye while I read.'

She curled up in the railway carriage, pillowed her head on her arm, the little book in her hand. It was bitterly cold. The girl felt suddenly exhausted. It was the Fellow Passenger's comment upon her nervous, shaky hands. She had not quite got command of herself. She could not quite see the future. Felt suddenly that she had plunged into a sea without the slightest idea as to whether she was swimming towards land or quicksand, or mirage. Now this Fellow Passenger, her assurance, her laughter, the very way she powdered her face, all seemed to speak of success and experience. The girl felt crude beside her, longed suddenly to speak of a dozen vague fears. But she fell asleep and did not wake until the train stopped at Rouen. It certainly was bitterly cold. The Fellow Passenger was tugging a long fur out of her rug-strap.

'Felt I couldn't do without my little piece of dog,' she said.

'Have I been asleep?' said the girl.

'Asleep, my dear, like a baby, with your eyelashes curled on your nice little pink cheeks – most fascinating to a "Young Lady's Companion" – That's a neat way of expressing a fact, isn't it. I've got a gift that way.' She picked up the red book that she had been reading. 'I say, there's a photo pasted in here of a kiddy – who is he?' And the girl answered 'Oh, that's my brother.'

A wave of colour seemed to flood over her whole body. She did not want this woman to look at him, to speak laughingly of him. Felt almost ashamed for one moment of her sentimentality, that she could snatch away the little photograph and hide it in her bosom.

But the Fellow Passenger did not laugh. She spread the page out on her lap. 'Oh, so that's your brother. My word, he looks fine – a regular boy, and yet . . . there's something so sensitive and splendid in his face – spiritual – my dear.'

'Yes, that's just it.' The girl sat upright, her hands clasped on her knees 'he's a marvellous child.' Her heart warmed to this other woman, she could have kissed her.

'Well, nurse, your night-duty now,' said the Fellow Passenger, her voice regaining its flippant tone. 'I'm going up the wooden lane. Send me to sleep with a story – about your little brother.'

The girl smiled, but the Fellow Passenger nodded gravely.

'Across my heart' she said, 'I'd really love to hear anything, it's so refreshing.'

She wound her fur twice round her throat and lay down to sleep.

'When I last saw him,' said the girl, 'he was thirteen – very young, you see, but tall and splendidly made, broad shoulders and slight of hip – you know.'

She was speaking to nobody really, only thinking aloud, her head raised, in her eyes almost a prophetic sweetness. The light fell upon the yellow braids of her hair. 'I felt maternal towards him. As a baby he clung to me, and all the years after – I could still when I looked at him, feel those little hands round my neck, on my face, blindly feeling. And through all the sadness of my girlhood that child brought me light and sweetness. He had a little habit of bringing me flowers – a rose, some violets, a spray of apple blossom – yes, he was always coming to me with his hands full of flowers. I have so many pictures of him,' said the girl, 'in my mind you know. He will be the finest man on earth. Oh, I see him as a little child sitting on the table while I scrubbed his grubby knees, and after his bath in my room in the morning in his pink pyjamas, his hair curling all over his head, standing on one leg and flicking the towel and crying "It's a lovely day, dearest". And at night after he had gone to bed we had a mysterious game called "Pyjama arm". I used to go in the dark and lie down on his bed, my head pillowed on his arm while he told me all his thoughts, his growing ideas, his strange little fantastic conceptions, questioned me, implicitly believed in me. In the dark even now sometimes I hear that little high voice. And then, particularly after he had been playing cricket, I could hear him stumbling up the stairs, hot, out of breath, his shirt collar unbuttoned, his hair on end, damp with perspiration, and mopping his face with an indescribable handkerchief.'

The girl laughed suddenly. 'He was so absent-minded, too. Often I would go into his room when he was half an hour late for breakfast – "I can't find my braces anywhere, sister, I've been looking and looking" and they'd be buttoned to his trousers all the time, trailing on the floor. Then he used to stand on a chair and part his hair before my mirror, called it a "bug-track" after he'd been to school. He read too, everything I gave him, good things you know, the very best always. Oh dear, what didn't he exact and demand of me in those days. I remember very well saying Good-bye to him. He was going to school, and we kissed for a moment and then I leaned out of my window. It had been raining – the air was very cool and clean. He waved to me from the gate and I listened, hearing the glad, little footsteps die down the street, fainter and fainter, so fast. . . . out of my life.'

She stopped speaking a moment. The Fellow Passenger was lying with her hands over her face. Blue light flooded the windows of the carriage and the girl, rubbing a place in the glass saw in the gloom a green tree white with frost.

'He is going to be a splendid man' she said suddenly, 'Oh, one of the best – a wonderful man. Yes, you were right – spiritual is the word. He needs the very best influences. . . . Are you laughing?'

She thought the Fellow Passenger stirred. No answer. The train throbbed on and the girl, tired out, lay down in the corner. Then, the Fellow Passenger suddenly sat up, and to her amazement the girl saw that her face was wet with tears. She was twisting her handkerchief in her hand, dabbing her eyes with it, the powder and rouge smudging her face, and she suddenly slipped down to the floor of the carriage and pillowed her head in the girl's lap.

'Oh, listen' she said. 'I too, had just such a brother, just. The world to me, you understand. We lived just so together. I was his sister and his mother. On him I based all the hopes and aspirations of my life. Unhappy at home, too, you know, and he my ideal – but we did not part, oh no. We were twins, that was the great difference to you, so *although* I felt older and he always came to me I had not felt him as a child in my arms. That does make such a difference – absurd how we love the helplessness, but we do . . . I gave up my life for him. Put him, if you like, upon a pedestal, made him perfect man, and he you know took such care of me, watched over me so. We decided that when I was old enough we should live together. I did not wish to marry, he filled my life, and I was sound asleep, really, you know. Well, one day, I had to go to London. We lived in the country and at that time my brother was living in London sharing a small flat. I was to stay several days with an aunt of mine. My train was very late, and when we reached the station Aunt was not to be found. I waited on the station – all alone – and by and bye a woman quietly dressed came up and asked me if I was waiting for anybody – You know I was young. All I said to her was "Have you come from my Aunt, Mrs —— oh, well the name's nothing – and she said Yes, there's a cab waiting." My aunt was engaged and would meet me at the house. So we walked along the platform, it was six o'clock, a winter day and quite dark. I remember several people looking at us closely – I had my hair down still you know, in a long plait. A carriage was waiting, we got in. The woman gave no address, but we drove a long distance. During the drive she was silent and I, thinking her a maid of my aunt's, looked out of the window. We drove for what seemed an interminable distance, and then at last the carriage stopped in a quiet street, a large grey stone house before us. Though I had never been to stay with her before, the house did not look at all as I had expected, but still I was unsuspicious. The woman had a key, and I remember standing on the steps and looking down the lighted street as she fitted it into the lock. Then she turned round – "Well, come in miss, your aunt will be waiting for you." So I walked into the hall and the door was shut to. I wonder if you can imagine my feelings at seeing a great heavily furnished hall with a gilt mirror and in the glass visiting cards – the names most curious to me. The woman with me took off her hat and cloak.

'I'll have your things taken to your room, Miss,' she said. "I'm afraid your Aunt won't be able to see you to-night. You will find some supper ready – this way."

I followed her up the stairs along the passage and into a bedroom. She turned on the light, the room was large and ugly, but I was too tired and hungry to care about anything except that there was some supper on a table by the fire. The woman stood by me while I ate, and, I cannot tell you why, I think it was the strange silence of the house, of this woman – even the room seemed curiously expectant – I was frightened and after all I could not eat.

'If you will send up my boxes I will go to bed,' I told her.

'Yes,' she said, moving towards the door, the supper tray in her hands. "I'd go to bed now, if I were you, and have a nice long sleep."

Something in her voice ... I turned round, but she was out of the room, the door shut and I heard the heavy key grate in the lock.

'Locked in! I ran to the door, pulled it, shook it, beat upon it with my hands – it was no use. Silent a moment, terror choking me, I heard in the passage outside a woman laughing – such stupid, senseless laughter – it rose and fell ... Who was laughing like that – why? I cried out and screamed – nobody came. Stories I had overheard from the servants, newspaper reports that I had half read, vague transitory thoughts I had imagined almost obliterated – they trooped before me now, a hideous procession of hideous realities. There was a bell push in the room above the electric switch – I rang and rang – still silence.

Then I thought of him – my splendid brother. What would he think or say to know his sister. . . And he was in the same city, visiting Aunt, maybe. His horror and terror at learning the awful truth. I remembered our conversations together – his high ideals – his reverence for women.

At the thought I cried anew, flinging myself down upon the bed, my hands over my face. Finally, do you know, I fell asleep tired out – and woke, to find the room in darkness – someone was kissing my neck and throat, someone was whispering to me to . . . think of it, my dear, his arms round me, a country girl, filled with a white heat of reserve and terror –' The Fellow Passenger laughed bitterly, her voice full of tears.

I struggled like a little wild cat, shook him off me, rushed to the bell push, and groping for it, in the darkness my hand touched the electric switch instead. I turned round – and it was he – the idol, my brother. *Sic transit gloria me'* said the Fellow Passenger.

We both left that room, but I went into another.'

The girl stared, sat up, and rubbed her eyes. The carriage was full of light. Out of the windows a sky like steel, and on both sides quaint, small, grey-built villages, miniature fields, girt with Noah's ark trees. And now and again the river, like a silver ribbon through the green tapestry of the fields.

At last dawn came. In the sky hung a pink banner of cloud. It grew and widened until at last it touched the houses and fields and peered into the silver mirror of the river.

She looked across at the Fellow Passenger who lay still as before, her hands over her face. A strange, terrible dream, thought the girl.

They were nearly there. The girl gathered together her wraps, pulled down her hat, then tapped the Fellow Passenger on the shoulder.

'We're there,' she said, 'nearly.'

'Oh all right my dear, half a shake.' She sat up and felt again for her powder puff – applied it with renewed vigour. They did not speak again until the station was reached. The Fellow Passenger got out first, greeting gaily a man whom she called Bertie. As she stepped from the carriage the girl saw her drop her handkerchief – it lay on the floor. The girl picked it up – a little damp ball – and handed it to her.

'Oh thanks' said the Fellow Passenger carelessly. 'Bye bye dear.'

In the cold of the winter morning the girl stumbled out of the train, her bag and rug and umbrella in her hand. A man came up to her gladly, quickly, but she almost ran past him and out alone into the street.

K. MANSFIELD
1909

Note Apart from obvious typographical errors, the author's typescript has been reproduced unchanged.

Notes

Preface

1. Letter to Anne Estelle Rice, January 1921.
2. Kate Fullbrook, who alone amongst earlier critics recognises the technical aspect of the 'layering' in Mansfield's writings, observes of one story in the *German Pension* collection, 'The narrative itself, with its sympathetic, revelatory, outraged view of Frau Brechenmacher's trouble, exists on a completely different ideological plane from that of the world it describes. The method is related to irony but goes beyond it to suggest a fracturing in the realm of values that is signalled by the distance of the ethical commitment of the narration from the world it realistically describes...' (*Katherine Mansfield*, Brighton, 1986, p. 56). Some of the Freudian traces in Mansfield's writings are suggested in C.A. Hankin, *Katherine Mansfield and Her Confessional Stories*, London, 1983, and Sydney Janet Kaplan, *Katherine Mansfield and the Origins of Modernist Fiction*, Ithaca, 1991.
3. The Hogarth Press brought out first two volumes of the *Collected Papers* in November 1924.
4. The son–mother relationship in Lawrence's novel *Sons and Lovers* (published 1913), though based in the first instance on the author's own early life, was clearly influenced by Freud's works, and the later *Psychology and the Unconscious* (published 1921) demonstrates influence by reaction through its attack on the Freudian conception of the unconscious. During her first marriage Frieda had an affair with a German disciple of Freud, and she and Lawrence are known to have debated the master's views together.
5. It is now generally acknowledged that literary Modernism was often as much a matter of re-visioning its nineteenth-century inheritance as of overthrowing it: see, for example, Malcolm Bradbury and James McFarlane, 'The Name and Nature of Modernism'; in *Modernism*, eds Bradbury and McFarlane, London, 1976, p. 46, for a list of the critics who have so regarded it. See also *The Struggle of the Modern*, London, 1963, p. 72, in which Stephen Spender observes, 'The modern is the realized consciousness of suffering, sensibility and awareness of the past.'
6. *Short Stories and Short Fictions 1880–1980*, London, 1985; *Katherine Mansfield*, op. cit.; and *Katherine Mansfield and the Origins of Modernist Fiction*, op. cit.
7. Virginia Woolf, *Diaries*, ed. Anne Olivier Bell, London 1977–84, II, p. 227 (16 January 1923).
8. Even those writers who pay tribute to Mansfield's general contribution to the Modernist movement tend to underestimate her innovative brilliance with respect to her better-known contemporary and

friend Virginia Woolf – usually by making only tentative acknowledgement of parallels between their writings: 'Both women were
aware of the similarities in their writing' (Fullbrook, p. 19); Mansfield's
'innovations in the short fiction genre . . . preceded Virginia Woolf's
use of them' (Kaplan, p. 3). Besides Fullbrook and Kaplan, see Antony
Alpers, *The Life of Katherine Mansfield*, Oxford, 1980, p. 345, and
Clare Hanson and Andrew Gurr, *Katherine Mansfield*, London, 1981,
p. 14. However, in her *Virginia Woolf*, London, 1994, p. 147, Hanson
does suggest that Mansfield may have influenced Woolf. (NB Woolf
showed Mansfield her 'Kew Gardens', often considered seminal in
this respect, on 18 August 1917: but by this time the first major
experimental Mansfield work, 'Prelude' – delivered to the Hogarth
Press for publication the same August – was largely complete.) There
remains of course the fact that both writers were subject to the same
influences, aestheticist and otherwise. Either this or a reciprocal influence of Woolf upon Mansfield may for instance account for the sim-
ilarity in subject and mood, and the general prose-poem effect, in
'Kew Gardens' and Mansfield's later stories 'Miss Brill' (1920) and
'Bank Holiday' (c. 1920).

9.   Mansfield's review of *Night and Day* originally appeared in *The Athe-
     naeum* of 21 November 1919, and is reprinted in Katherine Mansfield,
     Novels and Novelists, ed. J.M. Murry, London, 1930, pp. 107–11: the
     relevant passage is on page 111.
10. For a study of Mansfield's Symbolist connections see Clare Hanson
     and Andrew Gurr, *Katherine Mansfield*, op. cit.

1 Alienation

1.   See 'Enna Blake' and 'A Happy Christmas Eve'; published in Antony
     Alpers's edition of *The Stories of Katherine Mansfield*, Oxford, 1984,
     pp. 1–3.
2.   She was then a pupil at Wellington Girls' High School. The maga-
     zine's farsighted editor commented in a note that the first of the tales
     showed 'promise of great merit' (ibid., p. 2).
3.   No date. The notebook in which it is recorded is dated 1903. It was
     first published in *The Idler*, March 1910.
4.   Op. cit., p. 664.
5.   *Journal of Katherine Mansfield*, ed. J. Middleton Murry, London, 1954,
     p. 102.
6.   Marion C. Ruddick, 'Incidents in the Childhood of Katherine Mans-
     field'; unpublished typescript in the Alexander Turnbull Library, Wel-
     lington, New Zealand.
7.   Op. cit., p. 661.
8.   Quoted by Tom Mills in a letter in the Alexander Turnbull Library.
     Mills was a journalist and friend of Harold Beauchamp's. It was he
     who helped Mansfield to place her first-published stories.
9.   Manuscript papers 119 in the Alexander Turnbull Library, Welling-
     ton, New Zealand; written 1903.
10. It may as well owe a specific debt to Dante Gabriel Rossetti's

'Willowwood' sonnets, nos 49 to 52, from the sequence *The House of Life*.

11. Typescript in the Mansfield Collection of the Newberry Library, Chicago.

12. Mansfield's own words, recalled by Tom Mills, a reporter whose advice led to the printing of her first-published stories; see Claire Tomalin, *Katherine Mansfield: A Secret Life*, London, 1987, p. 45. Mansfield's friend Edith Bendall confirmed the report by characterising the Beauchamps as 'bridge and golf people' (Jeffrey Meyers, *Katherine Mansfield: A Biography*, London, 1978, p. 23).

13. *Turnbull Library Record*, III [n. s.] i, p. 8.

14. See Rachel Bowlby, *Just Looking*, New York and London, 1985, a literary–sociological study of the consumer society. Note in particular her reference to department stores as 'exhibition palaces' (p. 21).

15. To Sylvia Payne, 4 March 1908; quoted by Antony Alpers, *The Life of Katherine Mansfield*, Oxford, 1980, p. 60.

16. *Journal of Katherine Mansfield*, p. 42.

17. See e.g. *Katherine Mansfield and Her Confessional Stories*, op. cit.; and *Katherine Mansfield and the Origins of Modernist Fiction*, op. cit.

18. Op. cit., p. 112.

19. Compare also the reference to 'your English play' in 'Germans at Meat', p. 686. This is glossed by Alpers in his *Stories of Katherine Mansfield*, op. cit., p. 547, as a reference to 'the box office sensation of January 1909, *An Englishman's Home*, which portrayed an England that was hopelessly unprepared, being invaded in a surprise attack by efficient, Prussian-sounding soldiers'.

20. Ref. Alpers, *The Life*, op. cit., pp. 96–7 and 99.

21. Antony Alpers in a Commentary on his collected edition of *The Stories of Katherine Mansfield*, op. cit., pp. 547–8.

22. See Mary Burgan, 'Childbirth Trauma in Katherine Mansfield's Early Stories' (*Modern Fiction Studies*, XXIV, 1978, p. 399) for a discussion of Mansfield's association of gluttony with the assertive male.

23. A similar episode occurs in 'Frau Brechenmacher Attends a Wedding', where a coffee-pot is handled 'as if it were a baby' – and is also found to contain objects associated with babyhood.

24. Antony Alpers, op. cit., pp. 3–4 and 124.

25. See ibid., pp. 2, 12, and 124.

26. The Child's reference to how she 'once heard of a baby that died, and they found all its teeth in its stomach' – p. 745 – strengthens the connection.

27. See e.g. Elisabeth Schneider, 'Katherine Mansfield and Chekhov', *Modern Language Notes*, June 1935, pp. 394–7; R. Sutherland, 'Katherine Mansfield: Plagiarist, Disciple, or Ardent Admirer?', *Critique*, V, ii, Fall 1962, pp. 58–76; and Claire Tomalin, op. cit., pp. 72, 80, 210. See also Tomalin's Appendix 2 (pp. 261–72), which reprints the *Times Literary Supplement*'s correspondence on the subject. Kaplan's comment on the relationship between Mansfield's tale and Chekhov's is illuminating: 'Like much feminist writing, Mansfield's story is an attempt to deconstruct a phallocentric myth by retelling it' (op. cit., p. 202).

28. Consider, for example, the three poems, two by Wordsworth and one by Shelley, entitled 'To a Skylark'; also Blake's Prophetic book *Milton*, passim.

  An earlier version of excerpts from pp. 43–57 appeared in my article 'The Female in Katherine Mansfield's Colonial Tales', *Commonwealth and American Women's Discourse*, ed. A.L. McLeod, New Delhi, 1996.

29. In the first-published text of this tale (*Rhythm*, Spring 1912) the gender-specific pronoun 'she' is not used: nevertheless there is evidence in the rest of the tale to indicate Mansfield's preoccupation with the problematic nature of the Narrator's sex, and hence with the issue of gender construction.

30. See Alpers, op. cit., 1984, p. 551. Like the use of 'she' referred to in note 29 the name 'Jim' employed in the Constable text appears to be an unauthorised emendation of Murry's.

31. In a seminal article on the colonial tales, Lydia Wevers points out that 'If colonial romance signifies a discourse of racial and territorial appropriation, then the colonial fear of being in turn appropriated is typically represented in a displacement onto women' ('How Kathleen Beauchamp was Kidnapped', *Women's Studies Journal* (New Zealand) IV ii, December 1988, p. 16); article reprinted in Rhoda B. Nathan, ed., *Critical Essays on Katherine Mansfield*, New York, 1993, pp. 37–47.

32. *The Letters of Katherine Mansfield*, ed. J.M. Murry, London, 1928, II, p. 160; 5 December 1921. (The exhibition was in fact held not at the Goupil but in the Grafton Galleries.)

33. Van Gogh once declared in a letter, 'I have tried to express the terrible passions of humanity by means of red and green.' (*The Complete Letters of Vincent Van Gogh*, Greenwich [Connecticut], 1959 [2nd edn], III, p. 28; 8 September 1888.)

2 Isolation

1. Alpers, *The Stories of Katherine Mansfield*, op. cit., p. 3.
2. Ibid., p. 5.
3. For an illuminating study of the psychical pattern of adolescence, see Julia Kristeva, 'The Adolescent Novel'; in *Abjection, Melancholia and Love*, ed. John Fletcher and Andrew Benjamin, London, 1990, pp. 8–23.
4. *Novels and Novelists*, pp. 128–9.
5. *Letters*, 1928, op. cit., II, p. 88; 17 January 1921.
6. *Katherine Mansfield's Letters to John Middleton Murry 1913–22*, ed. J.M. Murry, London, 1951, p. 393 (to J.M. Murry, 16 November 1919). Her comments were provoked by reading Virginia Woolf's *Night and Day*: see my Preface.
7. Ibid., pp. 380–1.
8. Toby Silverman Zinman ('The Snail Under the Leaf: Katherine Mansfield's Imagery'; *Modern Fiction Studies*, XXIV, 1978, p. 463) observes that the missing word in the Boss's unspoken words of encouragement to the fly, 'Never say die; it was only a question of . . .' (p. 417), is undoubtedly 'time': his belief has again proved false.

9. *The Life of Katherine Mansfield*, op. cit., pp. 356–7: 'any role in its conception (i.e. that of 'The Fly') that Chekhov's cockroach may have played seems merely trivial.' 'Small Fry' was translated by Constance Garnett in 1920.
10. Leslie Beauchamp was killed on 7 October 1915; in February 1922 Mansfield was writing 'The Fly'.
11. *Letters*, 1951, op. cit., p. 116 (11 January 1918).
12. 31 December 1918. Manuscript in the Alexander Turnbull Library.
13. See *Letters*, 1928, op. cit., II, p. 190; 26 February 1922: 'I think my story for you will be called *Canaries*.'
14. Letter to J. Middleton Murry, 12 December 1915; *The Collected Letters of Katherine Mansfield*, ed. Vincent O'Sullivan with Margaret Scott, Oxford, 1984–, I, p. 210. Ref. also a letter from Mansfield to Dorothy Brett, 12 May 1918: 'My poor dear Prelude is still piping away in their [the Woolfs'] little cage and not out yet' (ibid., II, p. 169).
15. See also the letter to Dorothy Brett, 26 March 1920; ibid., III, p. 262: 'We must ... offer up ourselves as a sacrifice. You as a painter and me as a writer.'

3 The Self

1. Letter to J.M. Murry, 23 and 24 May 1918; ibid., II, p. 188.
2. In his edition of the *Stories*, op. cit., pp. 571–2, Alpers suggests – contrary to an earlier view – that 'A Married Man's Story' was 'wholly written ... in late August 1921': see also the *Life*, op. cit., p. 340n.
3. See e.g. her letter to Murry, *Collected Letters*, op. cit., I, pp. 125–6, ?May–June 1913.
4. *Between Two Worlds*, London, 1935, p. 464.
5. Mansfield recorded in a *Journal* entry for 1921, 'March 9 "I chucked the thing behind the fireplace. It wasn't even clever." Mr. Harold Beauchamp on *Je ne parle pas français*' (op. cit., p. 240).
6. Letter to Murry, 10 February 1918; *Collected Letters*, op. cit., II, p. 66.
7. April 1920.
8. 'Katherine Mansfield'; 1920, p. 274.
9. The story was printed unexpurgated in *The Stories of Katherine Mansfield*, ed. Antony Alpers, op. cit., Auckland and London, 1984. The most significant of the restored passages are to be found on pp. 281 (sentence beginning, 'And then with a soft growl ...') and 299 (last four lines).
10. Letter to Murry, 6 April 1920; *Collected Letters*, op. cit., III, p. 273.
11. Antony Alpers ed., *The Stories of Katherine Mansfield*, op. cit., p. 281.
12. Middleton Murry was the first to compare 'Je Ne Parle Pas Français' with *Notes from Underground*: 'my sensation is like that which I had when I read Dostoyevsky's *Letters from the Underworld*. ... It's utterly unlike any sensation I have ever yet had from any writing of yours, or any writing at all except Dostoyevsky's.' (*Between Two Worlds*, op. cit., p. 464). Saralyn R. Daly, *Katherine Mansfield*, New York, 1965, pp. 73–4, highlights the similarities in characterisation and structure between the two works.

13. See C.A. Hankin, *Katherine Mansfield and Her Confessional Stories*, op. cit., pp. 160–1, for a discussion of the literary relations between Raoul Duquette and Mouse.
14. See *Journal of Katherine Mansfield*, op. cit., p. 205.
15. See Alex Calder, 'My Katherine Mansfield'; *Landfall*, 172 (December 1989), p. 494; article reprinted in *In from the Margin*, ed. Roger Robinson, Louisiana, 1994, pp. 119–36. The figure of Hahnemann was first identified by Antony Alpers in his *Stories of Katherine Mansfield*, op. cit., p. 572.

4 Couples

1. In 'Katherine Mansfield – A Lesbian Writer?', *Women's Studies Journal* (New Zealand), IV ii, December 1988, pp. 48–70 (passim).
2. The term was Mansfield's – though ironically used.
3. Manuscript Papers 119, Alexander Turnbull Library, Wellington.
4. Ibid.
5. Ibid.
6. *Turnbull Library Record*, III (n.s.) iii, p. 134.
7. Ibid., p. 134.
8. Ibid., p. 134.
9. The rata is a native New Zealand tree.
10. Ibid., p. 135.
11. Ibid., p. 135.
12. Thus anticipating Julia Kristeva's interpretation of adolescence: op. cit. Chapter 2, n. 3.
13. *Katherine Mansfield: A Secret Life*, op. cit., p. 42.
14. *Turnbull Library Record*, III (n.s.) i, p. 14.
15. Ibid., p. 10.
16. Ibid., p. 25.
17. Ibid., p. 20.
18. Identified by Margaret Scott, ibid., p. 6.
19. Op. cit., p. 125.
20. *Journal of Katherine Mansfield*, op. cit., pp. 184 and 332.
21. The typescript is in the Mansfield Collection of the Newberry Library, Chicago; call no. MA. I. 20.
22. Ibid., p. 1.
23. The ideal that motivated the leading sharacter in the polemicist Russian novel *What Is To Be Done?*, the main target of satirical attack for Dostoevsky, one of Mansfield's literary mentors, in his *Notes from Underground*.
24. See e.g. Sandra M. Gilbert and Susan Gubar, *No Man's Land*, New Haven, 1989, vol. II, passim (but especially Chapter VII).
25. *Katherine Mansfield and Her Confessional Stories*, op. cit., p. 176.
26. An alternative, though similar, explanation for Bertha's switch of attention from Pearl Fulton to Harry is offered by Saralyn R. Daly, *Katherine Mansfield*, op. cit., 1965, pp. 85–6, who argues that Bertha is subconsciously aware of her husband's relationship with Miss Fulton. So Pearl Fulton's attraction to Harry provokes Bertha's desire for him.

27.	See Helen E. Nebeker, 'The Pear Tree: Sexual Implications in Katherine Mansfield's *Bliss*', *Modern Fiction Studies*, XVIII (1972–73), pp. 545–51.

28.	There are also hints in it of the Genesis myth of the Fall – another tale of innocence and sexual knowledge pertaining to a garden. In Mansfield's Modernist, and socialised, version of the story, however, the heroine's sexuality is more circumspect than Eve's, and her fate harsher: this time the hero gets off with the Serpent.

29.	See e.g. Walter Allen, *The Short Story in English*, Oxford, 1981, pp. 169–70, and Claire Tomalin, *Katherine Mansfield: A Secret Life*, London, 1987, p. 170.

30.	Letter to J.M. Murry, 28 February 1918; *Collected Letters*, op. cit., II, 98.

31.	See *Katherine Mansfield*, op. cit., p. 62: 'Her suppressed but real sexual force is indicated in the fire and sun imagery which dominates the first half of the story.'

32.	Mansfield's attitude towards rampant sexuality is evident from her comment on D.H. Lawrence's *The Lost Girl*: 'His hero and heroine are non-human. They are animals on the prowl. . . . They submit to the physical response and for the rest go veiled – blind – *faceless* – *mindless*. This is the doctrine of mindlessness.' (*Katherine Mansfield's Letters to John Middleton Murry 1913–1922*, ed. John Middleton Murry, London, 1951, p. 620 (December 1920).

33.	The parallel was suggested to me by Jeremy Treglown.

34.	'Bliss' is a 'sophisticated failure . . . the discordant combination of caricature with emotional pathos spoils the story' (John Middleton Murry, *Katherine Mansfield and Other Literary Portraits*, London, 1949, p. 9); 'I threw down *Bliss* with the exclamation, "She's done for!" Indeed I don't see how much faith in her as a woman or writer can survive that sort of story. I shall have to accept the fact, I'm afraid, that her mind is a very thin soil, laid an inch or two deep upon very barren rock. For *Bliss* is long enough to give her the chance of going deeper. Instead she is content with superficial smartness; and the whole conception is poor, cheap, not the vision, however imperfect, of an interesting mind' (Virginia Woolf, *A Writer's Diary*, op. cit., p. 2); 'In *Bliss* the moral implication is negligible: the centre of interest is the wife's feeling, first of ecstatic happiness, and then at the moment of revelation. We are given neither comment nor suggestion of any moral issue of good and evil, and within the setting this is quite right. The story is limited to this sudden change of feeling, and the moral and social ramifications are outside of the terms of reference. As the material is limited in this way – and indeed our satisfaction recognises the skill with which the author has handled perfectly the *minimum* material – it is what I believe would be called feminine' (T.S. Eliot, *After Strange Gods*, London, 1934, pp. 35–6). On the charge of cruelty, see Elaine Showalter, *A Literature of their Own*, London, 1982 (revised edn), p. 246; and Margaret Drabble, 'The New Woman of the Twenties: Fifty Years On', *Harpers & Queen*, June 1973, pp. 106–7 and 135; on that of incoherence, refer note 29 above.

35.	*Journal of Katherine Mansfield*, op. cit., July 1921.

36.	Ibid., July 1921.

37. The highly ambivalent love-poem which underpins Mansfield's story of the same name: see my discussion earlier in Chapter 4.
38. Letter to J.M. Murry, end November 1920; *Letters*, 1951, op. cit., pp. 604–5.
39. Henry Vaughan, *The World*, lines 111–12.
40. Entry for 1 January 1920; *Journal of Katherine Mansfield*, op. cit., p. 192. 'The Exile' was a working title for 'The Man Without a Temperament'.
41. Ibid., p. 158.
42. *The Stories of Katherine Mansfield*, op. cit., p. 570.

5 The Family

1. Reprinted in *Undiscovered Country: The New Zealand Stories of Katherine Mansfield*, ed. Ian A. Gordon, London, 1974, p. xviii.
2. Op. cit., revised edition, p. 34.
3. C.A. Hankin, op. cit., p. 84, notes the reference: Sydney Janet Kaplan, op. cit., p. 201, indicates the sexual significance of the fairytale to Mansfield's story.
4. London, 1978, p. 172; first published 1975.
5. Ibid., p. 172.
6. Letter to Ottoline Morrell, 22 February 1918; *Collected Letters*, op. cit., II, p. 86.
7. 10 November 1919; ibid., III, p. 82. See also ibid., III. p. 97 (letter dated 16 November 1919).
8. *Journal of Katherine Mansfield*, op. cit., pp. 93–4; entry for 22 January 1916.
9. Ibid., p. 98; entry for 16 February 1916.
10. Ibid., p. 90; entry for November 1915.
11. Letter to Dorothy Brett, 11 October 1917; *Collected Letters*, op. cit., I, p. 330.
12. *The Aloe*, ed. Vincent O'Sullivan, Manchester, 1983, p. 35. All extracts from 'The Aloe' are taken from this edition.
13. The title-heroine of *Anna Karenina* by Tolstoy, one of Mansfield's favourite authors, also interprets her own sense of duality in moral terms; and in 'Je Ne Parle Pas Français' Mansfield makes a similar association.
14. See Valerie Shaw, *The Short Story: A Critical Introduction*, London and New York, 1983, pp. 196–7.
15. See e.g. Sydney Janet Kaplan, op. cit., pp. 115–16.
16. Quoted by Alpers in *The Life*, op. cit., p. 193.
17. Reprinted in *Undiscovered Country*, op. cit., pp. 299–303.
18. Letter to J.M. Murry, 10 and 11 February 1918; *Collected Letters*, op. cit., II, p. 66.
19. *Letters*, 1928, op. cit., II, p. 87.
20. Josephine was modelled on Mansfield's cousin Sylvia Payne, whose nickname Jug she borrows; Constantia upon the author's lifelong friend Ida Baker, whose second name was Constance. Both Baker and Payne were at Queen's College with Mansfield: indeed the story was originally entitled 'Non-Compounders', a Queen's College term

for those students not taking the full, or 'compounded', course of lectures. The Colonel of the story was drawn from Ida Baker's father, a retired Indian Army doctor, although he bears a generic resemblance to Mansfield's other paterfamilias figures.

21. See Don W. Kleine, 'Mansfield and the Orphans of Time', *Modern Fiction Studies*, XXIV, 1978, pp. 423–38, for a detailed discussion of the narrative structure of 'The Daughters'.

22. 23 June 1921; *Letters*, 1928, op. cit., II, p. 120.

23. In their *Katherine Mansfield*, op. cit., p. 99.

24. Ibid., p. 99.

25. Claire Tomalin, op. cit., p. 200, also detects Mansfield's influence in *Jacob's Room*.

26. *The Life of Katherine Mansfield*, op. cit., p. 343.

27. 11 October 1917; *Collected Letters*, op. cit., I, p. 331.

28. 11 October 1917; ibid., p. 331.

29. *Letters*, 1928, op. cit., II, p. 134; letter to the Hon. Dorothy Brett, September 1921.

30. In 'The Aloe', Nan, another friend of Beryl's, is also associated with cross-gender behaviour – thereby showing a more or less explicit attraction towards Beryl herself.

31. Alpers, *The Life*, op. cit., p. 42.

32. *Letters*, 1928, op. cit., II, p. 196; 13 March 1922.

33. *Journal of Katherine Mansfield*, op. cit., p. 268; 27 October 1921.

34. Op. cit., pp. 219–20.

35. The analogy was Mansfield's own: see *Letters*, 1928, op. cit., II. p. 96; 1 March 1921.

Select Bibliography

Unless otherwise indicated the place of publication is London.

I. WORKS BY KATHERINE MANSFIELD

The Collected Short Stories of Katherine Mansfield, 1945 and 1981.
The Aloe with Prelude, ed. Vincent O'Sullivan, Manchester, 1983.
The Collected Letters of Katherine Mansfield, ed. Vincent O'Sullivan and Margaret Scott, 3 vols, 1984–93.
Journal of Katherine Mansfield, ed. J. Middleton Murry, 1927.
Journal of Katherine Mansfield, ed. J. Middleton Murry, 1954.
Katherine Mansfield: Dramatic Sketches, ed. David Drummond, Palmerston North (New Zealand), 1988.
The Letters of Katherine Mansfield, ed. J. Middleton Murry, 2 vols, 1928.
The Letters and Journals of Katherine Mansfield: A Selection, ed. C.K. Stead, 1977.
Novels and Novelists, ed. J. Middleton Murry, 1930.
The Stories of Katherine Mansfield, ed. Antony Alpers, Auckland and Oxford, 1984
Turnbull Library Record [Wellington] III [n.s.], i and iii.
Undiscovered Country: The New Zealand Stories of Katherine Mansfield, ed. Ian A. Gordon, 1974.

II. BIOGRAPHIES AND BIOGRAPHICAL ESSAYS

Alpers, Antony. *The Life of Katherine Mansfield*, 1980.
Baker, Ida. *Katherine Mansfield: The Memories of L.M.*, 1971.
Boddy, Gillian. *Katherine Mansfield: The Woman and the Writer*, Ringwood (Australia), 1988.
Mantz, Ruth Elvish and John Middleton Murry. *The Life of Katherine Mansfield*, 1933.
Meyers, Jeffrey. *Katherine Mansfield: A Biography*, 1978.
Murry, John Middleton. *Katherine Mansfield and Other Literary Portraits*, 1949.
Murry, John Middleton. *Katherine Mansfield and Other Literary Studies*, 1959.
Tomalin, Claire. *Katherine Mansfield: A Secret Life*, 1987.

III. CRITICAL WRITINGS ON KATHERINE MANSFIELD

Berkman, Sylvia. *Katherine Mansfield: A Critical Study*, Oxford, 1952.
Cather, Willa. 'Katherine Mansfield'; *Not Under Forty*, 1936.
Daiches, David. *The Novel and the Modern World*, Chicago, 1939, pp. 65–79.

Daly, Saralyn R. *Katherine Mansfield*, New York, 1965; revised edn 1994.
Fullbrook, Kate. *Katherine Mansfield*, Brighton, 1986.
Gubar, Susan, 'The Birth of the Artist as Heroine: [Re]production, the *Kunstlerroman* Tradition, and the Fiction of Katherine Mansfield'; in *The Representation of Women in Fiction*, ed. Carolyn G. Heilbrun and Margaret R. Higgonet, Baltimore, 1983, pp. 19–59.
Hankin, C.A. *Katherine Mansfield and Her Confessional Stories*, 1983.
Hanson, Clare, and Andrew Gurr. *Katherine Mansfield*, 1981.
Kaplan, Sydney Janet. *Katherine Mansfield and the Origins of the Modernist Movement*, New York, 1991.
King, Russell S. 'Katherine Mansfield as an Expatriate Writer'; *Journal of Commonwealth Literature*, VIII, i, June 1973, pp. 97–109.
Kobler, J.F. *Katherine Mansfield: A Study of the Short Fiction*, New York, 1990.
Modern Fiction Studies, XXIV, iii, Autumn 1978 (Mansfield issue).
Nathan, Rhoda B., ed. *Critical Essays on Katherine Mansfield*, New York, 1993.
Nebeker, Helen E. 'The Pear Tree: Sexual Implications in Katherine Mansfield's *Bliss*'; *Modern Fiction Studies*, XVIII, 1972–73, pp. 545–51.
Robinson, Roger, ed. *Katherine Mansfield: In from the Margin*, Louisiana, 1994.
Schneider, Elisabeth. 'Katherine Mansfield and Chekhov'; *Modern Language Notes*, June 1935, pp. 394–7.
Sutherland, R. 'Katherine Mansfield: Plagiarist, Disciple, or Ardent Admirer?'; *Critique*, V, ii, Fall 1962, pp. 58–76.
Women's Studies Journal (New Zealand), IV, 2, December 1988 (Mansfield issue).

IV. OTHER WORKS

Abel, Elizabeth. 'Narrative Structure[s] and Female Development'; *The Voyage In*, ed. Elizabeth Abel and others, Hanover, NH, 1983.
Allen, Walter. *The Short Story in English*, Oxford, 1981.
Bettelheim, Bruno. *The Uses of Enchantment*, 1976.
Bowlby, Rachel. *Just Looking*, New York and London, 1985.
Eliot, T.S. *After Strange Gods*, 1934.
Ellis, Kate Ferguson. *The Contested Castle*, Chicago, 1989.
Gilbert, Sandra and Susan Gubar. *The Madwoman in the Attic*, New Haven and London, 1979.
Gilbert, Sandra and Susan Guber. *No Man's Land*, vol. ii, New Haven and London, 1989.
Girard, René. *Deceit, Desire, and the Novel*, Baltimore, 1965.
Hanson, Clare. *Short Stories and Short Fictions, 1880–1980*, 1985.
Kristeva, Julia. 'The Adolescent Novel'; in *Abjection, Melancholia and Love*, ed. John Fletcher and Andrew Benjamin, 1990.
Murry, John Middleton. *Between Two Worlds: An Autobiography*, 1935.
Shaw, Valerie. *The Short Story: A Critical Introduction*, London and New York, 1983.
Showalter, Elaine. *A Literature of Their Own*, 1982 (revised edn).
Woolf, Virginia. *The Diaries of Virginia Woolf*, ed. Anne Olivier Bell, 3 vols, 1977–80.

Index

Note: References to Katherine Mansfield's short stories are listed under her name.

Index